Paula Allardyce was born in London of a
Hungarian father and a Scottish mother, and
studied at the London School of Economics
and Oxford. Her jobs have included running a
refugee children's scheme and teaching
English to commercial students. Her ever-
popular historical novels include *Adam's Rib*,
The Ghost of Archie Gilroy and *Miss Jonas's
Boy*.

Also by Paula Allardyce

Paula Allardyce

The Respectable Miss Parkington-Smith

Mayflower

Granada Publishing Limited
Published in 1977 by Mayflower Books Ltd
Frogmore, St Albans, Herts AL2 2NF

First published in Great Britain by
Hodder and Stoughton Ltd 1972
Copyright © Paula Allardyce 1972
Made and printed in Great Britain by
Richard Clay (The Chaucer Press) Ltd
Bungay, Suffolk
Set in Monotype Plantin

ONE

Miss Parkington-Smith lived in a small two-storey house, in Paradise Row, which lies halfway down Tottenham Court Road, the market road running from St. Giles to Hampstead, Kentish Town and Highgate.

It was a hot summer day in the month of June – and many said that this summer of 1750 was the warmest on record – but her parlour windows were tight shut, for the smell from the Rookeries next-door was enough to choke her, besides it was rumoured that some of the children were suffering from a dangerous infection.

'Which,' remarked Miss Parkington-Smith primly to Polly, her maid, 'is scarce surprising, for they are so dirty I cannot endure to be near them, and as for their clothes —'

She closed her eyes in rather an affected fashion, and indicated by a movement of her small hand, which was swollen and knotted with rheumatism, that she would like her vinaigrette. But Polly had suffered many years of grumbling from her mistress and habitually heard her without listening; she was now in the kitchen, sorting out the linen and washing the best cups and saucers for tomorrow's visitation.

Miss Parkington-Smith, whose Christian name was Arabella (after the sister of the great Duke of Marlborough, under whom her father had served throughout the campaigns in the Low Countries) was sixty-five years old, but she had been trained to remain upright, so her back was still as stiff as a poker. She did not care much for children, and, unless they were in the army, she disapproved of men. Indeed, she did not like anyone very much, not even the handsome young Mr. Francis Shelbrooke, who had married an actress six months ago, and who tomorrow afternoon was coming to take tea with her, together with his wife, Cassandra, and James, aged fifteen, who was his half-brother and Miss Parkington-Smith's nephew.

'No good will come of such an unsuitable marriage,' she had told Polly at the very beginning. 'Besides, from all I hear, he is a wild young man, he has had no army training, and they say he spends most of his income on the tables.'

'She's very handsome,' Polly said quite crossly then, though she was by no means timid, eyed her mistress with some apprehension, for Miss Parkington-Smith, being as she was, would probably regard this remark as grossly impertinent.

But Miss Parkington-Smith only said, 'Handsome is as handsome does,' and this being one of those meaningless remarks that sound profound, yet permit of no contradiction, there seemed nothing left to say, and the beautiful Mrs. Shelbrooke, who had been born Miss Cassandra Brydges and who was just nineteen, was not mentioned again by either of them, though at the time of her wedding she had been discussed extensively.

Polly, still washing the precious china, and muttering to herself as she did so, remembered that wedding and sighed.

She had not, of course, been invited to the reception, which must have been a magnificent affair. And precious odd Miss Parkington-Smith must have looked at it, thought Polly, surrounded by all the fine ladies and gentlemen, and her in her unfashionable clothes some thirty years out of date, her face prim and disapproving, her eyes riveted in the utmost distaste on all the glasses of strong liquor that were being passed around.

But Polly, unbeknown to her mistress, had stood in the crowd to watch the bride arrive, and the first sight of Miss Cassandra had taken her breath away, then brought the tears to her sentimental eyes. Oh she was a wild one too, if all the stories they told about her were true, and God knows, those stories were fantastic enough. They said she had driven her own phaeton at breakneck speed through Hyde Park at four in the morning, and they said too she adored dressing-up as a boy, using the costumes she had worn when she played Rosalind and Viola. There was one occasion, before she met Mr. Francis, when she swaggered out of the house as a young man, drove herself to Vauxhall Gardens, and behaved in so lunatic a fashion that she involved herself in a brawl with some drunken gallants, and was actually challenged to a duel.

The story perhaps was much exaggerated, for it was hard to imagine anyone mistaking young Miss Cassandra for a boy, but it was in all the gossip columns next day. They said the seconds came to call on her next morning, to be greeted by a sleepy young woman, her red hair soft and wild, with little on but her morning wrapper and that unfastened. They said she looked up at them drowsily, yawning and stretching out her arms. They said she asked if a sewing needle would serve as weapon, for faith, she could not trust herself with pistols, she might shoot down an innocent bystander. They said a great many things, and referred to her great outburst of dramatic, roaring laughter as the offended gentlemen hastily withdrew. The story went buzzing round the town for weeks, losing all resemblance to the original happening, and then, when it was dying down, she did something even more reckless and extravagant. The world in which she lived, laughed, swore or turned up its eyes, according to its inclinations, and Miss Parkington-Smith, who had followed the stories avidly and always read the gossip columns, said it was deplorable, and the hussy should be locked up in her room on bread and water.

Well, all that was as might be, and certainly the girl was an odd choice for Mr. Francis, who was disreputable enough himself to have, one would have thought, chosen a safer and staider wife, but Polly could only remember that she had never in her life seen anyone so lovely: she would always see before her eyes that vivid, gloriously amused face, with the mass of scarlet-red hair piled high under her veil.

She remembered something else too, something that she had never told Miss Parkington-Smith. After the ceremony, as they were all leaving in their carriages, and the music was playing, Miss Cassandra – only of course by then she was Mrs. Shelbrooke – had slipped her hand out of her husband's arm and come up to Polly who, amazed, had gaped at her, thinking she must have gone mad. 'You are Polly, aren't you?' she said, smiling and taking her hand. 'Now why didn't you come into the church, you silly girl?' And then she had said, waving imperiously at Mr. Shelbrooke who, not unnaturally, wished her to be at his side, 'Now you are going to have a glass of

7

wine, Polly, to drink my health, for, faith, I do not see why Aunt Arabella should drink and you go dry.' And the wine was duly brought to her, and never had Polly, blushing to her hair, drunk with heartier feeling: brought up as she was, with the rigid class distinctions of the country in her mind, she thought this wonderful, and loved the new Mrs. Shelbrooke ever afterwards.

The nephew had been there too, the full nephew, Master Jack's son, young Master James, who looked as if he might be as wild as his half-brother, and who was at present at the Manor House School, Marylebone, a handsome boy, like Mr. Francis, and big for his years.

Miss Parkington-Smith liked James, because he was Jack's son, but unfortunately on the only occasion when they met, he fell into a fit of the sullens: this was really shyness, but as she had never considered other people's feelings and knew nothing of children, she did not recognize it.

'All the young people today,' said Miss Parkington-Smith, 'are ill-mannered. There is no discipline, no respect for older people, no proper gentility. I do not know,' she said, 'what the world is coming to. It was never like that in my young days.'

But her young days were gone long ago – indeed, Polly wondered sometimes if they had ever existed – and Miss Parkington-Smith sat there poker-backed at her window, in the little house that had belonged to her father, the Captain.

Her greatest pride was the Captain's portrait on the wall, gilt-framed, and painted by some minor artist in oils. The Captain looked down upon her, dressed in full regimentals, his hand on his sword, the other arm across his breast. The artist had done his best for very little money, but not even he could glorify that choleric, port-drowned countenance, not even he could put nobility into those small eyes, the mean mouth, the triple-chinned jaw. But to his daughter it was something sacred: she looked at it every night before she went to bed, and every morning she passed her finger over the frame to make sure that there was not a speck of dust. And then she would glance once, almost indifferently, at the room which was her castle: the ormolu clock, the chimney-piece with two peacock's feathers and a large shell above it, the pewter dishes on the wall, the blue and white Sèvres china in the cabinet, the large print of Hogarth's 'March to Finchley' and, most precious of all, papa's duelling pistols and small-sword laid out on a small table. Woe betide Polly if she moved one article half a millimetre out of place: it was almost as if there were chalk marks for everything, from chairs to sideboard, from linen-chest to the small mat placed near the door to save wear on the carpets.

And now she called out to Polly, tapping imperiously with her stick as she did so. 'I feel,' she said, 'that a bottle of wine will be required.' She added, primming up her lips, 'Young people today drink far too much, and if Francis wishes to over-indulge himself, he can do it in one of his nasty Clubs. He will certainly not do it here. However, I do not wish to appear niggardly, so you will please go across to the Tea Gardens, the moment you have finished washing the china, and ask them to sell me a bottle. Do you have the tea and biscuits, Polly?'

'Yes, ma'am,' said Polly snappily, for she had already prepared the repast – if such it could be called. It would certainly not be up to the standard of Hanover Square, where young Mr. Francis and his wife lived, but then their income would not be up to his standard either. The Captain had believed that he had left his daughter reasonably well endowed, and never knew till the end of his days that almost all his money had gone in the South Sea Bubble. It was the one and only time his daughter ever deceived him, starving and scrimping so that he should still have his port and the large meals which in the end brought on the stroke that killed him.

Since his death Miss Parkington-Smith had lived in genteel poverty, yet somehow contrived to give the impression that she was parsimonious rather than poor. She added, 'I will not provide coffee. I understand it is fashionable, but there is no nourishment in it, none at all. Dear papa always enjoyed his tea, and what was good enough for him must suffice these young people.'

Polly, who remembered the old days, could have pointed out that the Captain preferred a glass of wine, but she knew better than anyone how the departed gentleman had, since his death twenty-five years ago, assumed in the passing of time a god-

9

like aura, so she simply said, 'Yes, ma'am,' once again, which was what she said most of the time, for it saved trouble and argument.

She came out into the hallway, to walk up to the 'Adam and Eve' Tea Gardens at the corner of Tottenham Court Road, and the footpath that crossed it. She was only a few years younger than her mistress, though she would never have admitted to such an age, and she could remember how in her extreme youth there had been tales of a manor that had stood there, which once belonged to the Dean and Chapter of St. Paul's.

She paused for a moment in the doorway, staring out at the courtyard beyond; she thought that the Captain, if he could see his daughter now, would turn in his grave.

In the old days, back in the sixteen hundreds, when the young Captain Parkington-Smith brought his plain little bride to London from her country vicarage, Paradise Row had been small, select and genteel. Its houses – and then there were six of them – were well set back from the main road: it was quiet, decent and suitable for a young woman, whose husband was always away at the wars, to bring up her two children, Jack and Arabella.

But oh lord, how times change, thought Polly. Five of the houses had fallen into decay and been knocked down, while in their place the Rookeries had sprung up, like some monstrous foetid plant. The Church officially owned the land they were built on, but Polly knew, as everyone knew, that the landlord had nothing whatsoever to do with the Church. Nobody knew who he was, nobody ever saw him, but his fellows – strong-arm bullies – collected the rents, threw out those who could not pay, and did nothing else, so that everything around was crumbling to pieces. Half the rooms in the Rookeries were common lodgings, with mattresses thrown down from garret to cellar, and there the lodgers lived, coming and going, brawling and fighting, sometimes murdering each other, so that the nights were made hideous by drunken laughter, hysterical screaming, swearing and shouting and the thin wailing of under-fed children.

Here was the refuse of the city of London, spewed out over the Holborn boundaries. Here lived the cut-throats and footpads, the coiners and beggars; here were the pickpockets and highwaymen; these crept out at night to lurk in the Marylebone Fields, waiting for unwary travellers from the Pleasure Gardens, or for the gentry come to amuse themselves at the boxing booths that abounded in the neighbourhood, where they could watch Mr. John Broughton instructing pupils in the 'most successful method of beating a man deaf, dumb, lame and blind'. There was not an evening when one did not fall over some wretched creature blind on gin and sprawled across the cobbles, or run the risk of meeting some roaring boy almost too drunk to stand, who would come lurching up with a knife in his hand. And the ladies of the town lived there too, and indeed, there was only a wall between a roomful of them and Miss Parkington-Smith's parlour: sometimes they screeched and cat-called half the night, or had monstrous fights with the men they brought in, yelling the place down in drunken fury.

Polly had once and once only suggested that her mistress might try to find new lodgings. She never mentioned this again. Miss Parkington-Smith refused to go. Miss Parkington-Smith sat, when the weather was warm enough, by her window in the utmost gentility, and gazed out on this wild, savage, teeming jungle of a world with cool indifference: perhaps she lived so much in the past that she scarcely saw it. The wretchedness and despair of it: the ragged, gaunt children, the women, perpetually pregnant, with their gin bottles and fierce, haunted eyes, the country coneys, who had come to make their fortunes in the great city and turned highwayman and thief in sheer desperation – all this passed her by.

It was nothing to do with her, and she sat there in her own small square of personal and genteel sun, while outside three grim shadows fell blackly athwart the Rookeries: the shadow of hunger, the shadow of disease, and the shadow, not of a pale horse, but of a squat triangle, the gallows at Tyburn.

And Miss Parkington-Smith ignored this and continued to dwell in the regimental world of her youth, when papa went to the wars, mama held her tea-parties and card-parties, and the plain little daughter played badly on the harpsichord, stitched clumsy kerchiefs, and tried to look as if a suitor were turning

11

up the very next day.

The landlord – this strange, sinister creature whom no one could remember having seen – had once made an attempt to persuade her to go. A gentleman from Lincoln's Inn had called to see her. Polly had not been present at the interview, but she had shown the gentleman out, and she had seen the astonishment and exasperation on his face.

He had had short shrift from Miss Parkington-Smith. 'Why should I go?' she said. 'It is my home. The Captain lived here. The Captain would never have permitted me to leave.'

And so she stayed, but there was of course no money for repairs or renovations: the damp crawled down the walls, pieces of the ceiling fell down, the roof let in the water, and from the Rookeries next door, unpleasant night crawlers and creepers appeared from time to time, to be instantly drowned, or stepped upon by Polly's large, affronted feet.

I only hope, thought Polly, that Mr. Francis, when he sees how shocking this all is, does something for his aunt. After all, he was more or less related. Polly had never been able to work out the exact degree of kinship, but Master Jack had married Mr. Francis's mother, then a young and wealthy widow, and James his son, at least was a full relation; it made no sense that a young man, with so many fine friends and an admirable income, should leave the old lady in such lamentable circumstances.

I wonder, thought Polly, what Mrs. Francis will think of this.

She stepped out into the courtyard. A child lay asleep in the sun. His filthy shirt was up under his armpits; his legs were splayed out like sticks. Polly, who still remembered her youthful days in the country, when children were sturdy and pink-cheeked, with milk and butter to spare for everyone, averted her eyes and passed quickly on. Once she would have stooped down to speak to the child or offered him food, but she had long since learnt better. The inhabitants of the Rookeries were bitterly united in their wretchedness; they resented all interference, and if one of them were spoken to, the odds were that all the rest of them would come tumbling out, and it would all end in oaths and shrieks and blows.

So Polly merely nodded to the people she met: she was a friendly soul and inquisitive; unlike Miss Parkington-Smith she knew most of them by sight and a great many by name.

There was Old Jack, the Musical Shrimp Man, who sold his wares and sang as he did so; his real trades were trickery and begging, and he looked the rogue he was, with a roving eye and a slippery tongue. There was Simon, the beggar, with his one-eyed dog, who lodged under the staircase and sat by his master all night, as he pretended to sell old copies of the *Gentleman's Magazine* and odd scraps from Foxe's *Book of Martyrs*, while his withered hand was outheld for money.

And of course there was Zephaniah Clarke.

Polly greeted him now. He was the only person she could really speak to, and she thanked God she had someone to gossip with occasionally, for otherwise she felt she might have gone out of her mind: Miss Parkington-Smith either spoke of the past or complained of the present, it really was more than a friendly, good-natured countrywoman could be expected to endure.

'So the old lady has company,' said Zephaniah. He had a soft country voice that had endeared him to Polly from the very beginning; she did not like the harsh, whining London accent. He was a stocky fellow, not very old, and something of a dandy, with sixteen coloured ribbons dangling from his sleeves and breeches; he was always clean and well turned out. There was also something else about him that pleased Polly; from his manner and manners she knew that at some time in his life he had been in service: it seemed to her a bond between them.

She said sedately, 'They are relatives of her dead brother, Mr. Zephaniah,' for she always preserved the civilities.

He shot her a strange look. He said, smiling as if this were unimportant, 'Then tell them to get her away from here, quick, Mistress Polly, quick as hell.'

'I don't know why you say that,' returned Polly, 'but oh how I wish they would.' And she sighed and thought for one enchanting, dreaming moment of some pretty little house with roses in the garden, and air that one could breathe without choking. She added, 'But she'll never move, not this side of heaven. She's too old and too set in her ways. She'll stay here until they bring her out feet first.'

Zephaniah only repeated, 'You should get her away. This is no place for the likes of her.'

'This is no place for the likes of anyone,' snapped Polly, rather crossly, for it was all very well for Zephaniah to go on like this, he did not know this genteel little spinster who sat primly by her window and resolutely ignored the dirty, dangerous world a few inches from her eyes. Then she said in a brighter tone, 'I've not seen much of you lately. How are you these days, Mr. Zephaniah?'

'Oh, I come and I go,' returned Zephaniah then, as if the conversation no longer interested him, stepped quietly backwards, remarking idly, 'I drink a dram now and then with the stagecoach men in the way of friendship and intelligence, where I know there'll be passengers who're worth speaking with. I come and I go.'

And with this fair description of himself, he disappeared into one of the Rookeries' many entrances.

Certainly Mr. Clarke came and went, for he led a busy life: in the evenings he was to be found in Marylebone Fields on his own personal errands, and in the daytime perhaps did a little quiet coining in the room which, unlike most of the people in the Rookeries, he had entirely on his own. But if he were a rogue, he was a good-natured one, even jolly, with a red, round face and an amiable smile; once when he had met Polly out in the street, he had taken her into a tavern and given her a glass of porter.

Naturally she never repeated this to Miss Parkington-Smith. Miss Parkington-Smith would have been dreadfully shocked, though Zephaniah was one of the few people she knew by name; on the rare occasions when she stepped outside, he always offered to help her, called her 'ma'am' and expressed a great interest in her state of health.

'That is a good fellow,' remarked Miss Parkington-Smith to Polly, who choked a little and covered it up with a cough. The old lady, not remarking this, went on, 'Do you know what family he works for?'

'No, ma'am,' mumbled Polly, not wishing to say a word against this courteous highwayman, but baffled as always by

14

her mistress's extraordinary lack of perceptiveness with regard to her neighbours.

Miss Parkington-Smith's next remark took the wind out of her sails. 'He is a groom, of course,' she said. It was one of her more sociable days. She added in condescending tones, 'You will naturally have perceived his front teeth. They are filed away. That is because of the whiplash, you know. All grooms hold their whips between their teeth. I don't expect you knew that. But the Captain's grooms were all the same. It used to entertain me when I was a young girl. Indeed, once I remember trying to hold a whip in my mouth. I was very young, of course, and headstrong. It was a very unladylike thing to do, and mama gave me a great scold for such unseemly behaviour.'

Polly did not know whether to gasp or giggle: the thought of Miss Parkington-Smith with a whiplash between her teeth made her want to laugh hysterically. But she mentioned the matter to Zephaniah one day, and he listened to her with his bland smile, his rogue's eyes moving up and down her.

He said comfortably, 'Ay, that is right enough, mistress. I was a groom for many years. It has been a great help to me in my profession, for, you see, I learnt the roads and I learnt the ways of gentlemen; I know better than most which one of them will draw a pill on me, and which will show off in front of his lady. It never hurts to learn a useful trade, Mistress Polly – you can always profit by it.'

Polly did not repeat this to Miss Parkington-Smith.

She walked down Tottenham Court Road. At this hour in the afternoon it was almost empty. The market carts had long since gone, and the Rookeries only came to full life after dusk. Most of the inhabitants would be sprawled out on their mattresses, and the young women in the ground-floor room would be fast asleep. The boxers' booths were closed too, and Mr. Broughton, presumably educating the young nobility in how to black each other's eyes and smash each other's teeth in, was not to be seen.

On one of the booths was a notice of tonight's contest, and Polly read it with interest, thinking it would be fun to see it.

The notice ran as follows:

*'I, Mokasa, known for my vast strength, my intrepid man-
hood and bravery on and off the stage, accept the challenge of the Fighting Quaker, and shall, if he don't care,
give him the truth of a good beating which will convince
him of his ignorance in the art of boxing.'*

'Lord, lord,' said Polly aloud – for what with Miss
Parkington-Smith's genteel reserve, and the lack of sociable
neighbours, she had the habit of speaking aloud to herself –
'he don't think much of himself, that Mokasa or whatever his
outlandish name is, and that's a fact.'

She grew aware that someone was standing behind her. She
whirled round, then gave a great scream of pure terror, so
frightened that she thought she would swoon.

He must have been about six foot six, and he was coal-black,
with a great mop of frizzy hair, and eyes that, in Polly's aghast
vision, seemed to roll round in his head. She had never seen
anything like this in all her born days. She believed he was a
devil, and it was only when he gave her a great beaming smile
with an enormous display of white teeth, that she saw he meant
her no harm. But she still could not quite believe in a human
being with so ebon a skin: she knew there were black people,
but they were savages that ate human flesh, and they lived in
jungles a million miles from here.

She said weakly, her voice shaking, 'Oh sir, if you'll excuse
me —' but he still stood there, with his vast white grin, and
there was so great a friendliness to him that she began to
giggle, and at that he laughed too, and there they stood, roaring
with mirth as if they had swallowed half the Rookeries' gin.

Presently she said, gasping, the tears rolling down her
cheeks, 'Now that's quite enough of that, young man; I'm on
an errand for my mistress.' She added more composedly,
'There's company for tea tomorrow, you know. The young
nephew and his wife. They're real swells. I am buying wine for
them.'

But she thought he did not understand her very well, for he
only continued to smile so widely that she wondered a mouth
could extend so far, then he pointed an enormous finger at the
poster, and said, 'Mokasa, Mokasa,' bowing and beaming and

bowing again.

'Well, I don't know, I'm sure,' said Polly, but she was thankful she was not the Fighting Quaker. Then, wishing to be friendly, she said, 'I expect in your own country you live in trees, don't you?' – for she knew that black men were like monkeys and spent their time swinging from branch to branch. And she peered covertly at him to see if he had a tail, but could not discern it; indeed, apart from his colour and size, he looked as if he were a human being like everyone else.

She thought he could not speak her language, but then to her surprise he opened his mouth, and his next words came out in perfect English, the only peculiarities being that his voice was deep as the lowest note of an organ, and his vocabulary oddly old-fashioned, even poetic, as if he had learnt the language from the Bible or from old plays.

'I pray you, mistress,' he said, so strangely that it was all Polly could do to keep her countenance, 'I pray you, mistress, that you will attend this battle between me and the gentleman they name the Fighting Quaker, when I trust to smite him hip and thigh.'

'Lord, what next!' exclaimed Polly, open-mouthed. Then she added quickly, lest he should be offended, for there was so amiable an air to him that she did not want to hurt his feelings, 'I am an old woman, sir, and I don't go to suchlike things. It wouldn't be seemly, not at my time of life.'

But he only repeated, with more smiles and bows, 'I pray you, mistress,' and this he said twice more, until at last Polly shrugged her shoulders, saying, 'Oh, very well, then. Perhaps I will. If my mistress don't need me. But I've work to do, you know, I can't go on wasting my time like this.'

And with that, she bobbed at him, as she had been taught in her youth, and turned into the Tea Gardens, where she stayed for a while, to drink a cup of hot chocolate, and hear all the local gossip.

And Miss Parkington-Smith still sat at her window, dreaming of the past, while the Rookeries began slowly to stir, like some giant animal roused from slumber.

TWO

Young Mr. and Mrs. Shelbrooke were quarrelling.

Below stairs the servants listened. The house in Hanover Square was too solidly built for them to hear the exact words, but someone must have left the drawing-room door open, or else Mr. Francis, who possessed powerful lungs, was roaring out his temper, for the angry sounds rolled like thunder above the kitchen where Mrs. Bowes, the cook, the butler, the under-housemaid and young Jem, the groom, were gathered, ostensibly to eat their evening meal.

'I do declare it's like Bedlam,' said Mrs. Bowes. She looked at the butler as she spoke. They had always got on well, they had both been with Mr. Shelbrooke long before he married, and they had both seen him through all kinds of scrapes and a number of alliances, not so legal as his present one.

The under-housemaid and young Jem said nothing, for it was not their place to do so, but they showed no wish to leave the kitchen, and they pushed assiduously at their food, their eyes lowered and their ears wide.

The butler remarked, 'I wasn't sure it would last, Mr. Francis being as he is, but I must say, I didn't think this would happen so soon.' Then forgetting himself, he banged his fork down on the plate, and exclaimed, 'After all, Mrs. Bowes, she's a most handsome girl, and I could swear they're very much in love. It's not,' he went on, carried away by genuine emotion, for he was not an indiscreet man, 'as if it were that Miss —— or Miss —— or even that young female from the country, who lodged here for three days, then ran off —'

He checked himself, rather too late. He roared at Jem: 'You lazy good-for-nothing young bastard, what are you hanging around here for? Think you're a person of quality, do you? Well, you're not, I can tell you that. The master wants his carriage done special for tomorrow. He's calling on Miss Parkington-Smith, and if there's one speck of dirt, she's bound to

18

see it as plain as if it were the whole confounded kennel.' And he turned on the under-housemaid, prepared to deliver another broadside, but she, being a sensible girl, had already slid out, and Jem followed her, muttering various things under his breath.

Mrs. Bowes and the butler, now on their own, looked dismally at each other. Not only did they know Mr. Shelbrooke very well, but they were also fond of him, for he was in his own way a considerate master; they were dismayed by what was going on upstairs, for this was not just a lovers' quarrel, nor was it an isolated instance: it was something more serious and more sustained.

Mrs. Bowes said at last, 'They're both so young — It didn't ought to be like this. What's the matter with the pair of them?' Then she rose briskly to her feet, and began piling the dishes together. 'The trouble is they're both so headstrong. Like a couple of children. Neither of 'em will give in and say he's sorry. They need some sense knocked into them, something from outside to make them see how silly they are. I think they need something to *do*. Too much money, too much time on their hands, that's their trouble like a great many more I could name. If they had six children to bring up, they'd never carry on like this, they wouldn't have the time.'

The butler raised his hands. He could have remarked that the young couple had only been married for six months, and that it was therefore a little premature to foist so vast a family upon them, but with Mrs. Bowes in such a mood, there was no point in saying so, it would only provoke another brawl, downstairs this time.

He went out to his pantry. He remarked over his shoulder, 'They're like people in a play. Only they don't have the right lines. When they find a play to suit them, maybe they'll settle down and behave themselves.'

At this moment, both Mr. and Mrs. Shelbrooke did indeed look like characters in a play. It was five in the afternoon, they had eaten their dinner, and were now in the drawing-room. Young Mr. Shelbrooke sprawled in his chair, legs wide, looking remarkably like the husband in 'Marriage à la Mode', even to the silk handkerchief hanging from his pocket, and his wife's

19

little spaniel, who was undeservedly called Cheri, and who gazed remotely ahead, as if all this brawling were too vulgar to endure for a dog of such a high pedigree.

Cassandra lay full-length on the chaise-longue. She was tall for a woman, and covered the full stretch of it. Her red hair was out of its pins, she still wore her wrapper, she had kicked her shoes off, and her face was set in sullen resentment and boredom.

Yet even in this impossible mood, with her hair untidy and her face scowling, she managed to look beautiful, and every angry movement was made with instinctive grace: Mr. Shelbrooke eyed her with rage and longing, wanting to slap her and embrace her at the same time.

He did neither. He said, pulling at the handkerchief until it fell from his pocket, 'There's no pleasing you, is there? I said I would stay in. What more do you want?'

She struggled. A tangled swathe of hair fell across her cheek. She pushed it violently back.

'If you could bring yourself to dress your hair,' began Mr. Shelbrooke, then exclaimed in fury, 'You look like a slut. You look like some drab from the streets. Suppose one of our friends were to call —'

'There is little point in dressing my hair,' returned Cassandra, 'for we are not going out, and you, in spite of your protestations, are unlikely to stay in. There will, therefore, be no one to see me. And if I look like a drab from the streets, which is charming of you, Francis, that should suit you very well, for faith, I hear nothing but tales of your females, and each one more vulgar than the last.'

He rose to his feet. He was a tall young man, being well over six foot, and he was good-looking, like the mother who refused to remain widowed, who had had two husbands, and might well seek one more. So far he had only had one wife, but Cassandra sensing her accusation was unfair and quite probably untrue, knew within her heart that with a little more of this, their marriage would be broken beyond recall. She knew too that it was foolish to quarrel with a husband who pleased her more than any man had ever done. But what Mrs. Bowes had said was perfectly true: she was too proud to apologize and, though she knew that her words were unpardonable, she could not bring herself to retract them. So she bent over the chaise-longue, and called in cajoling tones, 'Cheri. Cheri darling, come to mama.'

Cheri, who was no lapdog, ignored this, but Mr. Shelbrooke broke into an exasperated roar. 'Oh, leave that damned animal alone! And why the devil do you call him Cheri darling?' He repeated with the sad over-emphasis of lost temper, 'Cheri darling, Cheri darling — Why not call me François Francis? Why not call the butler —'

Then he realized that he had no idea of the French for 'butler', and stopped.

Cassandra began to laugh, and it was her shattering stage laugh that she only used on these occasions: a sustained bell-like trill, which carried most effectively to the back of the gallery, but which was a little overwhelming in Hanover Square, with her audience only a couple of feet away.

Mr. Shelbrooke advanced upon her, and she at once gave a cry, putting out her hands. 'If you dare to strike me,' she said, 'I shall leave the house this instant. I am not after all entirely without resources. I can always go back to the stage, you know.'

'You are acting very prettily at the moment,' said her husband. 'I have no intention of striking you. I have no intention of satisfying your craving for drama. You wish me to, of course, and then you will doubtless sweep out of the door and parade Great George Street, clasping your cheek and weeping and wailing, so that all the world will know how you are ill-treated.'

Cassandra fell silent, shooting lowering glances from her green eyes, and at this Mr. Shelbrooke emitted a brief laugh, near as theatrical as hers, and returned to his chair, flinging himself down upon it so that it creaked in protest.

After a pause, he said almost entreatingly – and this was unusual enough to make her raise her head – 'For God's sake, Cassie, what have I done wrong now? You accuse me always of my past mistresses — No! Listen. This time you'll damned well listen. I dare say I've not always conducted myself as I should. I dare say — Well, never mind. Only since I've married you, there has been no one else.'

21

'That is wonderful,' remarked Cassandra to the ceiling, for she had now moved so that she was lying prone upon her back, her hands clasped at her breast as if she were some medieval effigy on a tombstone. 'We have been married for a full six months, and there is no one else. Who could ask for more? Such devotion. Such fidelity.'

'Oh God in heaven!' sighed Mr. Shelbrooke, and at this Cheri rose and walked from the room. 'Even the dog has had enough,' he said.

'You seem to forget,' said Cassandra, ignoring this last remark, 'that there are always in this town a great many people who have nothing else to do but spy and tell tales on everybody else.'

Mr. Shelbrooke, who seemed unable to keep still, jumped to his feet again, but he did not come near his wife, only moved across to the mantelpiece where he began fingering and shifting the various ornaments upon it. He said quietly, 'And what have these people been telling you?'

'Well!' cried Cassandra in a hurry, 'if you must spend all your evenings at the hazard table – I never can understand why men like throwing dice around, such silly things. And your mornings in the coffee houses —'

'I asked,' said Mr. Shelbrooke, 'what these people have been telling you.'

As she did not answer, he repeated the question a third time, with such insistence that she no longer dared ignore it.

She spoke very quickly as she had done when a child, saying something she knew she should not say. 'Her name is Jenny, is it not?' She saw the sudden flicker in Mr. Shelbrooke's cheek, and her voice came out full volume. 'A female from the country. A maidservant or something of the kind. They say you kept her once, and are now seeing her again. They say —'

She stopped. He did not answer for a moment, then said calmly, 'I never kept her, but it is perfectly true that I have seen her.'

'Is that all you have to say?'

'Oh, I think it's sufficient.' Then he said, almost sadly, 'I suppose I could reproach you with your own behaviour, but perhaps there is no point in doing so. Only you are not very discreet and your hair is very noticeable. I hope you amused yourself at that masked ball yesterday evening?'

Cassandra did not answer this at all. They looked at each other, and in both their faces was unhappiness, anger, shame and regret. They searched each other's eyes as if by that means they could find out where they had gone wrong, how it was that their love for each other had led to this wilderness where both had lost all sense of direction, where neither could see the way ahead.

And so she fell back against the cushions of the chaise-longue, her hair a scarlet splash against them, and he continued to stand by the mantelpiece, fingering pieces of porcelain, moving them from one end to the other.

Presently he said in a pleasant, conversational tone, 'To-morrow afternoon we are calling on James's Aunt Arabella.'

'That will be very agreeable,' said Cassandra.

'Well, I hardly think it will. She is a very stiff-necked old lady, and she has always regarded me with suspicion: it was bad enough of her brother to marry a widow, but for the widow to have a son already is not quite decent. I suppose she will do her best to be civil. She quarrelled with my stepfather, and from what he told me, lives in the house that my grand-father bought, and dwells entirely in the past, talking of nothing but the Marlborough campaigns in the Low Countries.'

'Oh, Marlborough,' said Cassandra. 'That was the General, was it not?'

Mr. Shelbrooke turned up his eyes, then gave his first spontaneous laugh of the afternoon. It was a pleasant and infectious sound, and Cassandra half smiled before she remembered what had passed between them. She immediately looked grave again.

'Oh be careful,' he said. 'There's already been enough of a family feud. Don't offend Aunt Arabella. You had best memorize a few of the battles, my love. Say to yourself a dozen times before you go to bed: Ramillies, Blenheim, Malplaquet and Oudenarde. Then you can throw the names into the conversation. It will serve to distract her from our misdoings, if nothing else.'

'Why do we have to go?' said Cassandra. 'She will not like

23

me at all. I have been on the stage. She is bound to think me most unrespectable.'

Mr. Shelbrooke preferred to ignore this challenge, though his eyes moved over his wife's sprawling, fiery hair, and the wrapper which had come open. He said, 'I am afraid we said we would call. She came to our wedding. Do you not remember her? The little old lady who would not drink or eat, who ignored practically everybody and would only speak to the parson.'

Cassandra was so interested in this that she forgot her sulks and sat up. 'Oh I remember her, Francis. Such a strange old thing. She had rheumatism, she used a stick. And her clothes were at least fifty years out of date. That hair. It was skewered up right on top of her head, under the strangest hat.' She suddenly put a hand to her mouth, like a frightened child. 'Oh God —'

'Yes, Cassandra?' said her husband, smiling rather grimly at her.

'It was I who said we'd call —'

'Yes, Cassie. It was indeed.'

'Oh lord, lord, lord!' said Cassandra, giggled faintly, then said in a loud, angry tone, 'Well, I was sorry for her. The poor old thing. Though I didn't like her very much. She was unkind to her maid. I heard her. I don't like people who are rude to their servants.'

'Well, we've got to go now,' said Mr. Shelbrooke shortly. 'You promised we'd call. You said you were looking forward to it. I thought you were a trifle unwise at the time. But I dare say she can't help her manners. She's old. She's eccentric. It cannot be lack of money, for her father left her everything, and she should have plenty for her needs. But at that age one tends to hoard, and one is no longer interested in clothes.' He added, 'You doubtless will be the same.'

'Never!' declared Cassandra fiercely. 'Oh, never, never, never. But surely we could have invited her here, instead of going all that dreary way. We could send the carriage for her —'

'She never leaves the house these days. I believe her rheumatics are worse,' said Mr. Shelbrooke. 'And she is expecting us. We have no choice. If you will indulge in these generous gestures, you must take the consequences – only what seems rather unfair is that I have to take the consequences too. However, we needn't stay long. An hour perhaps. And it will give the old lady great pleasure.'

'I don't see why it should. And certainly it will give me none. What do we talk about?'

'Marlborough.'

'Oh, those silly battles — How, pray, do you expect me to bring them in? Such delicious tea – Ramillies! Such a charming house – Malplaquet! Such seasonable weather — Ou – ou — Oh, I don't even remember. And it is not amusing, Francis. It is not amusing at all.'

For Mr. Shelbrooke, who was after all only twenty-five, and who had at this point almost forgotten their quarrel and the unhappy remarks that had passed between them, had spluttered into a rude laugh.

He said, when he had recovered himself, 'If it is any consolation to you, we are not the only sufferers. James, as the full nephew, is coming with us. I have spoken to his headmaster.'

'He won't like it,' said Cassandra. 'Boys of that age do not care for old ladies.'

'I dare say he'll not, but he is her nephew after all, and she may as well see the whole family at one blow. And James on the whole is a well-mannered boy. At least it gets him away from school for the day.'

'How is that dreadful Mr. Fielding?'

'Who's he?' demanded her husband in surprise, adding resentfully, 'Is that someone at the school? James always seems to confide in you.'

'We are very fond of each other. Are you jealous?' said Cassandra. 'He is, after all, only fifteen.'

'Of course I'm not jealous,' snapped Mr. Shelbrooke, and with a clumsy movement knocked a little porcelain figure to the ground, where it smashed into fragments.

He looked down at this, swore, then kicked the pieces away. Cassandra looked down too. They did not meet each other's eyes.

'Who is Mr. Fielding?' asked Mr. Shelbrooke again. His

bad temper had returned, and he asked the question with some violence.

'He is the senior master,' returned Cassandra, plucking at the fringe of the chaise-longue. 'He is a perfectly horrid man. He is always very sarcastic. He beats James.'

'I dare say James deserves it.'

'He likes beating his boys. James says he is always against him. I think you ought to take your own brother's part.'

'James is quite capable of standing up for himself,' said Mr. Shelbrooke.

'Oh, I dare say — I can see tomorrow is going to be quite delightful. Your aunt will detest me. James will say nothing. I shall be very polite and I shall be very bored. But as you say, it won't last long.' She yawned. 'Are you not going out this evening, Francis? There is no need to stay in for me.'

He hesitated. He wanted to say, No. He looked wretchedly at her as she lay there, her face averted, still plucking at the fringe. Her hair could scarce be more disordered, she had made no attempt to pull her wrapper together, and her whole attitude was one of weary indifference. He had a wild desire to rush over to her, take her into his arms, say, For God's sake, let's forget all our quarrels, let's forgive each other, I love you with all my heart – or something preposterous of the kind, and then forget about the Club, which bored him, and his gambling friends who were only there to rook him.

He said, 'Well, I thought I might spend a couple of hours at the tables. I owe a few return games. But it's not important, and, of course, if you'd prefer me to stay —'

'Oh no,' cried Cassandra to the fringe. 'No, no.' She raised her head and gave him a dazzling smile. 'You go and play hazard, Francis. And no ames-ace, mind. You will win a great deal of money, and then I shall buy myself a fine new hat to wear for tomorrow afternoon.'

And she was longing to say, Don't go, please don't go. Stay as you used to stay. We could walk together, or take a drive, or sit and drink wine by candlelight, we could be as romantic as if we were not married at all.

'Goodbye, Francis,' she said. She could not restrain herself from adding, 'You'll not be too late, will you?'

'Of course not. Are you – are you sure you wouldn't like me to stay?'

'I'm quite sure.'

'Goodbye then.'

But he hesitated at the door. He was remembering the time when he could not have endured to leave her, and she could not have endured to let him go. He was wondering what had happened to them that there was now between them not the distance of the room, but that of the whole ocean. He said nothing more. He sighed, bowed and shut the door behind him.

The moment he was out of the room, she ran to the window. She watched him striding down Hanover Street, turn into Great Swallow Street and make for St. James. She watched until he vanished from view. Then she sank to her knees by the window sill, and the angry, self-pitying tears began to creep down her cheeks.

How did these things happen? But of course she knew the answer well enough, she was neither so stupid nor so self-deceiving that she could not know it. Marriage had not been quite what she thought it would be. At first it was wonderful, a miracle. A handsome husband she adored, a magnificent London house, as much money as she cared to spend, and the entrée into a society of which until then she had only touched the shabbier fringe.

It was not really like that. Cassandra adored drama, she had to have drama, and after the first glory, there was a sad, relentless respectability to it all that made her tap her foot, grow crosser and crosser as the days went by. Marriage was not just making love and romance and moonshine; it involved housekeeping and drudgery, and, what was far worse, the entertaining of quite remarkably dull people who did not approve of her and did not hesitate to show it: the endless round of assemblies, balls and parties grew a little frightening for she never quite knew where the next snub or patronizing remark would come from.

And the quarrels between them, which had once been amusing and followed so swiftly by glorious reconciliations, were now not amusing at all, and since last month there had

27

been no real reconciliation, and every day made it more un-likely.

'I believe,' she had cried, when he had complained about something – oh, she had forgotten what it was now, perhaps a coldness towards some high-flown and high-blown lady who had chosen to denigrate her – 'I believe you only married me, because I refused to be your mistress: if I had complied, I should probably by now be another of your cast-offs.' She had added, the wilful tongue that would never learn wisdom, run-ning away with her, 'Of course I am only an actress, and as such, easy game.'

She had been shocked by her own stupidity and by the look on his face. Sometimes he could look very formidable: this time he terrified her. 'You will apologize for that,' he said, and walked out of the room.

Cassandra, being Cassandra, had not apologized, and Cas-sandra, being Cassandra, regretted every passing day that made the apology more and more impossible. And Francis slept in his dressing-room, and went out at nights as he had done when he was a bachelor, and what had been a stone cast between them, grew to an insurmountable wall.

Cassandra made now for the first time in her life a genuine effort to grow up; kneeling there, with her wrapper dusty and the tangled hair hanging about her face, she struggled to think of some way of making up which would not humiliate either of them.

She could think of nothing, and despairingly called Cheri, in a faint, appealing voice. But Cheri was a sensible dog, far more so than his lop ears and silky coat indicated. He had learnt early on that this particular tone of voice went with hugs and tears, and he had no mind to be clasped to Cassandra's bosom, and have his curly coat crushed and wet. He heard her well enough, and at once slunk down to the kitchen where Mrs. Bowes might be prevailed upon to give him the scraps he yearned for, infinitely preferring these to the delicate portions served him on his official platter.

So he tucked into a delightful mess of bones, fat and gristle, while Cassandra called once again, 'Oh Cheri,' then forgot him.

She had never been a good actress, as she knew very well.

28

She was, despite her vivid looks, a provincial girl, brought up in a small town; except where Francis was concerned, she had a strong character and plenty of good sense. She had only achieved success through her quite remarkable beauty; one glimpse of her flaming hair and enormous, dark-fringed green eyes was sufficient to stir any audience, even the ribald souls in the gallery.

No eggs were thrown at Cassandra, for in addition to her looks she had a full, rich, seductive voice excellent for covering up the fact that she usually fluffed her lines. The running footmen were sent well in advance to book boxes when Cassandra was billed, though it was mainly the gentlemen who came to see her and afterwards besieged her, entreating her to take supper with them.

Cassandra took supper with a great many of them, accepted their flowers and gifts, flirted entrancingly with them and, when they had escorted her home, shut her front door in their face. Her eyes were keen as well as green, and she had seen what happened to her fellow-actresses when they did not shut the door.

If in addition to her looks, her wit and her virtue, she had had the faintest acting ability, she would have shot Kitty Clive, Peg Woffington, Mrs. Abington and Mrs. Pritchard straight off the stage. But she had none, only self-confidence and personality, she could only be herself, and it was simply Cassandra Brydges, (the 'y' was an after-thought, it looked more stylish) as Rosalind, as Polly Peachum, and a variety of provoked wives, saucy maidservants and lovelorn heroines. She always forgot her lines halfway through, but she always giggled so charmingly that it became part of the show, the audience expected it.

Only sometimes she lost her temper, for this was her greatest failing, and when she hurled a book at the great Mr. Garrick and cut his cheek open, that was virtually the end of her career. Only Cassandra had always fallen on her feet, and when at this point Mr. Francis Shelbrooke appeared in the wings and swept her into marriage, all within the space of five weeks, it seemed as if she were settled happily for life.

But oh how she missed the exciting, naughty episodes, such as the celebrated one at Vauxhall. Cassandra longed to wear her boy's clothes again, even wished passionately to lure amorous gentlemen on, and then at the last minute slam the door on them. But Francis was so stuffy, considering the fact that his own private life had been much more lurid than hers, and now he was drinking too much, gambling too heavily, and even apparently visiting this horrid female who had already caused so much scandal.

Cassandra rose to her feet and began to pace up and down the room, kicking the skirt of her wrapper aside as she did so. She could not act, but she never stopped acting, and she walked now as an actress, casting disdainful glances from side to side as if the gallery and pit were already applauding her.

Of course Francis was perfectly right about last night's ball. But then if he had been beside her, instead of drinking too much wine with the other gentlemen, the whole thing would never have happened. And the gentleman who danced with her most of the evening had been remarkably attentive. His eyes were concealed by a mask, but what she could see of his features was young and personable; he seemed to be wealthy, and the servants addressed him as 'my lord'.

He had made his intentions clear enough. 'When shall I see you again?' he said, and Cassandra who had shut so many doors on so many ardent young men, had stared up into the eyes looking through the slitted mask, and suddenly shuddered, as if this somehow were the beginning of an end she did not wish to contemplate.

Only she was so lonely, so bored and so very unhappy.

'In a week's time you will have made up your mind,' he said – it was very ham really, but there was in this world even an etiquette for infidelity – 'I will send you flowers every day. I do not intend that you should forget me.'

And while Mr. Shelbrooke was playing abominably and losing more than he could afford, brooding as he drank too much wine on the beautiful and infuriating young wife at home, Cassandra went on pacing up and down until the butler appeared in the doorway.

He expressed no surprise at the sight of his young mistress in *déshabillé* at six in the evening. He merely said, 'These have just come for you, ma'am,' and put into her hands a silk-wrapped trio of roses, one red, one yellow and one white.

Cassandra had never received anything quite like this, even at the height of her door-slamming career. She looked down at the roses, and idly, as if it did not matter, abstracted the note that lay pinned to them.

'Shall I put them in water for you, madam?'

'Oh,' said Cassandra – the Provoked Wife, perhaps, or Katharine at her most scornful – 'Oh, the scent is too strong. It gives me a headache. No. I shall throw them away.'

But she did not throw them away. She put them, still wrapped, into the drawer with her gloves and stockings. And the note which said simply, 'This is the first day,' she slipped down the bosom of her wrapper, then sat by the window, gazing out into the darkening street. So intent was she on her thoughts that when Cheri, well fed enough to feel indulgent towards his mistress, pushed a cold nose into her hand, she did not caress him, she did not even notice.

The first day — The gentleman had presumably summed up her taste for drama, as well as noticing when Francis was out before delivering his flowers. There were six more days in which to make up her mind.

And tomorrow she and Francis would pay their duty visit to Miss Parkington-Smith; it would all be very tedious, but Cassandra had always believed that events to some extent resolved themselves, and perhaps this strange and foolish old lady might by an idle word or an unintentional remark, give her some pointer as to what she was to do.

THREE

James Shelbrooke sat alone in the classroom of the Manor House School, Marylebone, with an exercise book on the desk in front of him, and Book Four of the *Aeneid* at his side.

There was more than a hint of a resemblance between James and his half-brother, a touch of the handsome, husband-loving mother who had bequeathed to the pair of them the same arrogant features, dark colouring and sensitive mouth, yet James was also like Miss Parkington-Smith's brother, as she had remarked the first time she saw him.

He was fifteen years of age, and a good-natured boy, not nearly as wilful and brooding as Francis, but at the moment he looked aggrieved, with resentment and anger bursting from every inch of him.

He was so angry that he could not bear to stay still. He wandered out into the hall, knocking half deliberately against the parrot-cage there, and the bird at once broke out into its usual squawk: 'Pray come into the parlour and take a glass of wine.' It belonged to the headmaster's wife, Mrs. Fountaine, and it was so old it had lost all its feathers and had to wear a red flannel jacket. This was its inevitable cry: it never said anything else, though various disrespectful boys had tried to teach it more interesting phrases, and with a pleasing lack of class consciousness, it extended this invitation to anyone who passed by, whether master, pupil, parent or tradesman.

James glowered at it, and the parrot shrugged its scaly neck into its shoulders, peering back malevolently out of reddened eyes.

'Confounded bird!' said James, came back into the class-room and flung himself down at the desk again.

The school was empty, except for the servants, the parrot and Master Shelbrooke. All the other boys had gone to the Marylebone Pleasure Gardens on one of the very rare evening outings organized by Dr. and Mrs. Fountaine, who were known to the boys respectively as Bushwig and Rainbow, the latter because the lady in question, though by no means youthful, had a passion for dyeing her hair. No one, not even presumably the Doctor, knew what colour she would be next: on Monday she might be golden, on Wednesday raven, and on Friday a brilliant red.

The school specialized in nicknames. Mr Fielding, damn his beastly eyes, was known usually as Beau Frog. James at that particular moment was calling him a great deal else; he saw a certain amount of his elder brother, and his vocabulary had increased accordingly.

They would all be sitting in the Gardens now, including Toady Tom, that abominable little sneak from some country house in Sussex, with his spots and slippery manner and fashion of telling tales. They would all be gaping at Mr. Taylor, as he sang about 'The young butcher and his mistress', they would be listening to the Pariton, an instrument hitherto unknown to mankind, and they would be stuffing themselves like the pigs they were on the provisions set out for them by Mr. Trusler of the 'Rose of Normandy'. And it was a hot, sweet-scented June evening, and the lanterns would be shining in the tree-iined walks, and all the town would be there except James Shelbrooke, James Shelbrooke who had been beaten with unnecessary violence by that bloody-minded swine, Beau Frog, and who was now expected to sit here alone, supperless and sweating in the heat, translating a dozen pages from a wretched book about some confounded female called Dido who seemed to be as silly as her name. He almost wished it were tomorrow when he was to visit this old aunt in the Tottenham Court Road: God knows, that would be tedious enough, but at least it would get him away from school and Mr. Fielding, that son of a bitch, that son of whatever you liked, that —

James embroidered on this theme for a while. He had not even started his translation. He was so hungry that it was almost impossible to work: he was big for his age, promising to be as tall as his brother, and his belly was screaming out for the supper that had been denied him.

'The son of a whore!' said James aloud, settling on this as a fitting conclusion to his philippic. The Fountaines would prob-

33

ably have expelled him for saying this, unless of course he had translated it into French. There was great emphasis on this language in the school curriculum, and one day in every week was set apart for French conversation; during that day no English must be spoken at all. Even Jim, the Yorkshire footman, had leant to say in his comical accent, 'Venny shurshay, measter, venny shurshay!'

But this appellation of Mr. Fielding was a sound, honest English phrase, learnt of course from Francis in one of his unguarded moments – 'Don't let me ever catch you using that!' – 'No, Francis' – and James, finding the sound of it soothing to his ill temper and sore bones, said it again more viciously, then suddenly wished that his darling Cassie were here. He was devoted to Cassandra, and tended to follow her around far more than the ungrateful Cheri ever did: she was no prissy, missish girl, she was gorgeous to look at, and the greatest fun when she mimicked people and struck attitudes: he only hoped that one day he would marry someone half as wonderful.

'The damned son of a whore!' said James for the third time, throwing in the adjective for good measure, then he fell into a sombre brooding on Mr. Fielding.

Mr. Fielding was, as Cassandra had told her husband, the senior master at the Manor House School, and spoke perfect French, for he had as a young man done the Grand Tour, and had lived in Paris besides. It was for this reason and also because he was something of a dandy that the boys had bestowed on him the sobriquet of Beau Frog.

Mr. Fielding might have been described as a fine figure of a man, a little corpulent now in his forty-fifth year, but still well-set-up with a high forehead and rather fleshy lips, and a nose resembling that of a Roman emperor. If a difficult mother arrived at the school with a complaint about her son, she was at once led into Mr. Fielding's study, where he dealt with her most tenderly, eyeing her as if she were the most beautiful creature imaginable, interposing the odd French phrase in his compliments, and all the while making soothing gestures with the long-fingered, beringed hands of which he was so inordinately proud.

It never failed to work. The mother might arrive furious, but

34

half an hour of this treatment was enough to send her away smiling, flushed, and probably quite forgetful of her son's problems.

If, however, it was the father who came, Mr. Fielding at once changed personality: this time it was the man-to-man and boys-will-be-boys approach: it worked equally well, and Dr. Fountaine, though in most respects a kindly and conscientious man, had learnt long ago to leave complaining parents to his senior master.

Mr. Fielding dressed surprisingly well for a man in his position, and was addicted to a discreet and expensive perfume which was ironically the saving of many a young delinquent: he walked as softly as a cat, but could often be smelt before arriving. Both the dress and the scent went oddly with a schoolmaster's salary. The boys, with the customary crudeness of their age, had the story that he was a kept man, with a rich elderly widow who adored him, and whom he was poisoning by slow degrees. There were naturally no grounds for this, for Mr. Fielding had never been seen in public with any kind of female, old or young – but it had become by now almost a school tradition, and new horrifying details were added term by term so that some of the newer and more innocent boys really believed it.

If Mr. Fielding himself knew the story – and probably, with his following of spies and toadies, he did – he blandly ignored it. He merely stroked his pencil-thin moustache, and examined his spotless nails, yet there was a certain perceptiveness to the boys' stories, for it was, to put it mildly, unusual in a schoolmaster to have his coat seams braided with rich lace, to wear costly, chased buttons and lace ruffles to his shirt, and to carry a gold fob loaded with seals which knocked together in time with his dignified steps. He was a staunch Tory, wearing at any moment of political crisis a spray of oak tied with green ribbons, and the rings on his fingers, which numbered four, were all of diamonds.

James had been largely responsible for the elderly widow who grew older and uglier term by term, and who was by now dying of at least six different poisons. He had his reasons for this, for he detested Mr. Fielding as a hypocrite and a bully, yet

35

sometimes he eyed his enemy with a genuine bewilderment. He had more idea than most of what clothes cost, for he had seen the bills from his brother's tailor, and he could not help wondering occasionally if the fellow had a private income and if so, why the devil he was a schoolmaster.

His dandyism, and even his hypocrisy, might have been forgiven Mr. Fielding, but he had other traits which were less desirable, notably a real and perceptible pleasure in flogging insubordinate boys, and his own long-drawn-out method of procedure, which made it plain that he was savouring every minute of it.

The Doctor himself was a gentle, academic bore, too absorbed in his books of philosophy to worry his head over disciplinary matters, and Rainbow, though harmless, was a feather-headed place-seeker, more interested in procuring invitations to Ranelagh than her students' welfare. It was Mr. Fielding, therefore, who held the reins of authority, and he made it plain that the whip went with the reins; as, in addition to his love of administering chastisement, he possessed a smooth and vicious tongue, he was detested by everyone except the few who acted as his spies and were as a result in his favour.

Toady Tom was one of these, and what his real name was is unimportant, for that was how he was universally known. He was a small, delicate boy with a puny body and intelligence above the average; he had soon found out that his only chance of survival was to be Mr. Fielding's ally, and being unusually clever, he was a very adroit one.

James, who was in some ways old for his years, as in others he was still childish, did not entirely blame him for this, though he was fully resolved to seek the traitor out and punish him. He was by temperament incapable of being a bully, and being broad and strong and trained by his brother in the art of self-defence, he had never suffered from the bullying of others. He had indeed found himself almost forced into the role of protector, for the new boys, milky from mother-love and home, soon learnt that it was far wiser to go snivelling to young Shelbrooke than write despairing letters. The letters would only be opened, and the result would be appalling and systematic persecution from Mr. Fielding who never forgave or forgot what he considered to be treachery.

James, therefore, understood very well why Toady Tom behaved as he did, but – and this was the childish side of him – could not see why his handsome appearance and his fashion of shrugging away trouble should arouse such hatred. However, that was the way it was, and it was because of this that he now found himself alone, with the *Aeneid* lying beside him.

It was natural enough that the boys should be forbidden the Fields around the hamlet of Marylebone. They were desolate and dangerous, infested by the highwaymen, footpads and cutthroats who lurked there, waiting for the quality to return from the Pleasure Gardens. But James was fearless and inquisitive; besides, not caring much for learning, he was bored, and sometimes he would contrive to steal out at nights and stroll through the Fields, wondering if he would meet a highwayman and what he would do if he did. But highwaymen were not interested in a fifteen-year-old boy, and James took to wandering farther and farther afield, until last night he had arrived at the 'Farthing Pye House', not far from Tottenham Court Road, where Aunt Arabella lived.

He had no intention of going in, but the sounds inside attracted him, and he was hanging around, forgetful of the time, when to his astonishment he saw a face he recognized. It was not easy to be certain in the half-light, but then the swinging lantern over the tavern flashed full on the fellow's face, and James, certain now, leapt forward with a glad cry.

'Zephaniah!' he exclaimed, 'Zephaniah!'

The gentleman thus addressed turned slowly round and stared at him. Something in his way of staring chilled James who backed a little; the eyes were cold and wary, the head inclined as if in suspicion.

James said, *diminuendo*, 'Don't you remember me, Zeph? I'm James. James Shelbrooke. You used to take me out riding.'

It was a round, red face that looked down into his. Zephaniah, if indeed this were Zephaniah, had come up in the world, for he no longer wore a groom's uniform, but was dressed almost as expensively as Mr. Fielding and far more brilliantly, for he wore bright-coloured ribbons at wrist and knee, and sported an enormous jewelled tiepin.

Then suddenly the suspicious look was transformed into an enormous grin, and he raised his hand to clap the boy on his shoulder.

'Why, Master James,' he said in the same country accent he had always had, 'what be you doing here? This is no place for a young lad. Why, there are desperate characters around here, highwaymen and the like.' And as he said this, he gave James an enormous wink that twisted his face as if he had had a seizure.

James had been about to inquire if he were still a groom in some rich household, but after this changed his mind. He remarked that he had lost his way, and added that he was a pupil at the Manor House School. And while he was speaking, he eyed Zephaniah thoughtfully, noting the business-like brace of pistols he carried, and a certain raffish, dangerous air to him that was new. He made no further inquiries as to Zephaniah's employment, but absent-mindedly followed him into the 'Farthing Pye House' where he sat down with a glass of ale in front of him, while Zephaniah, now in the best of tempers, talked of old times.

'Do you remember, young master, when you got lost on the hills? Do you remember when your brother took up with the young lady at the schoolhouse? And —'

The country voice bumbled on, while James, what with the ale, the warmth of the tavern and the lateness of the hour, grew a trifle sleepy, but sleepiness did not prevent him from observing the company, which seemed to him strange, interesting and not of a kind he had often met.

They were all, however, very civil to him, and presently Zephaniah escorted him back to the village, leaving him on the outskirts of the street for, he said, 'If I go farther, I might end up by being frummagemmed, young master, there's a deal of nosy, uncharitable folks around that won't leave a man be to go about his business. Prodigious meddling, that's what folks is, Master James,' and along came the wink again, suggesting, in defiance of the bright, shrewd eyes, that Zephaniah was the jolliest, most honest man alive.

James, interested, repeated, 'Frummagemmed?' and Zephaniah laughed.

'Scragged, sir,' he said, and he drew a hand across his throat with an unpleasant choking sound that made his meaning very clear.

'I think it's I who'll be frummagemmed Zeph,' said James, turning to go, 'especially if that stinking old Frog finds out where I've been.' He added, 'That's what we call Mr. Fielding. He's our senior master. I detest him.'

At the name Zephaniah's face changed. He had been lounging there, drawing one of the long coloured ribbons through his teeth. The teeth were filed, as James remembered them. But if he had intended to say anything, he changed his mind. He bade James a hearty farewell, entreated him to call in again at the 'Farthing Pye House', and vanished into the shadows, moving silently for so heavily built a man.

James had little time to reflect on how his father's groom had changed his profession. As he slid in through the ground-floor window, Mr. Fielding's hand came down on his collar, and Mr. Fielding's voice said, 'So, sir. And may I inquire where you have been?'

James was of a philosophical turn of mind. He knew he had done wrong, and would not normally have resented the flogging he received the next morning. But the brutality of it seemed to him unfair, and he stood there staring up into Mr. Fielding's face which, as always on these occasions, looked a little blown with over-bright eyes.

'I have no doubt,' said Mr. Fielding, moving one white hand across his moustache, 'that you consider yourself too important to be punished.'

James said nothing. He knew perfectly well that the information had come from Toady Tom, but it was not Toady Tom he longed to hit, it was Mr. Fielding: at that moment the sum total of his ambition was to bring his fist down on that smooth white face.

'A young gentleman such as yourself,' said Mr. Fielding, 'with a brother who moves in such fashionable circles, will doubtless consider himself immune from the rules and regulations that govern the lesser fry here, the boys who may not be so well-off nor so well-connected, yet who in their vulgar way manage to speak a recognizable French and attain a certain scholastic standard.'

James noted that Beau Frog in a rage was incapable of using a short word where a longer one would serve. How Cassie would love to mimick him, the pompous ass! But he did not answer, only looked back with a steady contempt, and then Mr. Fielding, smiling at him, raised one perfumed hand and struck him across the cheek.

James only winced because it was so totally unexpected: he made no sound, and he continued, after that brief, unavoidable flicker, to stare, his face a little white, his body stiff with hatred and rage. He was thinking, I'll get even with you for that, you dandified bastard, if it's the last thing I do, and the words came clearly out of his eyes for all he did not say them, so that Mr. Fielding, suddenly convulsed with an almost maniacal fury, stooped to pick up the rod again.

James was reflecting on this episode, which seemed strange to him, for Mr. Fielding must be perfectly aware that such conduct, if reported, would not improve his position, when he realized that someone had come into the hall.

He was delighted at the thought of any distraction. At least it would not be Mr. Fielding, who would now be sitting with his boys in the Pleasure Gardens. He ran out into the hall, then stopped astonished, to stare.

It was a young woman he had never seen before. She was certainly not a parent, for she was not much older than himself, and for some indefinable reason she did not look like a sister.

She was small, very pretty and extremely young. She was dressed in poor if flamboyant taste, she was not very clean, and her face, which in normal circumstances must have been very pleasing, was smudged with a mixture of tears, grime and paint, so that she looked like a small, incompetent clown.

She gazed at James, almost in panic, then dropped him a curtsey, much to his surprise. When she spoke, it was in a thick cockney accent; her voice was not as pretty as her face. He saw that she was very ill at ease, even frightened: she kept on glancing over her shoulder.

'You one of his boys?' she said.

'I am one of the pupils here,' said James. 'What do you

mean? Whose boys?'

She shot him a sideways look. She really was charmingly pretty, despite the harsh, common voice, but it was a pity that no one had taught her how to paint her face, and there was something about her that went oddly with her obvious youth, a kind of defensive knowledgeability. He noticed too that her gown was cut much too low, displaying youthful, immature breasts, and this embarrassed him, made him avert his eyes.

She did not answer his question. When she spoke again, she was smiling. It was a wide, painful smile. 'You're a handsome kind of fellow, ain't you?' she said. 'Bit big for schooling like.'

Then he understood. He was amazed, a little scared, for nothing like this had yet happened to him, and also bursting with curiosity. He forgot his smarting back and the resentment which had been smouldering inside him. He said, very cautiously, 'Oh, I shall be going to the university soon.' Then, 'But you didn't answer me. When you said was I one of his boys, who were you talking about?'

'Oh, Mr. Fielding,' she said, as if this were obvious. 'Don't you know him?' She came a little closer, with a confidential air. 'He works here, don't he? Mind you, he didn't tell me. Oh, not likely! He don't tell anyone nothing. But I found out. I ain't such a fool as he thinks I am.'

James's eyes opened very wide. He only just stopped himself from whistling. He managed with an effort to banish the excitement from his voice, and said quite casually, 'Oh, him. Yes. I know him.'

'He's out, ain't he?'

'I believe he is. Perhaps I can give him a message for you?' suggested James politely, while behind the words, his mind was seething with all kinds of wild ideas. This was no elderly widow, certainly, but how strange for the handsome and arrogant Beau Frog to involve himself with this little night-walker, and what on earth was she doing here, was she his cast-off, was she perhaps dunning him? None of this was much tribute to the education the good Doctor believed he was giving his boys, but James had always been observant, and certain incidents in his brother's life had not passed him by as completely as Mr. Shelbrooke might have wished. However,

41

he concealed all this beneath a reasonably impassive exterior, only was startled to the extent of flushing when, without answering him, she exclaimed, her voice quite shrill, 'Ain't I seen you somewheres before?'

'No!' cried James, with more vehemence than was polite, then he added quickly, 'I don't think so, ma'am,' for he did not wish to hurt her and despite all the paint and the arch, sideways glances, there was something vulnerable about her that moved him in just such a way as when some scruffy, snivelling little boy came whining to him for help and protection.

He saw that she was studying him as much as he was studying her. She had decided, he noted with relief, that he was too young to interest her professionally, but there was plainly something about his face that intrigued her, and James was young enough and fastidious enough to wriggle a little beneath her reflective gaze.

He said, in a more schoolboyish tone than the one he had previously adopted, 'Of course you've never seen me before. How could you?'

But she only shrugged saying, 'Well, I dunno. I see lots of folks. It don't matter. You're only a baby. But you can tell him something from me, see?'

'With the greatest of pleasure,' said James, recovering himself, and uttering these words with a suppressed melodrama that would have delighted his sister-in-law.

'Tell him it's Jenny,' she said, jabbing a finger at him. 'Jenny. Got that, young cocky?'

'Yes, ma'am,' said James, and something – perhaps it was the odd appellation – made him grin, at which she cried out, 'I have seen you before. I know I have. I never forgets a face.'

This seemed unimportant to him, as well as nonsense. He persisted, 'It's Jenny then. What next, Miss Jenny?'

She hesitated. She looked suddenly very frightened. Whatever it was between her and Mr. Fielding, it was certainly not love, in any sense of the word. She said, her husky voice cracking a little, 'Tell him this, boy. From me like. Tell him this. I am not staying in the Rookeries. Tell him that. I don't want his bloody room. I don't like it.' She straightened herself. Her eyes grew bolder. 'Tell him I've got a protector. There's a gentle-

42

man as'll help me to set myself up, and not in the way his dirty mind'll take it, neither. Tell him there are some real gentlemen in the world, and I'm a respectable girl, and I don't want no trucks with the likes of him.'

She began to move away. There was a glisten of sweat on her forehead. The evening was warm, but it did not seem to James she was sweating on this account.

'Tell him I'm moving from the Rookeries,' she said again. 'And I'm not taking the old lady's house. I don't want it. I tell you.' Her face crumpled up as if she were about to burst into tears. 'Oh, I've had my bellyful, I have. It's all his fault.' She gave a harsh, theatrical laugh that hurt James because there was no amusement in it, only pain. 'Fancy him teaching you! Gawd! I wouldn't have him near any brat of mine, I'd kill it first. I came up here to go into service. You wouldn't believe that, would you, cocky? But I did. You ask him, the son of a bitch.'

As she spoke she was sidling towards the front door, still eyeing him. Suddenly she exclaimed, 'I know who you are. You're his brother.' As she said this she brushed against the parrot's cage, and the bird at once squawked, 'Pray come into the parlour and take a glass of wine.'

She gave a shriek. 'Christ!' she said. Then she looked wildly around and, before James could stop her or even utter a word, had fled from the house, slamming the door behind her.

He called after her. 'Jenny!' he called. 'I say, Jenny!'

But whether or not she heard him, she would not answer. He saw her from the window, running as if for her life; she ran like a girl, kicking her heels out, with a great whirl of petticoats. In a minute she was out of sight.

James drew in a deep breath, and for a while stood there in a daze. He did not understand all of what she had said, especially the remark about his brother, but one thing shone out like a black star: Mr. Fielding was everything he had suspected, there was some very dirty work afoot, and he, James Shelbrooke, had plainly been created to foil the villain and bring him to justice.

'Polly,' he said sternly, pinching a nut from the parrot's cage and popping it into his mouth, 'we'll get even with him

43

yet. He'll be sorry, he'll be sorrier than he ever was in his life.'

He dodged the avenging beak, snatched at another nut and grinned at the parrot, which shifted like a stiff old woman on its perch and squawked again, 'Pray come into my parlour and take a glass of wine.'

'He'll come into my parlour,' said James, 'but he'll get no wine. Not if I can help it.'

Then he sat down again at his desk and, with a grand flourish, drew the exercise book towards him. He did not pause to reflect if he were being wise. He was aglow with battle, he had lost all sense of caution. Francis would have warned him. It had been the same with boxing. 'Think,' Francis had said, 'Think! Don't just shoot your fist out and leave yourself defenceless.' James had refused to think, had shot out his fist, and landed on his back with a bleeding nose, while Francis stood over him, saying, 'I told you. Why don't you listen?'

James was not thinking now.

'Mr. Fielding, sir,' he wrote. 'A young lady named Jenny called on you. She informs you, sir, that she does not require either your house or you, as she is now provided for.'

He thought this sounded very distinguished, and calculated to put Beau Frog into enough of a bait to burst him. Then he went on:

'And I am desirous to inform you, sir, that I am leaving this school. I do not feel you are a suitable person to instruct me, and I shall make this plain to my family.'

Here he did hesitate. An alarming thought had struck him. Suppose Francis insisted on sending him back. James was no coward, but he knew what Mr. Fielding was capable of, and he felt suddenly cold, despite the heat. Then he was furious with himself. After all, if the worst came to the worst, he would just run away. He would join the navy. Or perhaps old Zeph would help him — There were endless possibilities for a boy of spirit, and having committed himself so far, he might as well continue to the bitter end.

'I think,' wrote James in conclusion, 'you are a blackguard and a bully, sir, and I think you are not at all what you pretend to be.'

Then he signed this with his full name, in a grand flourish, kicked the *Aeneid* to the floor, and walked out of the school; he did not dare risk going upstairs for any of his belongings.

He missed Mr. Fielding by five minutes. By the time the gentleman had found his note and absorbed its contents, James was walking rapidly through Cavendish Square.

FOUR

Miss Parkington-Smith was eating her soup in the parlour. This was her regular evening meal; her supper was always a light one, for papa liked to dine at two o'clock, and she chose to keep exactly the same hours.

She sat, very upright, at the table, dimly lit by two tallow candles. Wax candles were well beyond her means. At the beginning, when the money was lost, Polly suggested that she had her supper in her bedroom, which would have been warmer and more comfortable, especially in the winter, but Miss Parkington-Smith's outraged indignation had ensured that she never proposed this again.

'The Captain,' said Miss Parkington-Smith, 'always dined in this room, and he always dressed for dinner. He would never have countenanced any slovenly behaviour. Why, to the end of his days he always had the family silver out, the full array of china, and he drank two kinds of wine with every meal. He always said it was our duty to set an example to the lower classes, and if we ever let our standards drop, we should be inciting revolution of the worst possible kind.'

Polly had heard this a thousand times before, and now scarcely listened when Miss Parkington-Smith held forth in this style. She knew that to the late Captain the world was divided like armies into two camps: in one were decent, honest folk, and in the other a horrid wild mob like the fiends in hell, who were only waiting for the slimmest chance to dash out, shrieking, and cut every throat in sight.

Polly often wondered what he would say if he saw his daughter now, with only the wall of her house between herself and just such fiends as he had envisaged. Perhaps, like her, he would simply ignore the drabs and cut-throats who squawled and bawled and brawled beside them. It really was fortunate that he was not alive; he had always been a violent-tempered man and – though Miss Parkington-Smith must genuinely have forgotten this – tyrannized with the utmost brutality over wife and daughter, and sent his son running after a quarrel that all but had the whole of Tottenham Court Road up in flames.

But young Master Jack – for so Polly still thought of him – was like his father dead and gone, caught by a summer fever that extinguished his breath in a matter of days. He had been the odd man out of the family, a good-humoured, jolly, rather dissolute boy who preferred the gaming-tables to the barracks, who consorted with the people his father despised, and who had nothing in common with either the surly, blustering old man or the two irreproachably genteel females who seemed to regard him as a being from another, not quite nice, world. Polly adored him, as most women did, apart from his own family. But after the quarrel he had never set foot in the house again; he pocketed the proverbial shilling and walked away. He should by rights, according to the Captain, have come to a bad end, but being as he was, he did nothing of the kind, he found himself a rich widow with one son, married her and gave her another, ending up as a country gentleman. But he never forgave his father, and so bitter was the feeling between them that he dropped his own name and took his wife's name of Shelbrooke in its place.

They said that Mr. Francis Shelbrooke was the image of his mother, but that young Master James had something of his father in him.

Polly was trembling with excitement at the thought of to-morrow's tea-party. She looked at her mistress with compassion, as she sat there in the dinner dress that had never been fashionable even twenty years ago, supping the thin soup which was all she could afford, yet still surrounded by the family silver, a decanter with no wine in it, and the Sèvres china plates.

After tomorrow there would be no meat for several days, only fish or eggs and vegetables: Miss Parkington-Smith might revile her brother, but she was determined to make a brave display for his family, and some three days' housekeeping money was going to that end.

Poor, proud old soul, thought Polly, a little wryly, for there was no denying that at times Miss Parkington-Smith was ex-

47

cessively tiresome; no one could term her a dear old lady, with her vinegar tongue, and her biting condemnation of everyone who had youth, looks, wealth or happiness. Perhaps if she had married, it might have been different, thought Polly, removing the soup bowl and placing a small plate of biscuits on the table. But it was quite impossible to imagine Miss Parkington-Smith as a wife, and though numerous young subalterns and ensigns had been invited to the house, they had never expended more than one brief, sideways glance at the thin, prim young woman who never troubled to make herself pleasant, and who seemed from the first moment to disapprove of them.

'Is all the best china washed?' demanded Miss Parkington-Smith: she was nibbling her biscuits like a mouse, for her side teeth had long since vanished and she could only chew with the front ones.

'Yes, ma'am,' said Polly, with some irritation.

'And you have, I trust, procured the wine?'

'That's what I went out for, wasn't it?' cried Polly, then more calmly, 'Yes, ma'am. Mr. Trusler from the "Rose" was at the Tea Gardens, and he sold me a bottle from France. A real bit of the old stuff, he says it is.'

'I hope it is a good vintage,' said Miss Parkington-Smith, finishing the last of the biscuits. 'The captain had such an excellent taste in wine. He always ordered special port from Lisbon, you know. He had it shipped over here.'

'Yes, ma'am,' said Polly resignedly.

'Naturally,' said Miss Parkington-Smith, wiping her fingers fastidiously on the napkin, 'we cannot provide the delicacies to which these young people will be accustomed, but I wish them to see that I still keep a genteel table. We will naturally have the best tablecloth. The one mama embroidered, you know, with the silken roses in the corner, and that fine lace that papa brought back from Ghent.'

She rose as she spoke, a tiny little person, hobbling because of the rheumatics in her joints, yet always holding herself upright. She walked towards the door, supporting herself on the chair-backs, then paused before the Captain's portrait.

As she did so, raising her bespectacled eyes to that fierce and apoplectic countenance, there was a crash from the Rookeries on the other side of the wall, followed by a screeching outburst of abuse.

It was the girls next-door, summarily woken up. There was plenty of this kind of thing in the evenings, but the words that flew in at the half-open window were such that Polly went a little pink, eyeing her mistress in trepidation.

Miss Parkington-Smith, for all the emotion she showed, might not have heard. She continued to survey the Captain, and ran her knotted finger along the bottom of the frame.

'This has not been properly dusted,' she said. She hobbled away to the door. She remarked, 'My brother, of course, behaved so disgracefully that I would never have lowered myself by addressing one word to him, if we had met in the street. But it is not right to lay the blame for his conduct on these young people. I believe I have done my duty in inviting them. I am sure that in the circumstances, they must be a trifle bewildered by such condescension, but yet, it was my duty, I know that.'

Polly, not quite so innocent of the ways of the world as her mistress, suspected that the reaction of Mr. Francis and his beautiful young wife might be quite otherwise, but she merely lifted the plates on to her tray and said, 'Yes, ma'am.'

'And kindly dust that picture,' said Miss Parkington-Smith.

The crashes and screams that half-drowned this sentence were so cataclysmic that even Miss Parkington-Smith's determinedly deaf ear was not proof against them. She was clutching the door handle: now she stood still, her head a little on one side.

There must be a devil of a brawl going on in the Rookeries – Polly found that the hands holding the tray were shaking. It was not rare, God knows, to hear such cries and oaths, but this tended to occur much later on, for at this hour the occupants were usually preparing for their nocturnal business. The little hussies would be decking themselves out, Zephaniah, the good fellow, would be pocketing his pistols, preparing in his amiable way to relieve travellers of their money and jewels, Old Jack would be making his way towards Holborn, and Simon would be limping forth with the faithful mongrel at his heels.

So all-enveloping was the noise that for a moment neither woman stirred. Then Miss Parkington-Smith said in a voice that was less assured than usual, 'Our neighbours are a little noisy, are they not?'

Polly for once did not give her inevitable assent. She simply stood there and, when a thundering knock came on the front door, she gave a gasp, and the tray slipped from her hands, with plates and silver falling to the floor.

Miss Parkington-Smith cried out pettishly, the fear plain to hear, 'Oh, really, Polly, you are too stupid and careless for words. Why, you have broken a plate. I shall deduct it from your salary.'

But Polly still did not answer, though she had not been paid a penny since the Captain died, and then the knocking came again as if whoever it was was fully prepared to batter the door down.

Miss Parkington-Smith said in a sudden voice of authority, 'Oh, what a stupid girl you are. I just do not know why I put up with you. We have visitors. Are you so deaf that you do not hear? We have visitors, I tell you. Answer the door at once.'

'Ma'am!' pleaded Polly. She made no attempt to pick up the tray. She was pleating her apron. Her eyes were showing their whites like those of a frightened horse.

Miss Parkington-Smith banged on the floor with her stick and, as if in mockery, the crashing on the door began again. 'Answer the door!' she commanded. Her voice was shrill. 'Don't let me have to tell you again. Do what I say.'

'Yes, ma'am,' said Polly, almost inaudibly, and came out into the hall.

Crash, crash, crash, went someone's fist on the door, and at this Polly, though her knees were giving beneath her, recovered some of her spirit. She called out, 'There's no need to break the door down, is there? I'm coming.'

She flung open the door. She had no idea who it could be. Perhaps someone was ill next-door. Perhaps it was the watch. She met the eyes of the two men who stood there, and opened her mouth to demand their business, but they shoved past her with a cursory, 'Out of the way, you old bitch. What the hell do you mean by keeping us waiting like this?' – and stamped into the parlour where Miss Parkington-Smith was still standing, holding on now to the Captain's picture, as if her departed father could somehow support her.

They were as rough and disagreeable a couple as either lady had ever seen. Polly at least had seen plenty of the Rookeries in her time, but Miss Parkington-Smith had scarcely set foot outside for the past three years, and certainly nothing in life with papa had prepared her for this.

They were squat fellows, both with tough, surly, brutal faces. One of them had a broken nose, as if he were a prize-fighter, and the other much smaller, appalling teeth which were nothing but rotting, mildewed stumps. Both stank of drink and dirt and sweat, both carried pistols and knives, plain to see in their belts, and the big one held a cudgel in his hand which he thwacked against his thigh.

Polly suddenly remembered Mokasa, and wished to God he were here. Then, noticing the armoury of weapons, she was thankful he was not, for these rogues would have shot down their own mothers, and never had she beheld countenances so devoid of humanity or compassion.

The fellow with the cudgel spoke first, and his voice was as rough as the rest of him, thick with drink and straight from the London gutter.

'You!' he shouted, jabbing his cudgel at Miss Parkington-Smith. 'You old faggot there! Are you the owner of this house?'

Polly sprang forward. 'Don't you dare speak to my mistress like that,' she began, her voice shrill with outrage, but he only turned his ugly face upon her, and gave her a push that all but sent her flat on her back.

'Shut your mouth, you old cow,' he said, then again to Miss Parkington-Smith, 'Well, old girl, and what's the matter with you? Can't you speak? I asked you a question, didn't I? You'd best answer, or it'll be the worse for you.'

The smaller rogue, with the rotting teeth, grinned widely at this, revealing enough to turn the stomach, and began to giggle a little, stepping forward, grabbing in the air with his hands, but his companion caught at his arm, restraining him.

Polly had a deep if unwilling affection for Miss Parkington-Smith, whom she regarded as a difficult child, and for a long time now had put up with her silliness, her tempers, her auto-

51

cratic ways and her incessant fault-findings. But now, for the first time, she was filled with a genuine admiration.

Miss Parkington-Smith was not the Captain's daughter for nothing. The Captain, God rest his soul, had not been much of a man; he had blustered and drunk and sworn, and his military exploits existed mostly in his daughter's mind, but now this frail old lady, so crippled with rheumatism that she could scarcely move, so tiny that she did not come up to the ruffian's shoulder, took papa's mantle upon her, and surveyed her opponent with a coolness that took Polly's breath away.

She said in a clipped voice, 'I am indeed the owner of this house,' and her demeanour was entirely composed, only her colour had faded, and the rouge she diligently applied every morning, stood out harshly on her cheeks.

He interrupted her. 'Oh, no you ain't. You thinks you are, don't you? But you're not, not by a long chalk, and I'm here to give you your notice to quit. By the day after tomorrow. Got that, old girl? Quit. That's the word. Quit.'

The smaller fellow began his giggle again, surveying Miss Parkington-Smith with such a wild leer that Polly perceived he must be gone in the wits: the eyes sparkled in a glassy way that held the brightness of lunacy.

Miss Parkington-Smith said, 'I do not understand you, fellow —'

'Fellow she calls me!' He gave a brief bellow of laughter. 'Fellow! Damn your blood, ma'am, you speaks to me with proper respect or else —'

But she went on, and Polly dared not interrupt; indeed, her tongue seemed stuck somewhere in her throat and she was almost choked with fear.

Miss Parkington-Smith said, 'This is my house. It belonged to my father, and —'

He roared at her, 'Oh — your father!' and at this she fell silent, her eyes staring, for never in her life had anyone used such an expression to her. She did not of course fully understand it, but the violence of the phrase and the spittle which spattered against her cheek, compelled her to see that this was something against which she was powerless.

The little fellow was giggling meanwhile, and the meaningless idiocy of that sound made Polly almost faint, for it chilled the blood. But she could not endure that her mistress should be so insulted, and she managed to stumble up so that she could put a protecting arm round her.

Miss Parkington-Smith shook the arm off. 'Really, Polly,' she snapped, 'you forget yourself. You know I do not permit anyone to handle me in such a fashion.' And still upright, though the hand clutching the picture frame was white at the knuckles, she looked disdainfully at the bully confronting her, and said, 'My father was a very gallant gentleman who died in defence of his country. Kindly do not insult his memory.'

And this was such a colossal lie that something of Polly's terror was lost in even greater admiration: the Captain had died long after the Treaty of Utrecht, and he had died of an apoplexy after too much food and wine. But Miss Parkington-Smith uttered these words with a complete conviction, and for the first time the bully was sufficiently taken aback to gape, while the giggling one stopped his dreadful laughter, and peered at her, screwing up his eyes as if he had never seen anything like this in his life.

But the rogue soon recovered himself, and began to bellow, hurling the words at her, his face and voice thick with violence.

'Lookee here, ma'am,' he began, 'this house ain't yours, not by a long chalk. It's been bought up, see, by a gentleman, and the gentleman wants you out instanter so that he can let it to his special customers.' He emitted a sudden hoarse laugh, and the little one at once started his giggling again. 'Them customers of his,' he said, 'ain't your sort, old girl, you wouldn't do with them here at all, you're too old, you're nearly in your grave anyways, you'd make any man puke to look at you. You got to get out, do you hear? – and damn my soul, if you don't, I'll pick you up by your ugly, scrawny old neck and throw you out. See? Out! That's what I said. Out!'

Miss Parkington-Smith had begun to tremble. She was old after all, she had spent her life avoiding life, and this sudden, violent manifestation of everything she had taught herself to ignore, was enough to break her into small pieces. She backed a little, still holding on. She spoke, her voice not quite so firm.

'I think you must be drunk,' she said. 'This is quite outrageous. But you'll not get away with this, my man. I have in-fluential relatives. I shall consult my lawyers tomorrow.'

'You got two days to quit. By the day after tomorrow you'll be out in the street,' he said. Then, 'Well? Going quiet, dear? You will, if you know what's good for you.'

'I am not,' said Miss Parkington-Smith, 'going at all. You cannot force me to move.' Then her voice cracked. 'This is my home. I've lived here all my life. It was my father's house, I tell you. He bought it.' Her voice was soaring now, her face puckered like a child's. 'It's mine by law. It's mine, I tell you. What right have you to come here, a disgusting creature like you, and tell me – me —'

'So I'm disgusting now, am I?' he said. 'I'm not good enough for the likes of you. I'm just a poor ignorant man, ain't I?' And he turned to his companion, nudging him so that the little fellow giggled fit to burst. 'I see as you're one of them as has to learn the hard way,' he said, 'I see as you'll have to be shown, ma'am. We'll show her, shall we? Shall we, you old dog, you old devil, you?'

The giggling one spluttered, 'Oh yes, yes, we'll show her, won't we just!'

'Dear God!' whispered Polly, and stared about with horri-fied eyes, but there was no one to help, and even Miss Parkington-Smith was dumb, brought face to face with some-thing before which her gentility and good breeding were helpless.

The two women were still for a second, then Polly opened her mouth to scream for help, only the bully roared at her, 'God damn you, if you squawl, I'll shoot you through the head,' and waved his pistol at her, while the little one shoved his giggling face close to hers so that the reek of him nearly made her vomit.

The bully moved back, raised his cudgel and brought it down against the cabinet, smashing the Sèvres china to pieces. Three times he did this, until there was not one whole piece remaining, then he turned his attention to the mirror, splinter-ing the glass across. He ground the fragments into the carpet with his heel, ripping it as he did so, then picked up a Chippendale chair and hurled it through the window. The

Hogarth print followed next, the clock, the peacock's feathers and the shell, then the little fellow wrenched the curtains down, stuffing the fragments through the broken window so that they fell into the mud outside.

Polly was sobbing, fit to break her heart, but Miss Parkington-Smith did not speak one word, only stood there face chalk-white, eyes dilated, as the two ruffians smashed everything within their reach. Only when the stick was upraised by the Captain's picture did she give a hollow scream.

'Don't touch that!' Then, frantically, 'Oh, don't, don't —!'

He swayed back on his heels. He was grinning from ear to ear, and so was the other, displaying all the monstrous remnants of teeth. He mimicked her, aping her prim voice. 'Oh don't, oh don't! But we do, we do, by Christ, ma'am, begging your fine ladyship's pardon, we do and we will, won't we, we will and all.'

And across the Captain's red and stupid face the cudgel swept, smashing the glass, and then the fellow, with the air of one drawing a chicken, put out his great fist and deliberately, chuckling all the while, his eyes on Miss Parkington-Smith's aghast face, clawed at the painting, screwing it out of the frame. Then slowly and deliberately, he proceeded to tear it across, so that the poor Captain's nose fell here, his chin there, one eye out of the window, another ground into the carpet, then as a final insult a portion was crammed into the charnel-house mouth, to be chewed and spat into the fireplace.

Polly could not speak. The tears were raining down her cheeks. The impotent rage and hate within her was so intense that she was sick and giddy with it.

Miss Parkington-Smith watched this dismemberment of her august parent as a dog will watch its master eating: her head swivelled first right, then left, up, then down, following each parental portion in turn as it was strewn about the room.

When it was all done, when there was nothing left of the Captain but a few shreds of oiled paper, the villain turned a beaming face upon her, made her a mocking bow, saying, 'That's for your ladyship's old pa. Next time it will be you, ma'am. Limb from limb. That's what we'll do to you, old girl, won't we?'

And the idiot companion, giggling like an hysterical girl, rubbed his hands together, squealing, 'Oh, won't we just, won't we just!'

Then Miss Parkington-Smith gave a great cry that was almost a howl, and roared out with a force that did not seem possible in one so frail and old, 'You wicked and abominable creature! Oh, if I had a pistol in my hand, I swear I'd shoot you down.'

And she turned passionate, frantic eyes on papa's duelling pistols which had been knocked to the floor with everything else, as if her poor, crippled fingers could have pulled the trigger, as if she had even had the strength to stoop down to pick the weapon up.

'Oh, so it's threats now, is it?' growled the ruffian. 'You're threatening me, are you, ma'am? I'll have to tell my employer that, won't I? He won't be pleased, I can tell you, he won't like an honest man like me being threatened in pursuit of his proper business, as you might say —'

'You disgust me,' said Miss Parkington-Smith. 'You stink.'

For some reason this went home, and nothing could have been more apt, for the pair of them smelt of the sewer, as if they had never washed in their lives. The bully reached back his fist and, through Polly's shrieks, gave Miss Parkington-Smith a great shove, his hand flat against her chest.

She went down like a ninepin, landing in a pile of scattered cushions, and at once Polly recovered the use of her limbs, rushed to her side and knelt there, sobbing wildly, calling out as she might have done fifty years ago, 'Oh, Miss Arabella, Miss Arabella, my little love, my darling, what have they done to you?'

The two ruffians fell silent, and Polly shrieked at them, 'Murderers! You've killed her. She's dead! Oh, you'll swing for this, if there's any justice left, you'll hang at Tyburn.'

Miss Parkington-Smith lay there, her eyes closed, her face dead white: she might well have been a corpse.

The men looked at her, then at each other, then the bully who seemed to be in charge, swore obscenely and ran from the room, lugging the other after him.

Polly could hear them battering and smashing as they went.

They were obviously going through her kitchen like Attila and his hordes. There would be nothing left of the house, and her mistress was dead. She forgot how impossible Miss Parkington-Smith had always been, forgot that she had not been paid for years, yet was treated like any serving slut. She stumbled to her feet. She moved towards the door so clumsily that it was as if her mistress's rheumatics had come upon her. She stood staring out and, when the two men crashed past her, out through the hall and slammed the door, still stood, her lips working, her hands clenching and unclenching as if she had the villains within reach of her nails.

She said aloud, 'I swear I'll kill them.'

Miss Parkington-Smith's voice came out, faint and querulous, yet bristling with disapproval, 'Really, Polly,' it said, 'I do believe you've taken leave of your senses. Am I simply to be left lying here?'

Polly swung round and, tripping and stumbling over the debris, caught her mistress in her sturdy arms, lifting her as if she were a child, sobbing over her, embracing her.

Miss Parkington-Smith whispered in petulant protest, 'Oh, don't do that — Upon my word, I don't know what's come over you. Put me down at once.'

Polly meekly sat her down in the only chair that still stood on its four legs, and Miss Parkington-Smith said, 'Surely you can see that there is a great deal of work to be done. You cannot wish for my nephew and his wife to find us in such a pickle.'

Then Polly's mouth fell open, so wide that it was as if her jaw had dropped for good, and at this Miss Parkington-Smith cried in a feeble whimper, 'Oh, how stupid you are. Really, it is more than anyone can be expected to endure. Have you forgot, you silly girl? Mr. Francis and his wife are coming to see us tomorrow.'

'But ma'am —!' Polly, speechless, could only flap her hands, while her eyes swivelled frantically around, seeing nothing but ruin and destruction, then fixed themselves again upon her mistress who, though too weak to raise herself, managed to glower at her in pursed disapproval.

'Certainly they are coming. Do you imagine I would go back

on an invitation? Oh, do get a move on, girl,' said Miss Parkington-Smith.

*

Polly managed to persuade her mistress to go up to bed, for the ruffians had concentrated on the ground floor, and the top was still untouched. There she brought her a hot posset. The fall, mercifully, had been broken by a couple of hurled-down cushions, but nevertheless it might well have killed a woman of lesser spirit, especially one of sixty-five. It was amazing to Polly that Miss Parkington-Smith, apart from a few bruises, seemed relatively unhurt: the brittle old bones had not snapped, and her heart seemed strong and steady as ever.

However, she was completely exhausted, and presently her eyes began to close, whereupon Polly, thinking the two villains would not return tonight, crept down the stairs and out into the Rookeries' courtyard.

When she saw Zephaniah, she gave a great cry of relief and ran up to him.

He turned a startled face upon her. She had no illusions about him, she did not think of him as a good fellow, but his countenance was not lacking in either intelligence or humour, and she did not believe he would beat up an old woman, nor would he wantonly destroy all her belongings.

But it was plain that he was impatient to be rid of her and, though he spoke good-humouredly enough, there was an edge to his voice. He would doubtless be involved in some ploy of his own; he was, like the cat, a creature of the night, and in the dark he was wild and fierce as he would not appear in the light of day.

But she was too desperate to concern herself with any of this. She stammered out her story quite hysterically, and it was such a tale that it received at last his full attention, and he stood stock still until she had done.

She concluded, 'They broke her goods to pieces before her face. They struck her. They knocked her down.'

Zephaniah did not answer for a moment. The one lantern hanging in the main entrance of the Rookeries shone its dusty light full upon his face. It was a powerful face with a great square jaw. Behind a pistol it must look more than formidable. If Zephaniah bade one stand and deliver, one would be brave indeed to refuse.

Behind and around him, a sombre backcloth, stretched the Rookeries. In the daytime they were filthy and squalid, but in the dark they assumed a certain dreadful majesty. They were grim and desolate as hell, the wan light reflected in the streams of dirty water that glistened on the pitted flags, with the black, hollow emptiness of unlit, gaping windows behind, and the fortress of the tall, steep walls. There was silence now, for the inmates, like Zephaniah himself, were night creatures, they were away. Only behind one of the windows a woman was crying, and the relentless, heavy, despairing sobbing with its utter lack of hope, drove a shudder through Polly so that for a brief second she felt she could bear it no longer, she must run away from this big city where people were of less value than the refuse that floated down the River Fleet.

Then she remembered Miss Parkington-Smith lying asleep, with her home in ruins about her, and she shifted her shoulders and spoke in a great, strapping voice, her country accent very pronounced.

'What,' she said, 'are you going to do about it?'

'Ma'am,' returned Zephaniah, 'Nothing. Nothing at all.'

'What do you mean? You should be ashamed of yourself! A poor, helpless old lady, so crippled she can scarce move —'

'Ma'am,' said Zephaniah again, 'do you imagine I don't know? Get your old lady away. Didn't I tell you? But you wouldn't listen. Well, I'm telling you again. Tell this nephew of hers to give her lodging in his fine house. Tell him to buy her a country cottage. She can't stay here. She's not got a chance in hell, Mistress Polly, not a dog's chance in hell, not a Tyburn gallows chance in hell. It's not as if it was just these two fellows —'

'They half-killed her!'

'Ach!' He turned and spat on the cobbles. 'Them! They're nothing, my lass. They're the kind I eat for breakfast. They're a couple of hired bullies. They'll end up dancing the Paddington frisk, and it won't be long, either. If it was just those two bloody bastards, why, I'd give 'em a pill for you, ma'am, I'd

59

blow their guts out easy as kiss your hand, and stow their corpses in the Marylebone Basin. But it's not just them, ma'am. If they're put out of the way, there's more in their place, and more and more, like bluebottles that feed on rotting flesh. Oh, you don't need to worry about them, ma'am. It's the fellow that employs 'em.'

'And who is he?' demanded Polly.

Zephaniah looked at her, then gave her his great, honest, beaming smile, so that she knew he was going to lie. 'Oh, I don't know, Mistress Polly. How should I know? It'll be some fine gentleman who don't wish to soil his pretty hands and gets rogues to do his dirty work for him. It's done all the time, ma'am. It's the way of the world, as the saying goes. The world is full of fine gentlemen who don't give a damn, they want their gold and they want their whores and they want their pleasures, so they tread folks for what they can get out of them, as them Frenchies tread grapes for wine – and they squeeze all the blood out of them, they throw the skins away, and they're as happy as the day is long. They say,' went on Zephaniah earnestly, for he was a great one for talking and always enjoyed the sound of his own music, 'they say the wicked don't flourish. If you believe that, ma'am, you'll believe anything. The wicked do flourish. It's poor honest folks like you and me, Miss Polly, who don't have a bloody chance, we're just kicked around, we get all the kicks and none of the pence, none at all.'

Polly looked into that sturdy face, with its charming grin. She did not take him up on this curious representation of himself. She only said grimly, 'There's one gentleman who's not going to flourish, not if I have any say in it.'

'But you haven't any say,' returned Zephaniah. 'Don't you know what he's after, this fine gentleman? He'll take possession of that house – oh, yes, he will, Miss Polly, that he will, don't delude yourself, my lass – and he'll fill it up with his doxies and send 'em out to work for him. That's what he'll do. He don't want an old lady like Miss Parkington-Smith. She's no use to him. She can't earn money for him. So —'

'Do you mean —' began Polly, outraged yet excited: this kind of thing was well beyond her range.

'Of course I mean it, you old fool.' Zephaniah spoke with

sudden roughness. 'He's a pimp and a ponce, your fine gentle-man, and he wants room for his whores, because they're useful to him, because they pay for his silk shirts and fine wine and brood mares. He wants to turn your pretty house into a bawdy-house, that's what he wants, and it's time you listened to sense, because I'm a busy man, and you're wasting my valuable time.'

Polly absorbed this in a kind of dazed bewilderment: the thought uppermost in her mind was that it would be quite im-possible to explain this to Miss Parkington-Smith.

She said at last, rather faintly, 'But she won't go.'

'She will,' said Zephaniah. He was no longer smiling. 'This is only the beginning, ma'am. She'll go. If she don't, they'll carry her out feet first. You don't know this gentleman.'

'Do you?' asked Polly.

He beamed again. 'Why, no. I tell you, I don't mix with the likes of him, except on business.'

'Do you mean,' said Polly steadily, 'that you'll let a poor old lady be knocked down so that it's a wonder she's still kept her wits, much less being alive, you'll let her be bullied and savaged by a couple of ruffians who should have had their throats cut the day they were born? Oh, I'm disappointed in you, Zephaniah, I really am. I thought you were my friend.'

'Did you now!' Then he suddenly snarled at her, all pre-tence of joviality gone. 'I got better things to do with my time. I've no mind to be scragged yet, Mistress Polly. Oh, I'm sorry about the old girl, I'll help you get her out if you want – but run my head into the noose I will not do, not if she was as beautiful as a queen. Not,' he added after a pause, 'if she was as pretty a young thing as this creature here.'

Polly, so angry with him she could hardly speak, followed his gaze.

A young girl was walking up the flags. Her head was bowed, and the light was too dim to make out her features, but her figure was charming, the line of neck and shoulder most grace-ful, and even in that graveyard light, her youth flamed about her. She did not look round at them. Polly had the impression she was weeping. She vanished into the buildings.

Zephaniah looked after her for a long time. There was a strange expression on his face. 'That's Jenny Trantum,' he said. 'That's a real pretty lass. That's one of the prettiest lasses I've ever seen, and good-hearted too. She's one of the new ones, God help her. She won't stay like that long. He picks 'em up, ma'am, as I picks up rings and watches. He meets 'em dewy-fresh from the country. It might have been you, Mistress Polly, ten years ago.'

Polly ignored this shameless flattery. She continued to stare at him.

He went on idly, as if it did not matter; only his flickering lashes betrayed some strong emotion. 'Country girls, that's what they are,' he said, running one of his ribbons through the filed teeth. 'They come up to see the streets as is paved with gold. They come up to find a job. Or a husband maybe. And – I don't know this, mark you, ma'am, I just suspicion it – I think a handsome gentleman meets 'em at the coaching inn. "Such a sweet girl," he'll say to them, or something of the kind, "I've the very job for a dear little thing like you." And he takes them off in his carriage, and he puts 'em in a nice room, all warm and cosy, only – only there's a couple of gentlemen seem to be thrown in with the room like – I don't know. It's not my trade. But I think they never go back to the country. I think they don't take no job neither. Only they need a room, and Paradise Row's a fine place, being near the town and nice and quiet, with no one to interfere.'

Polly said in a quivering voice, 'This is a terrible thing you're telling me. This – this gentleman don't deserve to live. I didn't know there was such wicked folk in the world, I didn't indeed.'

'Ah there's a deal of stuff we none of us know,' said Zephaniah. He looked over his shoulder. 'She's very young. She'll just have started.'

'Oh, never mind her!' cried Polly savagely. 'I'm not concerned with a slut like that. I'm concerned with my old lady. But you wouldn't care —'

'No,' said Zephaniah. 'I learned not to care a long time ago.'

And then he was gone, and Polly stood there alone, an old woman, defenceless, weak, with no spirit left in her, and to her the darkness of the Rookeries was now a tangible evil. There was silence now. The sobbing had stopped. The only sound was a steady drip-drip-drip from some leaking roof. It seemed to Polly like blood.

Then she stiffened her shoulders. The old lady lay asleep at home, and her house was wrecked, but she was stubborn as the devil, was Miss Arabella, always had been ever since a girl — no fine gentleman would shift her, and there was only old Polly, silly old Polly from the country, who could scarce write her name, to help her. This was no time for weakening. Zephaniah said he had learned not to care. But Polly had always cared, and there was a stubborn streak in her too. Maybe in the end the fine gentleman would have his wicked way. But not if Polly could help it. Oh, not if Polly could help it.

And tomorrow, Mr., Mrs. and Master Shelbrooke were coming to tea.

FIVE

By the time James arrived at Hanover Square, he was very tired and more than a little scared. The note which he had written Mr. Fielding, which had at the time seemed so exquisitely humorous and defiant, now assumed different proportions. No man, not even the Doctor himself, who was by nature tolerant and easy-going, could swallow such impertinence, and Mr. Fielding, who was not easy-going and who had detested his pupil from the start, was going to react like a naval gun.

James, walking down Little Holles Street, and with only a couple of hundred yards between himself and home, began to lag more and more, dragging his feet as if he were a little boy again and not a young man of fifteen summers whom naughty ladies made eyes at.

It was Francis who worried him, more than Mr. Fielding. There was, after all, ten years between them – 'You were an after-thought,' Francis said once, when he had lost his temper – but there had always been a great deal of sympathy as well. Only since his marriage, his elder brother had changed, becoming shorter in temper and in patience, more addicted to the bottle and a great deal less understanding with James.

He used not to be like that, thought James, gazing ahead at Hanover Square in the moonlight. Around him were the sounds of laughter and voices. Midnight was young for these parts: Hanover Square was the centre of the *ton*, and the *ton* never went to bed before dawn. It was said that Lady Mary Wortley Montague organized a private society which met in this Square: each gentleman came masked and brought with him one lady, either his mistress, another man's wife or perhaps a woman of the town, all masked. They were on oath not to divulge names, and continued masked till the very end.

James was still young and puritanic enough to find this silly and distasteful. In any case Lady Mary was one of those bluestocking women, which really was a contradiction in terms.

Cassandra now – Cassandra was not like that. Cassandra was a good sport. Oh, she had plenty of brains, and wit too, behind those enormous green eyes with the lashes that looked so false and were not false at all – but there was no blue-stocking nonsense about Cassie.

Dear Cassie.

But Francis —

Since papa had died, his amiable papa who, towards the end of his life had become so much the country gentleman, mama had stayed down in Buckinghamshire, and it was rumoured that she was about to marry for the third time. She was never the kind to remain a widow for long, even at her vast age of forty-three, and talk filtered through to the Shelbrookes in London of a retired General who was already making his intentions plain. James liked his mother, but wished occasionally she were more the traditional parent: somehow he felt it would be more decent for her to be sitting at home in her widow's weeds, instead of riding to hounds and dancing the dawn in, all of which must be most dangerous to a woman of her advanced years. But she had never troubled herself unduly about her sons: in a scrape she was wonderful, but for ordinary living she never seemed to be there: at times she swore and laughed and told stories like a man, all of which upset James's ideas of the conventions. He had, therefore, turned to Francis, but Francis now had grown moodier and moodier. Indeed, he might be described as cursedly bad-tempered, spending all his time in the Club, drinking too much wine, creating scandals and quarrelling incessantly with his handsome young wife.

They tried not to quarrel when James was there, but he was too perceptive not to see what was happening.

It's absurd, he muttered to himself. He was in Hanover Square now. He could see the Shelbrooke house plainly. The lights were still on. And as he stood gazing, trying to summon up his courage, a voice snapped down on his apprehensive soliloquy.

'What the devil are you doing here?' the voice demanded in annoyance and James, blinking, raised his head to meet his brother's angry eyes.

His immediate reaction was: He's foxed. And his heart sank,

65

for Francis with the wine in him was not a reasonable man.

He continued to stare, without speaking. Mr. Shelbrooke wore the air of one who was as elevated as he was dipped. There was ames-ace written across every feature. The eyes — his mother's eyes — were black with temper, the brows meeting, mouth set in a scowl. His wig was slightly awry, and there was a wine-stain on his cravat.

'Well?' said Mr. Shelbrooke. He was only a few yards from home, but he was plainly set on having this out here and now. His voice was raised sufficiently to carry to Piccadilly. A sedan chair passing him did not make him so much as shift his glance: they might have been alone in the world.

James said, very meekly, 'I've run away.'

'What do you mean, you've run away?'

'I've run away from school,' said James. He tried, rather unsuccessfully, to look like some persecuted apprentice who had escaped his master's cruelty. He was a handsome boy and large for his age: there was nothing persecuted in his appearance at all, and the absurdity of his own remarks suddenly struck him so that, what with the strain of it all and his over-excitement and state of apprehension, he burst into a loud laugh.

Mr. Shelbrooke did not laugh. He said, 'Well, you can run back again.' He added, 'You're too old for this kind of behaviour.'

James remembered quite clearly that Francis had once been rusticated from Oxford, for a whole term. He had never been told the whole story, but he had gathered that it was something to do with the local innkeeper's daughter. Mama, he remembered, had laughed, and papa had grown very stern. He opened his mouth to point this out then, thinking better of it, shut his lips tightly again.

'Don't stand there gaping like a frog,' said his brother. 'Go back to school immediately. I will not tolerate this behaviour. You've run away, indeed! I've never heard such gammon. Why, may I inquire, have you run away?'

'They beat me,' said James.

'I bet you deserved it,' said Mr. Shelbrooke. 'I hope they beat you again. They can depend on my heartiest approval.'

At this point James lost his temper. He did not know,

naturally, how this heightened the elusive family resemblance between them, but a passer-by noted the two dark, handsome faces, both ablaze with anger; they even stood in the same way, legs astride, and made the same gesticulations, long-fingered hands outstretched.

He was a respectable city merchant, and he perceived at once that these were fighting cocks of quality. And indeed, he thought, as he went home to his cosy little wife and well-behaved children, they were squaring up to each other like a couple of spurred Black-reds in an organized main. He shook his head, then strode on quickly, forgetting about them.

James shot out his fist, and his brother caught the blow on his forearm. He did not offer to return it. He only said, 'Well now!' and stared, eyes very wide.

James cried out fiercely, 'Oh, of course it would have your heartiest approval, I know that. If I were flogged to death, you'd shrug your shoulders and open another bottle of wine. It wouldn't matter to you. Why should it? Only I'm not a coward – I'm not, even if you think I am, and this fellow Fielding is a coward and a bully, and now he's driven me too far and I've let him see I know it, and if he gets hold of me, he'll probably kill me.' He paused, mainly for breath. Then he said in a quieter voice, 'Would you mind that, Francis?'

'It would cause something of a scandal,' returned Mr. Shelbrooke gravely. He was recovering his own temper; moreover, he was slightly ashamed of himself. He was, if he had chosen to admit it, extremely fond of his young half-brother, and he was wondering who Mr. Fielding was, for to the best of his knowledge he had never seen him, all his interviews having been conducted with Dr. Fountaine. Then he remembered that Cassie had mentioned him, and in no complimentary fashion. He hesitated, while James said nothing more, being by this time both exhausted and depressed: he supposed there was no hope for it, he would be sent back to school.

Mr. Shelbrooke said more amiably, 'Well, one thing is certain, sir, you cannot return tonight. Nor should we stand here, blowing our differences to the four winds. Come home, for God's sake. Cassie will fuss you and condole with you, then you can go to bed and we'll talk this over more reasonably in the morning.'

They started to walk on. James said, rather wretchedly, 'It's not only me. There was a little boy. He was new. Oh, he was mammy's pet, he had long, curly hair, he was always crying. But I don't think,' said James, staring up into Francis's profile, 'that makes so much difference. Old Beau Frog – Mr. Fielding, that is, that's what we call him – treated him in such a way that he became ill. He couldn't stay on at school. They had to come and take him away. We never saw him again. They say he's quite gone in the wits, he'll never be well again.'

Mr. Shelbrooke said nothing to this. They were at the house now. He searched his pocket for his keys.

'I think,' said James, 'it's not only that he likes beating us. He does worse things than that, I'm sure. I believe myself it's women —'

'Good God!' said his brother faintly, as he inserted the key in the lock.

'And I don't think it's *good* women either.'

'What the devil are you talking about?' demanded Mr. Shelbrooke, so astounded that he held on to the key without turning it round.

'In fact, I know it's not good women. I met one of them. Tonight. She said she came up here to go into service. She called him the son of a bitch.'

Mr. Shelbrooke said, after a pause, 'Do you mind not shouting that phrase round the whole Square?'

'You use it. I've heard you.'

'Don't be so damned insolent,' retorted Mr. Shelbrooke, falling into his parental *non sequitur* as easily as if he had been a father for years; this must have struck him, for then he laughed, saying, 'I see you are receiving an unusual kind of education. Perhaps we'll have to reconsider the matter after all,' and opened the door to step inside.

Cassandra called out to him from the drawing-room, 'Is that you, Francis?' Then, before he could answer, she came to the door. She did not at once see James who stood in the shadow. She was still in her wrapper, and her red hair was wilder than ever as if she had run her hands through it many times. It is a little unreasonable, reflected Mr. Shelbrooke, as he eyed her with the soft candlelight behind her – she should look like a slut, she should look like some drab from the streets, and she does not, though God knows why, she still looks infinitely more beautiful and infinitely more elegant than all the fashionable ladies strung together, with hours of grooming behind them.

Cassandra said in her rich, theatrical voice, her virago voice, her Regan-and-Goneril voice, 'And where have you been, Francis? With Jenny, I presume —'

James, who had not expected this, jumped, and in the movement Cassandra saw him. At once her whole manner changed, her voice sank softly down the scale. 'Oh, James,' she said, and ran towards him, holding out her hands.

James could not help but note the difference in the reception accorded to him and to his brother. He was too sleepy and too innocent to realize that he was being made use of, but somehow this offended his sense of fitness, he did not like it, and he said stiffly, 'I'm sorry, Cassie. I've run away from school.'

'Oh, you poor, poor boy!' cried Cassie, and then of course he forgot his resentment and could only adore her: he had been longing for sympathy, and this soft voice, the tears glistening in her eyes, the tenderness of her whole demeanour, quite overcame him.

Mr. Shelbrooke, during this interlude, did not utter a word: he looked from one to the other, his expression ugly.

Cassie noticed this, and at once the colour flared into her cheeks. She said in a quieter voice. 'We'll go into the drawing-room. We'll open a bottle of wine. How lovely that will be —' Her voice trailed off, then came out in a snap. 'Oh, don't be so stuffy, Francis. Do you expect us to stay standing here?'

'I was not sure,' said Mr. Shelbrooke, falling as was his wont into a lamentable sarcasm, 'if I was invited into my own house.' He added – he was after all very tired and more than a little drunk – 'After my rendezvous with Jenny.'

His wife fell silent, and suddenly James could no longer endure the pair of them: this hostility frightened him. He muttered, 'If you'll excuse me, Cassie, I'm so very tired – I think I would like to go to bed.'

For it seemed to him that they must hate each other to speak in such a way; this tore at his loyalties, for in his heart he was fond of both of them. He was thankful when his brother said calmly, 'Yes. You'd best sleep. And tomorrow we'll decide what we're going to do with you.'

'I'll bring you some hot milk,' cried Cassandra in a flurry, but Mr. Shelbrooke interrupted her, and with such authority that she dared not argue further, only bit her finger and glowered at him dramatically from beneath the fringe of her lashes.

'No,' he said. 'James, my love, is no longer a baby. Leave him be. From all accounts he has had quite a day of it.'

And he made a gesture of dismissal that was amiable but undeniable, so that James made a slow, drowsy progress upstairs, almost too exhausted to wonder what tomorrow held in store for him.

Casandra called after him, 'You're coming with us to your Aunt Arabella tomorrow. Don't forget now.'

He did not answer. He flung off his clothes, leaving them where they fell, and climbed into bed. The sheets were soft, cool and fresh, unlike the coarse things at school. He felt sick at the heart. But in a moment he was asleep, so heavily that he did not even dream, and as he lay there, looking young and lost, his brother downstairs was carefully shutting the drawing-room door.

'I gather,' he said, very carefully, 'that we are now in our fashionable way going to quarrel.'

'No,' said Cassandra. 'No.'

'No?' There was an astonished derision in his voice.

'Oh, why should we?' She stooped down to give Cheri a perfunctory pat. 'There's no point in it any longer. I don't know why it should be like this. I suppose it's my fault. Dear God!' cried Cassandra, her sense of drama overcoming her as usual, though heaven knows, she meant every word of it. 'What has happened to us? Tell me that, Francis. What has happened?'

'Exit Lavinia ravished, with both hands cut off, pursued by a bear,' said Mr. Shelbrooke and, at this, Cassandra, infuriated beyond all control, seized the nearest thing to hand, and flung it at his head.

It happened to be a group of Meissen figurines. It missed him by several inches. It broke to pieces, and Cheri, outraged, raised himself from the rug he was snoozing on, and retreated to the far corner of the room, where he lay down again, tucking his head into his paws as if the whole thing were too much for him.

'Mama gave us that,' said Mr. Shelbrooke. He surveyed the fragments for a while, touching them with his toe. Then, without raising his voice, he said, 'I think it is time I told you about Jenny.'

'Ah God!' cried Cassandra, raising her hands high. 'Do I now have to listen while you speak of your mistress?'

'No,' said Mr. Shelbrooke, 'you do not. You simply have to listen to what I propose to say.'

She said sulkily, 'I'm tired.'

'So am I.'

'I want to go to bed.'

'So you shall. In five minutes.'

Cassandra made the mouthing faces that were her speciality in moments of rage or emotion, then sank down on the footstool, her hands hanging at her side.

'Jenny,' said Mr. Shelbrooke, speaking in a level voice without histrionics, 'was sixteen when I first met her. I suppose she is now just over seventeen. She came up to the big city to find a job and, when she got off the coach, a kindly gentleman was waiting for her, to conduct her to a lady who would help her find employment.'

He paused. Cassandra said nothing.

'The lady lived in Covent Garden. She got Jenny her employment. You will understand what I mean. Such employment tends to be permanent. Oh, she was the silliest of girls, there was never much wit in her, she knew nothing of London life. All she had was a pretty body, and that would not have lasted long. When I came across her, it was in the small hours of the morning. I was, I believe, foxed. I was strolling home. I saw her just as she was about to throw herself in the river. I hauled her back. I told her off. And then,' said Mr. Shelbrooke, 'I took her home.'

He waited again, but Cassandra still was silent, her face hidden by the red hair.

'I suppose that's all,' he said. His voice had roughened; he half-turned his back on her. 'You'll not believe it, naturally, but she was never my mistress, though all the world believes it to be so. But then our world, no more than yourself, cannot conceive of a man sheltering a young and foolish girl without exacting payment of her. There was quite a scandal, of course, and one day, while I was out, a so-called friend of mine called upon her and explained how impossible the situation was for me. And Jenny ran away. You see, she was never quite devoid of heart. But by the grace of God I met her again. I scarce recognized her. She even has the London accent. But she's going home. I shall pay her fare. That's all. Once she has settled her affairs, she will, I trust, leave the city and never come back. Only this gentleman – I wish I knew who he was. He'll not let her go, if he can help it, and she won't tell me his name, she's too frightened. But I'm going to do my damndest to find out.' Then he said, almost in astonishment, 'You are very innocent, Cassandra. I swear in some ways you're as innocent as my aunt. All this is part of a trade, you know. There are far too many kindly gentlemen who meet the stagecoaches up from the country, and they all run brothels as sidelines. It is one of the ugliest fashions of our age, and God knows why Parliament doesn't do something about it. There is a name for such gentlemen, but I'll not offend you by uttering it. To my mind, it is one of the lowest and most disgusting things that any human being, man or woman, can do. You have in your time accused me of indifference, but here I assure you, I am not indifferent, as that gentleman will discover if ever I have the good fortune to meet him.'

Cassandra said, almost inaudibly, 'I think that was magnificent of you, Francis.' She rose to her feet. 'I admire you for it. Thank you for telling me.'

Mr. Shelbrooke, with for the first time an air of slight bewilderment, said, 'Thank you for listening.'

She walked towards the door, in her usual dramatic manner: this time it might have been Lady Macbeth in the sleepwalking scene. But the fatigue was plainly genuine, and there were great shadows beneath her eyes. She half opened her mouth to speak. She looked sideways at him out of the vast green eyes. She longed to say, Oh, Francis, this is all so silly, we've misjudged each other, can't we forget about it, can't we start again? But as she took a deep breath to utter these words aloud, he remarked casually, his back towards her, 'We must remember not to quarrel before my Aunt Arabella. She is such a very respectable lady. It will be a very respectable tea-party, with doubtless all the family linen and china, and what we will talk about, God only knows, but I suspect it will be the smallest of small-talk, and you and James must endeavour not to yawn. I,' said Mr. Shelbrooke, with a rather savage sigh, 'must not yawn either. I dare say we will discuss the variety of cousins I have never heard of and perhaps, if the atmosphere grows sufficiently intimate, we might bring ourselves to mention the weather.'

'Poor old lady,' said Cassandra, with one of her customary voltes-face.

'Do you call her that? My father always disliked her. People who pride themselves on their respectability invariably take the utmost delight in ferreting out in others the vices they deplore. I suspect,' said Mr. Shelbrooke with some bitterness, 'that it is easy to be respectable if you are dead plain. Aunt Arabella, both in feature and character, is one of those to whom nothing ever happens, and certainly at her age nothing now will.'

Cassandra said irrelevantly, as she had said before, 'I wonder what will happen to us.' She opened the door. She exclaimed, 'Oh, if only something would happen! Something exciting. Something dramatic.'

Then, as if afraid her husband might provide some unexpected drama, she slammed the door behind her; she remembered the sleeping James and apologetically opened it again to shut it very softly.

But Mr. Shelbrooke stayed where he was, and presently settled himself on the chaise-longue, leaning back, his arms beneath his head. Cheri emerged from his corner, and – though this was strictly forbidden – jumped up beside him, falling to sleep against his knee. Mr. Shelbrooke neither reproached him,

nor closed his eyes: he was still lying there when the dawn
light slanted through the curtains.

*

Mr. Fielding arrived at ten next morning. James saw him
arrive from the window. It astonished and mortified him to
realize how afraid he was of his master. The fear had nothing
to do with cane or birch. A flogging, even a savage one, was
merely a temporary inconvenience, and he was a healthy,
sturdy boy brought up to deliver blows as well as take them;
he had fought most of the school bullies in his time, received
black eyes and a bloody nose which he would have been
ashamed to make a sound about. He was not, thank God, like
that miserable, curly-headed little wretch, brought up so soft
that the brutality of the world drove the wits clean out of him.
James scowled at the memory. One day, oh, one day, he would
repay that — But it looked now as if the payment would be on
the other side, and James, raging at himself for being a bloody
coward, could not ignore the cold shudders that were running
through him.

There was nothing either extraordinary or repulsive about
Mr. Fielding's appearance. He strode down Hanover Square,
swinging his malacca cane: as usual he was immaculately
dressed and perfumed, the moustache was a neat, thin line
and his beringed hands were soft and white and spotlessly
clean.

Mr. Shelbrooke, not best pleased at so early a visitation,
strove to shake himself into wakefulness and received him in
the drawing-room. He found Mr. Fielding agreeable enough
in his fat, pompous way: the fellow seemed a gentleman, if
something of a bore. After all, he was only a schoolmaster.
Only he too remarked the elegant clothes and was faintly astonished. The schoolmasters of his own youth had, if he remembered rightly, been shabby, ink-stained creatures with
half-starved looks; certainly they did not wear perfume, and
such an expensive brand of it too. For in this kind of thing Mr.
Shelbrooke was remarkably knowledgeable; his dark eyes fixed
themselves momentarily on the silver snuff-box that was
offered him, and widened a little at the display of diamond

74

rings, which he could price almost to the last shilling.

'Such a foolish affair,' said Mr. Fielding with an understanding, yet contemptuous smile. 'But boys will be boys, will they not?'

'I suppose they will,' agreed Mr. Shelbrooke.

'James is your brother, I understand, sir?'

'My half-brother.'

'Ah!' Mr. Fielding by this somehow indicated in a flattering manner that this accounted for the unfortunate traits in James's character.

'What exactly has happened?' asked Mr. Shelbrooke. He could not say in all honesty that he found anything to dislike in his visitor, yet there was something about him that was displeasing, and a warning signal was flickering inside him.

'Oh, did James not tell you? The silly, misguided boy,' said Mr. Fielding, with another of his small, secret smiles. 'But I can explain it to you easily. It is really only a small thing. We do not allow our boys to walk in Marylebone Fields. You will naturally appreciate this, Mr. Shelbrooke, for we are after all *in loco parentis*. Forgive the tag! We schoolmasters are sadly pedantic mortals. But you, of course, as a man of the world, will understand perfectly the necessity for such a veto. There are, I fear, many unsavoury characters abroad these days, and the Fields have a sad reputation.' He paused to take a pinch of snuff. 'Young Master James decided to disobey us. Oh, it's understandable,' said Mr. Fielding, 'and your young brother is a manly boy, a very manly boy if I may say so, if one without – you'll pardon me, sir – much academic qualifications. But nonetheless, he is a fine lad, in need of discipline perhaps, but a fine lad, a fine lad, a credit to the noble name he bears.'

This particular form of flattery was not of a kind to appeal to Mr. Shelbrooke who, though possessing many faults of character such as hot-headedness and lack of tolerance, was not self-important and had few illusions about his own family. But what was really preoccupying him at this moment was a small, uninvited voice inside him which was saying quite persistently, There is something wrong with this man, he is bad, he is a bastard. It startled him. He cleared his throat. He said quickly, feeling as if he were a father, not a half-brother,

'Certainly I don't think there is anything womanish about James. I have always found him courageous and honest.'

'Oh, very honest, yes indeed,' said Mr. Fielding. He looked down for a moment. 'But foolish, even at times insolent.' He looked up again, fixing his prominent eyes unblinkingly on his host. 'And with a marked tendency to flout authority. That is something we cannot tolerate. You will appreciate that, Mr. Shelbrooke. There is no place in the Manor House School for disobedient, insubordinate boys.'

Mr. Shelbrooke had in his own youth flouted authority persistently, and still had a tendency to do so. He could find nothing to say to this diatribe, so merely inclined his head. He was beginning to find this enforced parental role not only tiresome but ridiculous.

'I was compelled to discipline him,' said Mr. Fielding. He was a man of iron self-control when this seemed to him necessary, but as he spoke these words, he quite unconsciously passed his tongue between his lips, and his eyes narrowed in a kind of intense, hidden delight.

Mr. Shelbrooke saw this. He was an observant young man, except naturally where his wife was concerned, and cards and dice had helped him to study his fellow men. He was aware of a hot upsurge of pure fury, yet this was preposterous, for this fellow was perfectly right: James had been disobedient and James must therefore be punished.

'I flogged him,' said Mr. Fielding. He surveyed Mr. Shelbrooke, his head a little on one side. 'Do you blame me for that?'

'No. Of course not,' said Mr. Shelbrooke.

'There was in the circumstances no alternative. I cannot but feel, sir, that you would have done the same.'

Mr. Shelbrooke did not answer this. He had never beaten his brother in his life: occasionally when he had aimed a clout at his head, James had always done his best to hit him back. It had all been on what one might term a friendly basis.

'The boy resented it,' said Mr. Fielding. He stood up, as if to emphasize the importance of these words. He was almost as tall as Mr. Shelbrooke, who was thinking that the fellow must wear corsets, there was an impression of grossness kept under rigid restraint.

'I am disappointed in the boy,' said Mr. Fielding heavily. 'I would be lying to you if I said otherwise. James should have learnt by now to take his punishment like a gentleman. I find this running away cowardice. I fear he will have to be taught a lesson. Disobedience, yes. Insubordination, yes. But insolence and cowardice I will not tolerate.'

He is a bastard, you know, said the small voice at the back of Mr. Shelbrooke's mind. His normal voice said, 'I think you might have misunderstood the situation. I cannot believe that James is a coward. Perhaps it is simply that he chose to come home tonight rather than in the morning, for he has, if you remember, permission for a day's absence. It's a question of a family visit. I discussed the matter with Dr. Fountaine last week.'

'I have not misunderstood,' said Mr. Fielding almost petulantly, adding quickly, 'I wish I had. Oh, how I wish I had. It grieves me to be disappointed in my boys.'

'Well then,' said Mr. Shelbrooke in a brisk, practical voice, 'what are you proposing to do with my villain of a brother?'

'He must be disciplined very severely,' said Mr. Fielding. 'I fear I must make an example of him in front of the whole school. I cannot countenance such behaviour. But,' he added with a flashing smile that revealed oddly pointed canines, 'we shall be good friends again afterwards. Very good friends. He is after all only a boy, a foolish boy, but still a boy. May I speak to the lad now, sir? I shall naturally be escorting him back to school. I —' He broke off. The smile flashed on again. A strange warmth and gentleness exuded from him as he bowed to Cassandra who, fully and elegantly dressed for the occasion, stood in the doorway, Cheri at her very high heels.

She made an inclination and permitted him to kiss her hand. She was looking at her most dazzling, dressed in the height of fashion so as to impress Aunt Arabella later in the afternoon. The bedraggled girl with unkempt hair and trailing wrapper had vanished; in her place was a beauty that would have brought the gallery roaring to its feet. Cassandra's taste in dress was as dramatic as the rest of her, and her husband blinked a little at the gown of green and silver worn over a black hooped

77

petticoat, and the rich brocade shoes to match. A plainer woman in such apparel would have looked like a lady of the town, but there was no denying that Cassandra carried it with an air: Mr. Shelbrooke felt, however, that Miss Parkington-Smith would view this with the utmost disapproval.

Mr. Fielding viewed it otherwise. Mrs. Shelbrooke's beauty brought out every speck of the Beau Frog charm: it was as well for his vanity that he did not see himself through Cassandra's eyes as the apotheosis of all the unpleasant gentlemen on whom she had once slammed the front door.

He began, 'Dear lady —' then saw James in the background, and stopped. A blown look came upon him, and his voice changed. 'Well, sir?' he said. 'I trust you have come to make me your apologies. What have you to say for yourself?'

James came fully into the room. Cassandra caught at his hand and pressed it: he snatched it angrily away. He adored Cassie, but no woman, not even the best of them, had any conception of the masculine decencies. He raised his head proudly and in so doing caught his brother's eye.

Mr. Shelbrooke bestowed on him a swift but unmistakable wink. He could not have said why he did such an unseemly thing. In all reason they were making a precious fuss about a naughty boy who fully deserved whatever awaited him, yet for some unknown reason James, who was almost as tall as himself, seemed to him at that moment like a small and frightened child.

That wink did more for James than anything else in the whole wide world. Everything came into focus again, and he saw his schoolmaster not as a monster but as a stupid, vicious and cruel person, less to be afraid of than despised. He gave Mr. Fielding a bold and contemptuous stare. He said, 'Nothing, sir. I have nothing to add to what I've already said.'

'I see,' said Mr. Fielding. His face had grown bland, expressionless. His voice was even. 'Well, we shall discuss this more fully later. In the meantime, I feel you have already put your kind brother and his charming wife to enough inconvenience. The sooner we leave, the better. I hope you will at least have the decency to apologize to Mrs. Shelbrooke. What a delightful little dog, ma'am!' And he stooped to hold out his

78

hand to Cheri, making the kind of noise that certain people consider due to animals and children.

Cheri backed from him, growling. He was a friendly dog, if a trifle self-opinionated, and Cassandra stared down at him in astonishment.

'Come, old fellow,' cooed Mr. Fielding, adding, 'I confess I have the greatest possible weakness for all our dumb friends.' And he laid his large white hand on Cheri's silken head, only to withdraw it with a yelp as Cheri's sharp teeth fastened themselves in the fleshy surface.

James burst out laughing. He knew this was outrageous, he did not even find the situation particularly amusing, but the strain of the past hours had been terrible, and he could no longer control himself.

His laughter ceased as abruptly as it began. There was a silence, and during that silence Mr. Fielding flashed him one look. It was his greatest mistake, for both Mr. Shelbrooke and Cassandra saw it; it was instantly replaced by a bewildered, deprecatory smile, and he had no idea of the impression left by that flash of vicious fury.

The next moment Cassandra was crying out in dismay, pretending to slap Cheri, offering Mr. Fielding her handkerchief, entreating him to let her bathe his wound.

'But it's nothing,' he protested, 'I assure you, dear lady, it is nothing. Just an excess of high spirits.' And indeed it was not much, for Cheri's teeth had merely grazed the skin. He went on, 'And now I must beg of you to excuse me. I am sure you have affairs to see to, and I myself am regrettably a busy man. Why, my pupils will be waiting for me. James —'

Mr. Shelbrooke said quietly, 'But I explained to you, sir. Dr. Fountaine has given permission for James to spend the day with us. I am afraid he cannot accompany you.'

'But surely, in the circumstances —' began Mr. Fielding, but he was never allowed to finish, for Cassandra broke in upon his words in an excited, dramatic fashion. She assured him that some aunt or other that he had never heard of would be mortally offended if James did not come, that it was a *promise*, she was so *sure* Mr. Fielding would understand, and of course James would go back later, it was so *kind* of dear

79

Mr. Fielding to have taken so much trouble, they were all *so* grateful to him, and really he was not to distress himself, *everything* would be arranged.

It was all third-grade stuff from a third-grade play, and Mr. Fielding was not to know that this was not Cassandra's normal way of speaking, but somehow in a remarkably short space of time he found himself outside the house, and no James.

He was so furious he could hardly contain himself. His farewell to Mr. Shelbrooke was barely civil, and even to Cassandra his acknowledgements were made in a chill, tight voice. He swept out of the house and into the street; when a small errand-boy crossed his path, he turned a savage face upon the wretched brat, and lashed out at him with his cane.

It did not help matters that the common little creature who should have been strangled at birth, dodged the blow, then yelled out after him, 'Gawd's truth, look at his little Froggy moustachio!'

It was definitely not Mr. Fielding's day.

Cassandra waited for a moment after he had gone. Then she drew herself up and folded her hands across her breast. 'I do not,' she said, 'like that man.'

James said nothing. He was breathing quickly. Mr. Shelbrooke smiled faintly and said, 'Neither do I.'

Cassandra looked a little taken aback, as she always did when her husband agreed with her. She said defiantly, challenging him with her eyes, 'James is not going back to that school. I will not permit it.'

James at this went suddenly white. The pallor was startling in his clear-skinned face. He stared from one to the other then, without uttering one word or even waiting for his brother's reply, rushed from the room.

They heard him tearing up the stairs.

'You see what I mean,' said Cassandra adding, 'That man is a blackguard and a scoundrel and a rogue.' She paused, waiting for the contradiction that did not come. She went on, 'Cheri didn't like him either. Dogs always know.' Then she said, almost coaxingly, her voice sinking down, 'Oh, Francis, you're not going to make him go back, are you?'

'I thought you said you would not permit it,' said Mr.

Shelbrooke. He added thoughtfully, his brows meeting, 'Strange. I wanted to punch him on the nose and before God, I do not know why, for he was perfectly civil, and you must admit, even though you're a woman, that James has behaved disgracefully and deserves everything the gentleman intends him to get.'

'Don't send him back,' said Cassandra.

'Are you entreating me, my love?'

'Oh, if you want me to — Please don't, Francis. That man frightens me. There's something evil about him.'

'You're always so dramatic!'

'But I mean it. Please promise not to send him back. Please!'

'I'll see,' said Mr. Shelbrooke, who was beginning to enjoy himself.

She hesitated, peering at him, trying to read his expression. She grimaced, but dared not mention the subject again. She said rather pettishly, raising her shoulders, 'I suppose we must all get ready for dear Aunt Arabella.'

'I suppose we must,' said Mr. Shelbrooke. 'You had best go up to James and see if he's over his fit of the vapours. Try him with a dose of rhubarb.'

Cassandra chose to ignore this. She remarked disdainfully as she sailed towards the door, 'Oh, I fear the afternoon will be prodigious dull.'

'Undoubtedly,' said Mr. Shelbrooke.

In that, however, they were both very much mistaken.

SIX

The parlour of Miss Parkington-Smith's house was ready for the guests, and the old lady sat at the table, waiting for them.

Polly had done her best. She had begged her mistress to let her set the tea upstairs. 'I can shift the bed,' she said. 'I can make the room look just like the parlour. They'll never know.'

Miss Parkington-Smith replied icily, 'Receive guests in my bedroom! Upon my soul, Polly, I am beginning to think you must be in your second childhood. What an idea! Why, my dear father would turn in his grave. It would be highly improper.'

Polly lost her temper. The sight of Miss Parkington-Smith was almost breaking her heart, for an old lady of over sixty, and one crippled with rheumatism at that, could not be expected to sustain a violent fall without showing some effects of it. Miss Parkington-Smith was grey-white, and the rouge looked ghastly and macabre on her ashen cheeks. She had grown a great deal thinner during the past year, and since last night seemed to have shrunk to dust: the black bombazine that was her best dress hung upon her like a shroud. Yet though she looked so ill, and ten years older than her age, her indomitable spirit sustained her like a corset, kept her back upright and her chin high: her voice was strong, and her expression as prim and disagreeable as ever.

All this was too much for Polly, who was a warm-hearted creature given to moods and impulses, and who had never learnt to restrain herself. She burst into a shrill flood of speech.

'You're nothing but a silly, proud old creature!' she cried. 'You'll be respectable on your death bed. I suppose you won't have the surgeon near you because it wouldn't be nice for him to see you lying on your bed in your shift. Improper indeed! Twaddle!' shouted Polly, quite beside herself. 'How do you imagine they're going to feel, Mr. Francis and that lovely girl of his, seeing you sitting there on a broken chair, with the table

82

certain to collapse any moment, and a few chipped cups and plates that don't match, for their tea? Do you think they won't notice? Of course they'll notice. And I'll tell you one thing more, ma'am, with your high and mighty airs. They'll think you mad. That's what they'll think you. A mad old woman. They'll probably have you shut up. In Bedlam.'

Miss Parkington-Smith stiffened visibly during this outburst; by the end of it her look of icy outrage was such that the aura about her was below freezing point. She spoke from her icicle, and her voice was stiff with incredulous distaste.

'You will take a week's notice,' she said, staring over Polly's head. 'You have been grossly insolent. I think you must have been drinking. You will leave my service next week, and I shall give you neither wages nor references.'

'Yes, ma'am,' said Polly resignedly, for the dismissal was as non-existent as her wages; she would never leave Miss Parkington-Smith, and by the evening Miss Parkington-Smith would in her genteel way have forgotten the whole matter.

She shot her mistress a look of exasperation not unmingled with wry humour, for the dear lord knew what the young gentleman and Miss Cassandra would think of this lunatic set-up; still they must do the best they could, and at least the blackamoor was there to help her.

She had in all the excitement forgotten about Mokasa. She had been far too upset over last night's happenings to bother her head with such nonsense as boxing, and it was only this morning when she went to the Tea Gardens to beg the loan of some crockery that she saw Mokasa again.

He was even bigger and blacker than she remembered, and his grin was as disarming as ever. He shook an arch finger at her, and the finger was like the branch of a tree. –

'Mistress,' he said, in that vast deep voice of his that reminded her somehow of the thundering of surf on shingle, 'mistress, you did not attend the fight, although you gave me your promise you would do so.'

'Lord!' said Polly. 'It went clean out of my mind.' She eyed him to see if the signs of battle were upon him. But his flat nose seemed unbroken, and there were no visible bruises, though with so black a skin it was not easy to be certain. 'Did you win?' she asked. 'Did you beat that old Fighting Quaker?'

He gave her so colossal a grin that she could have sworn it met his ears. He silently extended his hands to her so that she could see the knuckles.

Polly exclaimed in dismay and admiration. The knuckles were skinned and burst. Mr. Broughton next-door might be training his pupils to use mufflers, but Mokasa obviously belonged to the old school and employed his bare hands.

She said wonderingly, 'Your blood is the same colour as mine,' for she had always imagined the blackamoors to have blood the same colour as their skin, a kind of ink-like substance, in the same way as the blood of the highest nobility was reputed to have a bluish tinge. But she was not really interested in Mokasa's blood, nor even in his victory over the Fighting Quaker, for a wonderful idea had just come to her.

She continued to survey him in a speculative fashion. Really, once one grew accustomed to the colour of his skin and the wide, flattened features, one had to admit that the face was an amiable one, even kindly: there was nothing alarming in it, though possibly the Fighting Quaker might think differently.

'Mokasa!' she began. Then she paused, making a wary kind of face, for after all they were in enough trouble as it was, and you never knew with these savages: it stood to reason that living as they did on the top branches of trees and wearing no clothes, they must be different from the white people who had such lovely houses, and covered themselves in silk and fine linen.

He said nothing, only beamed and, as she paused, she had a sudden vision of the Rookeries, where the building was as beautiful and sweet as a sewer, and where most of the inhabitants wore nothing but filthy rags.

'Mokasa,' she said again, 'where do you come from? Why are you here? This isn't your country.'

'Mistress,' he replied in his strange, pedantic fashion of speaking, 'I was but an infant when they brought me here, they sought my people out to execute vengeance and punishment, they led my parents into captivity, and we sailed in a ship called the *Jesus*. We came across the sea, and I was put to work in the household of a fine lady. She called me her little black boy. Only as you will perceive, I grew.' He grinned suddenly. 'I am still a black boy, mistress, but little I am not. So I left the service of the fine lady, and now – why now, I do whatever work there is for the likes of me, and sometimes I fight – for God, mistress, has given me mighty powerful arms, mighty, mighty powerful.'

'That's what I was thinking,' said Polly, then in a hurry, 'Mokasa, I want you to help me. I can't offer you no money, because I ha'ent got any, neither has my poor old mistress, but I'll feed you, I'll feed you to the brim, and I'll find you somewhere to sleep. It's your powerful arms I'm needing, boy, because without them we shall be shamed before them all, and maybe worse will happen to us.'

She was thinking now, as they were all waiting for Mr. Francis, his wife and young Master James to arrive, that what they would have done without Mokasa did not bear thinking of.

Miss Parkington-Smith had shown no particular astonishment at the sight of her new servant. But then in her youth it had been common enough for ladies to have little black boys, turbaned and be-feathered, attending on them, and living as she did in her self-fortress, she accepted the fact composedly enough that this great coal-black fellow should arrive to do her bidding.

It was Mokasa who carried the furniture down from the top floor. It was Mokasa who somehow patched the table together. It was Mokasa who brought over the crockery from the 'Adam and Eve' Tea Gardens at the top of Tottenham Court Road. It was Mokasa and Polly between them who picked up all that remained of the Captain, the fragments of a Sèvres tea service, and the feathers from the cushions, who scrubbed off the marks of dirty feet and filthy hands, who restored a kind of barren order to the place.

But it was not as it had been. It never would be again. Polly, giving one last look at the parlour before she went into the kitchen to set the food out – the kitchen being full of pots and pans and china had in some ways suffered the worst of all – Polly, surveying her handiwork, choked then, once she was in the kitchen with only Mokasa to see her, wept bitterly and would not stop, though he patted her urgently on the shoulder, saying, 'There, mistress, there, God will provide.'

But Polly, who was of a practical nature and sadly concerned with material things, could only see that all the family possessions had been smashed beyond repair; she could not rid her eyes of the sight of her old lady sitting stiffly there, her poor face as prim and contemptuous as always, sitting by a broken, scratched table with a makeshift cloth upon it, a few shoddy cups and plates, and great dirty marks on the wall around her, where only last night there had been pictures, brackets and the various vases and pots and jugs and bric-à-brac that had been the late Mrs. Parkington-Smith's pride.

Miss Parkington-Smith had permitted them to arrange the room around her. It was almost as if the proceeding did not interest her. Only when Polly attempted to prop a plant of fern (brought down from upstairs) against the mournful, black-rimmed square where papa had hung, did she suddenly turn her head and raise a rheumaticky hand, saying in a loud voice, 'Stop!'

'But, ma'am,' protested Polly, who was sweating and exhausted and in no mood to put up with vapours, 'we can't leave it looking like this. Anybody can see there's been a picture there and, what is more, ma'am, anybody can see these walls ain't been papered for the past forty years.'

Miss Parkington-Smith merely said in a cool, distant voice, 'Ask the blackamoor to fetch me papa's sword and pistols. And you shall bring me his regimental badge, which is in the drawer of my dressing-table.'

Oh lord, what now, thought Polly, and wondered a little fearfully if Mokasa might resent his designation, but – as she was to learn in due course – he regarded most white people as harmless lunatics, and little they could say to him offended him.

He did as he was told, and presently the Captain's sword was hung across the space, with the pistols beneath it, and the regimental badge perched rather rakishly on top.

And Miss Parkington-Smith surveyed this and nodded proudly: it was chiefly the memory of this that made Polly weep so outrageously, sit down by what remained of the kitchen dresser and howl her heart out.

Mokasa repeated, rather desperately and for once not smiling, 'Oh, mistress, God will provide,' then, as her sobs increased in volume, appeared to decide that the Almighty needed a little assistance and produced a large, black bottle from his pocket.

'I pray you, mistress,' he said, touching her arm, first gently then more insistently, 'drink. The Good Book permits you to take a little for your stomach's sake.'

Polly raised a red, soaked face and looked first at the enormous black countenance so near hers, then at the equally black bottle extended in his hand.

'Lord!' she cried, 'I never touch the stuff,' then grabbed the bottle from his hand and swigged a great gulp of it from the neck.

It was undiluted gin. She nearly choked, coughing so wildly that the world split into stars about her. But Mokasa only nodded, saying, 'It is good. Drink more, mistress. It maketh glad the heart of man.'

And Polly, who had touched little but ale in her life, and who had always exclaimed against the inhabitants of the Rookeries who drank gin down as if it were water, broke into wild laughter through her tears and snatched the bottle back from Mokasa's hand.

* * *

Mr. and Mrs. Shelbrooke, with James facing them, set out in the carriage a little after four.

Cassandra had, in addition to the new gown, piled her red hair high, with a delightful little feather hat on top of it. She sat there, her hands lightly folded upon her knee, gazing ahead with an aloof, distinguished air. She was thinking of the second bunch of three roses which had been brought her after Mr. Fielding's departure: the messenger must have watched carefully, for this arrived while her husband was taking his morning stroll in the park. 'This is the second day.' That was all that was written on the card. Cassandra for the first time began to think this was a little foolish: she wished the persistent gallant would transfer his attentions elsewhere. But none of this showed on her face, and Mr. Shelbrooke, glancing sideways at her and noting her haughty and unapproachable expression, shrugged faintly and continued to stare out of his side of the window.

Only James could stay neither still nor silent. He fidgeted so badly that Mr. Shelbrooke exclaimed in irritation, 'Oh, for God's sake, James! If you're so ill-bred that you can't even manage to sit quietly for half an hour, it'll serve you right if I tell Jem to turn round and take you straight back to school.'

Cassandra leaned forward, opening her mouth to protest, but James at once lost his temper and shouted, 'Turn round and be damned then! Take me back to school in irons, if you wish. Hand me over to old Beau Frog and let him murder me. At least you'll have me off your hands. At least you won't have to bother about me any more – except,' added James, whose imagination sometimes went beyond proper bounds, 'to put a few flowers by my tombstone.'

'Such an interesting drive,' remarked Cassandra into the resulting silence. 'Oh look, James. This is Oxford Street. This is the Tyburn way, you know. This is where they bring the poor, condemned men on their last ride to the gallows.'

'James,' said her husband, 'has spent the greater part of his life in London. If, however, you think it an essential part of his education, we can always escort him to Tyburn itself, so that he may have the pleasure of seeing a handful of rogues turned off.'

'Scragged,' said James sullenly.

'Kindly don't use that thieves' cant,' snapped Mr. Shelbrooke.

At this Cassandra, suddenly scarlet, flung her arms wide, interesting several passers-by, and startling the off-side horse so that it swerved and nearly ran an inoffensive gentleman down.

'Oh, charming, charming!' she cried in a great voice, and Jem thought, She's off again, while he gazed stolidly ahead.

'Charming!' cried Cassandra for the third time, and her voice pealed out so that any gallery would have been delighted. 'Here we are on a little family visit, to see a sweet old lady who will be enchanted by our kindness, and what do we do?'

She paused, rather unfortunately, for Mr. Shelbrooke at once finished her discourse for her.

'We distinguish ourselves as usual by brawling,' he said.

'I am not brawling!' exclaimed Cassandra. 'I am the gentlest creature alive. I always have been since a child. I am perfectly prepared to be friendly and good-tempered. I'm sure I've done my best. I've put on my newest gown. I was even about to suggest that it would be a pretty gesture to invite your dear aunt to stay with us for a day or so —'

Mr. Shelbrooke cut across this with some vigour. 'I've told you, Cassandra, she is no dear aunt of mine. She is my step-father's sister, she is no relative, and from what I remember of her, she is disagreeable, poor-tempered and will entirely dis-approve of us. I have no intention whatsoever of asking her to stay with us, and confound your pretty gestures, Cassie – if you would only stop being so damned theatrical for once and drop this act of the little angel wife bent on succouring poor relatives — You know perfectly well that if I had made the suggestion, you would be screaming with horror.'

'This,' said Cassandra coldly, leaning forward to touch James's knee, 'this, dear James, is Rathbone Place. I remember how once – before I met your brother, of course – I had a beau who lived here. He was madly in love with me, poor fellow. I often wonder what became of him. I sometimes fear he might have done something desperate, for he was every night at the theatre with great armfuls of flowers, and he never – but never – ceased pestering me to give up the stage, marry him and be with him for ever.'

'I am beginning to wonder why you ever married me,' said Mr. Shelbrooke.

'You pestered me too,' said Cassandra.

At this her husband became silent, and meanwhile the carriage had reached the top of Oxford Street and turned into Tottenham Court Road.

James, making a great effort to behave himself, for he saw that Francis and Cassie were in a great tizzy with each other, noted Black Horse Yard and Stable Yard, also Windmill Street where the new Middlesex Hospital had recently come into existence. The road was in the main a country road, leading to the village of Highgate, and there were green fields on either side. James did not care much for the country, having had enough of it at Marylebone; when his eyes lit on a sprawling black building, he exclaimed, 'Oh, look! Isn't it ugly? That must be where the poorest people live.'

Cassandra, gazing at the Rookeries – though of course she did not know the name – looked unhappy. 'It's shocking,' she said, 'that people should live in such conditions. Why does no one do anything about it?'

'People do not have to live in such conditions if they don't want to,' said Mr. Shelbrooke shortly. 'They live there because they are too lazy to work.'

'That is simply not true,' cried Cassandra, and James too looked angrily at his brother who, seeing that he was generally condemned, reacted naturally enough by saying something even more outrageous.

'If,' he declared, 'you removed those people from their home, and placed them in a beautiful house such as the one we have in Hanover Square, you would find that within a couple of months they would have made our own home as filthy and degraded as that building over there. They are not like humans. They are like beasts, only beasts are not so nasty in their habits. I have no doubt, my dear Cassie and James, that you picture yourselves as noble reformers, visiting with a Bible in one hand and a bowl of soup in the other, with grateful, servile folk bowing and smiling and saying, God bless you for your kindness – but I assure you, the moment your back was turned, they would throw the soup out of the window and turn to their bottle of gin.'

He paused to smile into their outraged faces. He saw they both detested him. He went on blandly, 'Mr. Henry Fielding and people of his ilk talk of reforming the criminal classes and improving the conditions of the poor, but this is all a pretty fantasy, and for my part I wish Fielding would confine himself to his novels, which he does tolerably well, and not preach so much meaningless charity.'

Having delivered himself of this sermon, most of which he did not mean, he leaned back, only to discover that the carriage had stopped and the groom was opening the door.

90

'What the devil has happened now?' he demanded. 'Has the carriage broken down? I must say, Jem, you could have found a more salubrious place for this disaster.'

And he gazed out, his disapproval mingled with a faint horror, at the Rookeries. In the summer heat the filth in the courtyard stank abominably, and the odour came rankly to his nostrils so that he fumbled in his pocket for a handkerchief.

'This is Paradise Row, sir,' said Jem.

'Good God!' said Mr. Shelbrooke, and gazed at it afresh, in honest alarm, while the quizzing glass he had raised, slipped to his knee.

'I'm afraid, sir, you and the lady will have to walk. The path is too rough and narrow to get the horses down it.'

Mr. Shelbrooke was so startled that he half thought of directing Jem to take his family back home: he could not believe that his pretty wife in all her finery would contemplate walking through this putrid mess of garbage, especially as this was the dangerous season for fevers.

But Cassandra, her face alight, had already skipped out, and James leapt after her. Mr. Shelbrooke could see that she was delighting in the drama of it, and his young brother in the novelty; as he himself was by now intrigued, he was not entirely displeased to follow them.

They walked towards the Rookeries, and saw at once Miss Parkington-Smith's little house sandwiched between the two black wings of the Rookeries, like an innocent soul between two demons of hell. The house, even from the outside, bore little resemblance to the genteel residence of the Captain's day, but by contrast it seemed the primmest place imaginable.

By now Mr. Shelbrooke's curiosity was so much aroused that he would not have turned back, had both members of his family gone on their knees to him. He knocked on the door: when it was opened by a gigantic and beaming blackamoor, he scarcely blinked, only begged to know if Miss Parkington-Smith were expecting them.

Mokasa, smiling at them with the utmost friendliness, said in his great bell-like voice, 'The lady is attending your visit, dear friends, and better is a dinner with herbs where love is than a stalled ox and hatred therewith,' and bowed them into the hall and from thence into the parlour.

Mr. Shelbrooke did not answer this strange introduction, for he could think of no suitable comment. He stepped inside, with his family close to his coat-tails, their eyes round with astonishment. He was by now prepared for almost anything, but as he took in his surroundings, he began to wonder quite seriously if he had a fever.

Polly and Mokasa had, in the circumstances, worked a miracle. The room was no longer the shambles of last night. But at its best it was shabby and fallen into disrepair: now it was desolate indeed: it was even worse than desolate, it was deprived. There were great gaps on the walls, no window curtains, and the carpet was torn and stained. The furniture, such as there was, was battered, and everywhere there was a vast emptiness where, twenty-four hours ago, there had been little tables loaded with bric-à-brac, ornaments, pictures, footstools, embroidered screens, and all the impedimenta that had been collected first by Mrs. Parkington-Smith, and then by her daughter. It was all gone, there was nothing to replace it and, like an old woman at night shorn of wig, teeth and paint, the room was stripped of illusion and displayed its decrepitude and age.

Mr. Shelbrooke saw and could not believe his eyes. Then he became aware of the little old lady sitting on her hard-backed chair, and he stepped over to her with the utmost speed, for he resembled James in that he was instinctively courteous and compassionate; he talked a great deal of nonsense, especially when he was hurt or angry, but there was no meanness in him, and he was both shocked and angry that any member of his family should live in such circumstances, without his knowing.

'Aunt Arabella,' he said, with all the charm that had won Cassandra in the blink of an eye, and laying a gentle hand on her shoulder, he stooped to kiss her cheek.

He knew at once that his stepfather had not been unreasonable in his accusations. This was no dear old lady. Self-righteousness, intolerance and a most mortal pride had etched their lines in that face: the mouth was thin and querulous, the eyes cold, and she sat there with ramrod back as if nothing would ever make her bend or soften. But Mr. Shelbrooke saw also her frailty; in the awareness of his own youth and strength he winced, for there was almost nothing of her, and the hand held out to his was cruelly knotted with swollen joints and clawed fingers.

'Well, Francis,' said Miss Parkington-Smith, then she flushed a little, for no handsome young man had ever kissed her before. She turned to Cassandra, who came running to her at once, and knelt beside her in a pretty fashion that would have been hard to resist, quite disregarding the new dress which trailed behind her.

'Dear Aunt Arabella,' said Cassandra, kissing her also, and filled with emotion, for she too was horrified by the room and was already planning some enchanting country cottage that she and Francis would immediately present to this poor, lonely old soul.

'The Captain,' said Miss Parkington-Smith, rising with great difficulty to her feet, and ignoring Mr. Shelbrooke's protests, 'would be very pleased to see you in his house. I believe, young Master James, you have an air of him. I have no doubt you are wishful to go into the army. It is the only profession for a young man who wishes to make his mark in the world. Your grandfather of course was a great man, and it is but natural you should be desirous to emulate him.'

James wanted to be a great many things, including a surgeon, an explorer, an historian and a celebrated actor like Mr. Garrick, but he had not the least wish to die for his country. However, he too was impressed by the strange appearance of the room; it all seemed to him less like poverty than as if the Captain's regiment had ploughed through it; besides, he was sorry for this funny old lady who spoke such fustian. He bowed. He said, 'I should be very pleased, ma'am, to do what my grandfather did,' and this delighted Miss Parkington-Smith who smiled as she had not done for a long time.

She moved a little, leaning heavily on her stick. She pointed at the great, ugly, square gap on the wall, that the sword, pistols and badge could not begin to cover.

'Your grandfather's portrait hung there,' she said. 'It's a pity you cannot see it, but I have sent it to be cleaned.' The colour suddenly receded from her face as she spoke, and Mr.

Shelbrooke at once came up to her, to support her back to her chair.

She waved him away indignantly. 'I am perfectly capable,' she said, 'of moving without help. I may be old, young man, but I am not yet helpless.' Then she went on, 'I fear you are not seeing my room at its best. We are about to decorate the walls – a more fashionable new paper, you know, or perhaps silk hangings. A little extravagant, I know, but then we old folk must indulge ourselves, must we not? And, of course, new curtains,' continued Miss Parkington-Smith rapidly. 'Velvet. Purple. So tedious of the girl not to have finished making them. I told her you were coming. My brother's son, I said, and his half-brother together with his young wife. So essential to have the house looking at its best. But, of course, nothing has been done. It is always the same these days, is it not? People have no sense of duty. However, never mind, we will now have our tea. I will ring the bell.'

The Shelbrookes were, God knows, none of them silent people, all of them being very partial to the sound of their own voices, but this speech was so painfully embarrassing that they all sat down without a word. Miss Parkington-Smith perhaps did not realize how remarkable this was. She sat sedately at the head of the table, as Polly, very flushed and a little unsteady on her feet, set down a chipped plate with some biscuits on it, glasses of the kind to be found in a common alehouse, and wine that was still in its bottle, because the Captain's cut-glass decanter had been smashed to pieces.

There was a strong aura of gin around Polly, which Mr. Shelbrooke naturally noticed; he glanced at her, then away, thinking how disgraceful it was that this poor old lady had no one to care for her but a drunken maidservant.

'Pray let me offer you one of these biscuits,' said Miss Parkington-Smith, and she picked the plate up with such an air that it was a wonder it did not turn into Sèvres porcelain in her hands. 'Perhaps, sir,' she said, turning to Mr. Shelbrooke, 'you will pour the wine. It is after all the gentleman's privilege.'

And she smiled at him, motioning him to the bottle with the utmost dignity: it might well have been some precious vintage, instead of being a thin, sour wine that was all she had been able to afford.

'With pleasure,' said Mr. Shelbrooke. He was turning over in his mind the best beginning to what he was proposing to say. It was quite obvious that the old lady could not continue living in such appalling surroundings, but it was equally obvious that any suggestion must be made with the utmost tact. He was considering when and how he could introduce the subject, and absent-mindedly leaned on the table with one hand as he reached out for the wine.

Polly reappeared at this moment with a small tray of sweetmeats that she had made herself. As she stood in the doorway, wondering why she felt so strange, and wishing the walls would not sway in so disturbing a fashion, the table-leg that Mokasa had somehow put together, cracked in two again. Mr. Shelbrooke nearly fell flat on his face, James gave a wild, startled giggle, while the table lurched and collapsed, sending biscuits and bottle into Cassandra's lap and everything else rolling on to the floor.

It was too much for Polly. She had already had one fit of weeping and had not fully recovered from it, besides she was full of gin. She could only see that the beautiful Mrs. Francis's gown must be irretrievably ruined and that the whole situation was vulgar beyond words: how Miss Parkington-Smith could sit there as if everything were just as it should be was entirely beyond her. She burst into tears again, not caring that Mr. Jack's family was watching her, not even wishing to keep up any appearance of normality. It was all dreadful, nothing would be right again, the room looked worse than anything in the Rookeries, the cheap, chipped china affronted every instinct in her, and the gaps which had once been filled with all those pretty, genteel things, were as obscene to her as if each one were filled with a jeering face giggling like that terrible creature yesterday.

She wept and, through her weeping, bawled in choked, thick accents, 'Oh, ma'am, Miss Arabella, why don't you tell them? How can you sit there like that when any moment now they'll be back? Oh, I'm so ashamed,' sobbed Polly, twisting her apron into so frantic a tangle that she tore the pocket half off, 'oh, I'm so ashamed, I wish I was dead. To think that Master

Jack's family should be here, and see us without any furniture or any china, and nothing decent to eat or drink—'

'Go back to your kitchen at once, Polly,' commanded Miss Parkington-Smith. She was white to the lips, but from her way of speaking this might have been some foolish fit of the hysterics. She added as she always did, and quite unaware that for the first time her accusation was true, 'You're drunk.'

'Of course I'm drunk!' wailed Polly. 'You'd be drunk too, if you'd any blood in you. Half a bottle of gin, that's what I've had, a whole twopenny-worth, and I'd drink the rest of it if it didn't make me sick. How could I come in here if I hadn't drunk it? How could I bear to see *them* here, and you not turning a hair? It's not natural like. If I didn't take a drink, I'd go mad, upon my soul I would. I've taken a great deal from you, Miss Arabella, and lied for you, and pretended everything was as it should be, but this is too much to expect of anyone, and it's time someone spoke the truth.'

Miss Parkington-Smith was banging on the table with her stick-handle, trying frantically to interrupt, but Polly, who was long past reason, only shouted out, 'Mr. Francis! Get her away from here. They'll kill her. They've already struck her, a poor old soul who can hardly walk, and if she isn't gone by tomorrow evening, they'll murder her. She's a cursed, obstinate old bitch,' wailed Polly, so bemused by gin, exhaustion and despair that she scarcely knew what she was saying, 'and if her own flesh and blood can't persuade her, I don't know who can. Oh, make her go! If she won't, carry her out, sir, because if you don't, she'll be carried out whether she likes it or not, and feet first most likely. And I can't take any more, I can't, I can't, I think I'm going mad with it already.'

'This is outrageous,' whispered Miss Parkington-Smith, but she too had taken more than a much younger woman could have endured, and her voice failed her: she could only wave her hand feebly as her head fell back against the cushion.

It was Cassandra who swept to her feet, who, ignoring her ruined dress with the wine trickling down it, put an arm round her. Normally Miss Parkington-Smith would have rebelled against such familiarity, but she was so exhausted that she found the gentle touch comforting, and she leaned against

Cassandra's shoulder as the soft voice – and this time it was not for the stage patrons – spoke.

'Dear Aunt,' said Cassandra, 'for the love of God tell us what all this is about. We're your family, Aunt Arabella. We want to help you. Why, Francis is devoted to you, you know that, there is nothing he wants to do more than help. What has happened? Who dared to strike you? Who wants you to go? I swear I don't understand a word, it seems quite lunatic.'

James was sitting there with popping eyes, while he privately decided that his family was a great deal nicer than he had imagined. He gazed at Cassandra with open adoration, then his gaze swivelled with proprietary pride to his half-brother who, after a hopeless attempt to repair the table, had risen to his feet.

Mr. Shelbrooke glanced sideways at Polly, who had now covered her face with the mangled apron and was making enough noise to scare an army, then said as calmly as he could, forcing all the authority he possessed into his voice, 'I don't know what all this is about, Aunt Arabella, but your maid is perfectly right. You cannot stay here alone. Why —' He swept his arm round the deplorable room. 'Everything seems smashed to pieces. And for God's sake, what kind of place is this to live in? Why, next door you have dwellings of the lowest sort. You must be surrounded by thieves and murderers and worse. Your very life must be in danger. Now, what I suggest is this —'

But no one was to hear what Mr. Shelbrooke had to suggest, for at that moment there was a great crash at the door. Cassandra felt Miss Parkington-Smith stiffen in her arms. For the first time it seemed as if the old lady's courage was failing her. Polly had stopped her bawling. The apron had fallen from her face, which had turned a mottled, purple colour.

The knocking came again, then Miss Parkington-Smith spoke in a weak, high voice.

'I cannot endure any more,' she whispered. 'Papa taught me not to be a coward, especially in front of the lower orders, but I – I —'

A voice roared from outside. Both Miss Parkington-Smith and Polly knew that voice, and the rotting teeth in the mouth that produced it.

'Are you not gone yet, you old bitch?' demanded the voice. And at that Mr. Shelbrooke suddenly took on an air that his wife and brother had never yet seen: the gambling hells and certain insulting gentlemen might have recognized that cold fury, but his family could only stare at him.

'If you're not out by tomorrow, you cussed old cow,' bellowed Rotten Teeth, 'we'll be giving you another little taste of what's owing to you, only this time we'll burn the place to the ground, and you with it, you old witch. You ought to be dead anyway, you're too old to last much longer. You got notice to quit, ain't you? Then why are you still here?'

Mr. Shelbrooke said, 'It's all right, Aunt. I'll deal with this.'

'Oh, kill him,' whispered Cassandra, 'Francis, you must kill him,' while James cried out jubilantly, 'I'll come and watch this, this'll be something worth watching.'

But Mr. Shelbrooke, shooting one fierce glance at his gentle wife, gave his brother a shove back into the room, saying with a snap, 'If you take one more step, *I'll* kill *you*,' and strode into the hall, flinging open the door.

The two bullies had not expected to see a gentleman, and for a second they stared up at him, while Mr. Shelbrooke, still consumed with a murderous anger, surveyed two of the ugliest and most vicious countenances he had ever beheld. Then the bigger of the two, giving him a wide, mirthless smile, snarled, 'All right, cocky, you've asked for it,' and made a lunge at Mr. Shelbrooke with his cudgel, while his companion, with a high, lunatic giggle, drew from his belt a knife which he held in the manner of one well accustomed to using such a weapon.

Both, however, found themselves staring down the barrel of Mr. Shelbrooke's pistol, and at that they backed, the little one giggling in a kind of panic, while the other fell silent.

'If you're not gone in one minute,' said Mr. Shelbrooke, 'I'll shoot the pair of you. I'm a good shot.' And indeed he was, and he looked it, his face so savage with anger that even the bigger bully of the two hesitated.

'The minute's nearly up,' said Mr. Shelbrooke. He had never felt so enraged in his life. He moved his finger on the trigger, and at this the bully with the cudgel broke into a volley of obscene abuse, shouting, 'If you shoot, that's murder. You'll swing for that, cully, you will and all. Attacking decent citizens going about their duty—' His voice changed, became mild, oily. 'Now lookee here, sir. I dare say you're sorry for the old lady, and I'm sure it does you credit, it's only right and proper, shows you got good feelings, but be reasonable, sir, we got our duty to do like you have, and this house has been bought up, see, by a gentleman, and the gentleman wants to take over instanter, which is only natural, you got to admit it. He got a family of daughters, sir, real nice girls they are, and they got to have somewheres to live. So the old lady's got to go, poor soul, but after all she's near her end as you might say, and it's right the young folk should have first pluck. Now ain't it, sir? You look a reasonable sort of gentleman.' He eyed Mr. Shelbrooke's unmistakably unreasonable countenance, then, as inspiration came to him, gave him a leer. It was a pity that the leer was so unpleasing. 'The gentleman's daughters is real, handsome girls, sir. I dare say you and them would get on a fair treat. Now, why don't you persuade the old lady to go quietly, then come back here in a few days' time? I know the girls would like to meet you, and I'm sure you'd like to meet them. They're good girls, sir. They do what they're told, they're used to all classes of customers, as you might say, and they don't mind overmuch what you tell 'em. They're the sort of girls, sir, that know just what a gentleman like you wants—'

Mr. Shelbrooke had seldom been called a gentleman so persistently. Perhaps this influenced his resulting behaviour. He stepped swiftly out into the courtyard and kicked the bully in a manner that was not gentlemanly at all, then, as the rogue gave a yell of anguish, brought the pistol butt down on his head, and turned to deal with the giggler, only to find that he was running away as hard as he could: there was a great deal wrong with his wits but nothing with his legs.

The bully with the cudgel should by rights have been flat on his face, but he was seasoned to blows and, though he staggered, retching and groaning, he was upright: he leapt out of Mr. Shelbrooke's reach.

He spoke, and there was nothing mild or oily about him now: he spoke like the wolf he was. 'Right,' he said. 'That settles it, sir. My employer won't be pleased, oh, not at all. That bloody old girl's getting out – whether she likes it or she don't like it, it's all one to me. And by the time we're through with her, she'll be glad to be gone. If there's anything left of her. We've had this kind of situation before, sir.' He was retreating as he spoke. His voice was soft and he was smiling his wolfish smile. 'There was a fellow, sir, we had last year. He had a wife and a couple of beautiful children, fair broke your heart they did, lovely they was, just like your own, I dare say. They wouldn't go neither. Oh no. They wasn't going to move for anyone. I don't know, sir, but they was very misfortunate. They had their pretty home broke to pieces, sir, there wasn't a stick left. And folks – you know what folks are, sir – they threw all their slops in the window like, it was easy because the glass was gone, and they smashed the door down, and then they broke the banister so that one of the children fell through. I don't think he survived, sir. I think his poor little neck was broke. It's a dreadful story. And such noisy folk all around, too, singing they was the whole night, and beating drums and blowing trumpets, and the girls too – there was girls next door, you see – they had their friends in, and their friends got drunk. Oh, it was a shame, sir. What with the poor little baby being killed like, and the wife having another and being frightened out of her senses – but it would none of it have happened if the fellow had only done as he was told.' His lips parted. 'My heart fair bleeds for the old lady, but there's one consolation, sir, she's so old and frail, she won't last long.'

Mr. Shelbrooke received all this in silence, only he grew whiter as the speech continued. He had within his own circle led a by no means peaceful life. He knew very well how to stand up for himself: he had fought with sword and pistol and fists. He had met in his time a number of tough and unscrupulous people. He had known gentlemen who snatched other people's wives, and he had met ladies who were only interested in other people's husbands. He had had dealings with a great many night-walkers and several genteel ladies who only did not bear that name because they had a pedigree behind them. He had mixed with stable-boys, and rubbed shoulders with the gentry who went to cockings, boxing, wrestling and the gambling hells. He believed he knew the world. But this was new to him, and in a kind of sick disgust he raised his pistol again, to shoot the vermin down as if it were a rat running round the rafters.

But the bully was gone before he could press the trigger, and so he shut the door and walked slowly back to the parlour again, only to pause outside the door as Miss Parkington-Smith's voice came clearly through.

'I am not going,' she said. 'That is my final word. This was the Captain's, my dear papa's house. He would not like it if I retreated before such excessively ill-bred villains. He never approved of the lower orders. So that is all there is to it, and I beg of you not to refer to the matter again. Let us, pray, discuss something more pleasant, for I have made up my mind: I am not going.'

SEVEN

Mr. Shelbrooke opened the door very carefully, rather as if he were entering upon a wake. All sorts of foreign, disturbing emotions were churning inside him; as he stood there, his wig almost brushing the top of the lintel, his eyes wandering from one to the other, he was muttering to himself, I must keep calm, I must not lose my temper.

His wife, he saw with some satisfaction, was looking entirely dazed. He was glad that he was not the only one to find the situation beyond him : besides, it was not often that Cassie was set down. She had always been a self-confident, outspoken girl, afraid of no one. When they had first married, a number of fashionable ladies made the grave mistake of patronizing the new Mrs. Shelbrooke, who had after all been on the stage – and everyone knew what *that* meant – and who naturally could know nothing of the ways of the *haut ton*. They spoke to her with a kind of sneering amiability, being so sensitive of her feelings that they trampled on them in every other word. Not a sound was murmured against her profession, but the implication hung vast as a moon, and a mutter of Nell Gwyn and Peg Woffington could be heard on all sides.

Mr. Shelbrooke was prepared to fly to his wife's defence with every weapon at his command, but found almost at once that there was no need. Cassie had too much native wit to be snubbed with impunity : she had not slammed the door on a procession of minor peers for nothing. She was all charm and courtesy to the ladies, then turned her elegant back upon them and concentrated on their husbands, who fell instantly in love with her, encircled her for the rest of the evening, while the wives, cold and abandoned, were left tapping silk-shod feet and hissing to each other in pinched, chilly tones.

'They are bitches, the pack of them,' said Cassandra afterwards to her husband, in the ringing voice that she invariably adopted when pleased with herself, then she began to giggle and rocked shamelessly with laughter until, unable to endure it a moment longer, he caught her up in his arms and kissed all the breath out of her.

But that was long ago.

And now Cassandra sat on a small, broken footstool at Miss Parkington-Smith's feet, gazing up at her in bewilderment and exasperation. James too seemed baffled but, being as he was, was plainly delighted with the novelty of the situation. He really was behaving admirably, rushing forward to pick up his aunt's handkerchief when she dropped it, and rearranging her cushions for her. But Mr. Shelbrooke was not deceived: James was dying to interfere, and this must at all costs be prevented: the type of customer he had just encountered was no fit acquaintance for a young boy.

Whether Miss Parkington-Smith saw him come back or not, he was not quite sure: he suspected that she was very much aware of him, but she chose to ignore him and went on talking.

There was a flush on her cheeks, and her eyes shone. There was no trace of the frightened old lady who had whispered she could not endure it. She could never have been handsome, but when she was so animated, one could see that the blood of the old Captain stirred in her veins. And naturally it was of the Captain she was speaking; there was not one reference to the disaster, it was impossible to believe that only a few minutes ago she had been overcome with terror and defeat.

'The Captain,' she said, 'was of course in the 29th Regiment of Foot. He was with the Duke of Marlborough on his march across the Danube, which ended, as you will recollect, in the great victory at Blenheim.' Suddenly she shot a knotted finger at James. 'What was the date of that victory, nephew?'

'Seventeen hundred and four, Aunt Arabella,' returned James with composure. He had, as it happened, looked up Marlborough's campaigns before setting out, but from the calm indifference of his manner one might well have assumed he had known this since his cradle.

'Ah,' said the old lady, 'I am glad to see that it is still remembered. I never met the Duke, of course, but I was once honoured by meeting Prince Eugene of Savoy. Such a charming gentleman. I fear the gentlemen are not as they were in my young days. Of course, the officers all made quite a fuss of me when I was a little girl. I remember one of them told me such an amusing story. I will relate this to you, James, for it is instructive though, I fear, a little mischievous. But then young men —'

She paused, beaming at them all.

Mr. Shelbrooke, muttering a variety of unrepeatable blasphemies to himself, was listening less to her chatter than to the silence outside. He did not like this at all. He did not believe for one moment that the two bullies had abandoned their project. From the window he could see the shadow of the Rookeries. It was another world side by side with their own, a world alive with violence and brutality, crude with reality – and here in this pitiful, wrecked room, this sad memento of a time that was dead and gone, sat this preposterous old lady, smiling brightly and recounting anecdotes of her youth.

'It was two of papa's officers,' she said. 'Such naughty boys — They asked a leading clothier of the town to dinner, and then I fear they gave him a very great deal to drink, so that the poor fellow scarce knew what he was saying or doing. And before he knew what they were about, they pressed a shilling into his hand and enlisted him as a soldier.'

And she nodded at them in a genteel, quizzical way as if this scandalous story were the most amusing thing in the world.

'But how dreadful!' cried Cassandra. 'What happened to him?'

'Oh really, I do not know,' cried Miss Parkington-Smith crossly, finding this question quite irrelevant. She was silent for a second as if the interruption had offended her, and Mr. Shelbrooke, thinking this was his opportunity, began, 'Madam—'

But, confound the old girl, she was off again.

'If only you could have seen papa's regiment,' she said. 'They were so handsome, so very handsome.' And she clasped her hands at her breast as if she were a young girl again, not a withered old maid to whom men were merely clumsy, uncivil creatures, intruders in her neat, vinaigrette world. 'They wore broad-skirted, scarlet coats,' she said.

'They still do, Aunt,' said Mr. Shelbrooke.

She did not appear to have heard this. She went on, 'And

long, low-flapped waistcoats, breeches and long white spatter-dash gaiters reaching high up. And they all wore broad buff leather shoulder belts, and broad waist belts as well, and they carried sword and bayonet and musket. Oh, I dare say it was foolish of me, but young girls are always so feather-headed, and I vow I could scarce take my eyes off them.'

Cassandra could scarce take her eyes off Miss Parkington-Smith, for it was quite impossible to imagine her so girlish – but she like her husband was growing restless, and she turned a beseeching gaze upon him, making a small despairing gesture as she did so.

'Madam!' said Mr. Shelbrooke again, then very loudly, 'Aunt Arabella!'

Miss Parkington-Smith turned her head towards him. Suddenly the flame was extinguished, and she looked what she was, an exhausted old woman, who had never cared much for her fellow creatures and now found them more distasteful than ever. Her face grew sour, her thin mouth twisted down, and her voice when she spoke again was dry and dusty as a leaf blown along the cobbles.

'Oh really,' she said. 'Really, Francis! I dare say my foolish conversation bores you. I'm sure you have better things to do than listen to a poor old woman's reminiscences, but surely in the name of courtesy – if such a term is in use today – you could bear with me for a few moments. It is after all,' she said, gazing disapprovingly at all of them, one after the other, 'not often that you honour me with your company, and surely for the space of one hour—'

'If we have not been here often,' interrupted Mr. Shelbrooke, who was rapidly losing his temper, in defiance of his own admonition, 'it is because we have not been invited, Aunt. If you care to throw your mind back, you will remember that my stepfather – James's father – was forbidden to set foot in this house, and I am not aware that you ever pressed him to return, even after your father's death, when it would have been easy to make some gesture of reconciliation.'

'Francis!' said Cassandra entreatingly, but he paid her no attention. He was indeed badly frightened and therefore greatly out of control: like the mother, whose child runs across the road and who in her relief at once slaps him violently, Mr. Shelbrooke was filled with rage against this infuriating old lady who only looked backwards and refused to see the danger an inch in front of her nose.

'Jack behaved shamefully,' said Miss Parkington-Smith. 'He was most insolent to dear papa, and many's the time – I do not wish to cast aspersions on the dead, but I have always been truthful, I cannot change my ways at my time of life – many's the time I've seen him return shamefully the worse for drink.'

She paused so that these terrible words should sink in, always turning her head from one to the other of them, like some small venomless snake that wished it were a cobra.

Mr. Shelbrooke eyed her stonily. Cassandra shot one look at him, then hastily glanced away. James, who really had controlled himself very well up till now, exploded into a small, sharp giggle then, ashamed, got up and walked over to the window.

'He would frequently return late at night,' said Miss Parkington-Smith, 'scarce able to stand upright, and using the most shocking language. I used to lie in my bed, shaking, listening to him trying to get up the stairs.'

'You never thought to help him, I suppose?' said Mr. Shelbrooke.

'Help him! Why should I? He brought it all on himself. He had no right to be in such a condition. Naturally,' cried Miss Parkington-Smith, 'my father was extremely angry and one evening —' She broke off. She was shaking, her lips were writhing in that monkey fashion of hers when she was furious and at a loss. 'But it's no matter. It was over long ago. It's certainly not suitable hearing for this child here.'

And she sank back into herself again, still seeing that disastrous night when the Captain, shirted and capped, had emerged from his room, brandishing a horsewhip and cracking this at young Jack who was a head taller than he was and who, confronted with this parental vision, broke into a wild shout of drunken laughter. Young Arabella had peeped from behind her door, only to hear her brother say, 'You bloody old hypocrite! Do you think I've never seen you coming back from your regimental dinners, foxed to the wide? I mean you no harm, sir, and you're an old man, but I swear if you strike me, I'll put you back into your room and lock the door on you.'

There had been a long, dreadful moment – Arabella had hardly dare look, but could not drag herself away – when the two men had stared at each other, and she remembered now the strange family likeness between them for that brief passage of time, though the Captain had never been good-looking, and Jack had somehow salvaged every handsome feature from the family tree. Then the Captain had exclaimed in a voice hoarse with defeat and fury, 'Get out of my house! Get out, you young blackguard. I never want to see you again, and don't imagine you'll ever get one penny of my money, because I'll see the lawyers first thing tomorrow and cut you out of my will.'

'Do you mean that, Father?' said Jack.

The Captain made it plain that he did mean it, in a variety of words and phrases that were new to his trembling daughter, and Jack had laughed again and called out, 'Goodbye, Bella, you owe me a debt of gratitude, girl, because you're going to be a rich woman,' and stormed out of the house, without so much as packing a handkerchief.

And she had never seen him again. She remembered this now, as she remembered that he was the only person to call her Bella, and for some reason it seemed to her that with Jack's departure, the light and warmth had gone from the house, so that from that moment she was an old maid for all eternity, and her father a bad-tempered, liverish, autocratic old man. And this made her crosser than ever, so that she snapped, 'I don't know why you're all staring at me. You'd better say your say, Francis, and then you can all return to your fine home, and forget about an old woman like me. After all, you have now done your duty, have you not?'

And she smiled and nodded, thinking she had had the last word; she stared as Mr. Shelbrooke roared at her, in a fashion remarkably like her father.

'You confounded silly woman!' he said, and at that Miss Parkington-Smith exclaimed, 'How dare you speak to me like that! Kindly leave my house, sir. I suppose you think that because I have no one to protect me —'

107

'No one to protect you!' shouted Mr. Shelbrooke, advancing upon her. 'Did I not knock one of those bullies down for you just now? Did I not risk a knife in my guts on your behalf? Now you are going to listen to me and,' cried Mr. Shelbrooke, forgetting everything except the urgency of the situation, 'you are going to stop sidetracking us with these absurd stories of your old father who, from what my stepmother told me, was a sot and a tyrant who made your life hell for you, and who at the end hadn't a friend to come near him.'

'My dear father—' began Miss Parkington-Smith in a shriek of outrage, but he would not let her continue, nor would he heed James who, looking a little pale, had come up to him and was pulling at his sleeve.

'Francis,' he said in an urgent whisper, 'Francis—'

But Francis merely shoved him away, hard enough to send him reeling, so he looked in despair at Cassandra, who shrugged her shoulders and turned her eyes to the battered ceiling.

It was quite a typical Shelbrooke scene, only Miss Parkington-Smith did not know this side of the family, and could only believe they had all gone mad.

Mr. Shelbrooke said more quietly, 'I suppose I am in some way to blame. I did not know you lived here, nor did I know your circumstances. There has not been much friendship between the two branches of the family, Aunt, but I do not see at this point that there is any use in our railing at each other. The important thing is that you are in the greatest possible danger, and do not seem to have the sense to see it. No! Don't interrupt me. You will kindly listen to me, and never mind what happened twenty years ago, never mind if my stepfather drank – for God's sake, I drink, and my wife's helped me up the stairs before now, and put me to bed too, not to mention pulling my boots off—'

'Yes, Francis,' said Cassandra, and bestowed upon him so entrancing a smile that for the first time during this scene he became fully aware of her, made a half-gesture towards her and stumbled in his speech. Then he went on.

'Never mind all that. It's old stuff. This isn't a question of who was right or who was wrong, or what your father thought of mine. They're both dead, aren't they?'

'Oh!' cried Miss Parkington-Smith, and fumbled for a handkerchief in her string bag. But her eyes were dry as a bone, and her face quivered with temper.

'And don't pretend you mind, either!' exclaimed Mr. Shelbrooke, who had endured a great many theatrical scenes from his wife, and could sum up the value of a tear better than most. 'It's a devil of a long time ago, and if you were honest with yourself, which I don't suppose you ever have been, you'd admit that the day they carried the old boy out, you heaved a sigh of the utmost relief and drank a small glass of sherry to restore yourself.'

'I am going to swoon,' said Miss Parkington-Smith, but Mr. Shelbrooke only said brutally, 'Cassie, wave a feather under her nose,' adding to James who was still trying to attract his attention, 'and if you don't stop pulling at me, I'm going to box your ears. Now!' he said again to Miss Parkington-Smith,' who was not swooning at all, and who indeed wore the air of one to whom this scene was positively reviving, 'do me the courtesy of listening, without any stupid and irrelevant interruptions. You must know you are in grave danger. Your landlord, whoever the scoundrel is, wants to get you out so that he can set up a brothel here.'

Miss Parkington-Smith closed her eyes.

'And don't pretend you don't know what a brothel is,' went on Mr. Shelbrooke, who was growing desperate, and trying to find the means of shocking this obstinate creature into a state of reason. 'But if you wish to know, a brothel is a bawdy-house in which the girls are for hire, and your landlord, from what I can gather, is one who proposes to live on a proportion of their earnings. It is quite obvious,' said Mr. Shelbrooke grimly, wearing somewhat the air of a university lecturer dealing with an intractable student, 'that this is most remunerative, and the fellow stands to earn a great deal of money by it. He certainly earns nothing from you —'

'Francis!' said Cassandra again.

'Oh stop bleating my name,' cried Mr. Shelbrooke, 'and, James, if I have any more nonsense from you, I'm going to put you out of the room —'

James said a little hysterically, 'Look out of the window, Francis. Look out of the window.'

Mr. Shelbrooke gave him one look, saw that this was not impudence, but desperately serious, and stepped across to the window. Both Cassandra and Miss Parkington-Smith followed his gaze.

There was a small crowd assembled in the darkening courtyard of the Rookeries, outside Miss Parkington-Smith's window: there being no curtains to draw, they could stare in with impunity.

Polly would have known most of them. Zephaniah was not there, but several of the girls were, painted and plumed for their evening excursions, and half a dozen of the tougher bully-boys who later that night would be patrolling the Marylebone Fields. They were crouching near the house, carrying torches: the scarlet light on their faces made them look fiends in hell. One of them had flattened his nose against the window: as he met Mr. Shelbrooke's look of startled rage, he raised his hands above his head and made a rude, derisive gesture. This seemed to be a signal; the next instant a stone was flung which splintered the glass from top to bottom, and at that all bedlam broke loose: the whores shrieked with laughter, hurling filthy names at Miss Parkington-Smith, and extending lewd invitations to the handsome young man staring down at them, while the rest of them yelled and danced and catcalled.

And as Mr. Shelbrooke, frankly at a loss and clenching his fists, was swinging round, a bowl of stinking slops came through the broken pane, spattering him, then crashing on to the floor. This was followed by more shrieks and abuse, and then a deluge of objects showered through: refuse, rotten fruit, stones, bits of wood, and finally the corpse of a very dead rat – for the rats scurried round the rafters of the Rookeries, and their bodies could be seen lying in the courtyard any hour of the day or night.

Mr. Shelbrooke, white and with his fine ruffles befouled, raised his pistol and fired through the broken window. And in an instant the crowd was gone, and there was silence and darkness, with nothing left but the debris and a couple of torches spluttering on the ground.

He touched the dead rat with the toe of his boot, then stared stonily at Miss Parkington-Smith.

'That,' he said, 'is only the beginning. Charming, isn't it? But only the beginning, ma'am. They want you out by tomorrow night. Do you believe you can take much more of this? Your window is broken. Anyone can get in. These are gentry who will stop at nothing. Now it's only slops and fruit and rotting corpses. It'll be bullets next, and then it will be the men themselves. Perhaps the women. I think you'll find the women worse than all the rest put together. What do you propose to do, Aunt? Tell them of the Captain's exploits? Call them ruffians and scoundrels? Explain how you never really approved of the lower classes? There won't be much left of this little house, you know, and I'm afraid there won't be much left of you either. This is not a chivalrous place, and these people here are not afflicted with over-tenderness of heart. I do not think that empty bellies and soft hearts go together. Besides, I imagine this unknown landlord is behind them: either you are out, or they are. They are gone for the moment. A pistol is a fashion of communication that they understand only too well. It is a fashion they may be employing themselves shortly. What are you going to do? I cannot stay here to guard you, nor would it serve much purpose if I did. It is not even as if it were a question of one day or two. This will go on and get worse and worse until you are out, alive or dead.'

Miss Parkington-Smith said nothing. She was ghastly pale. She did not even look at Polly who, hearing the noise, had come running through again from the kitchen, and now hovered in the doorway, Mokasa a dark shadow behind her.

'I want you to come back with us now,' said Mr. Shelbrooke, and Cassandra cried out at once, 'Oh yes, Aunt Arabella, you must come – we have a lovely little room for you, and Polly shall come with you. You will be quite at home, and we shall all wait upon you.'

Miss Parkington-Smith still said nothing.

'You see how my wife makes you welcome,' said Mr. Shelbrooke, adding with a faint smile, 'We may not have spoken much to each other for the past few years, Aunt, but we are human in our own way, after all: we may drink and indulge in various excesses, but we do not care, oddly enough, to see a person victimized, especially when that person is old and alone. You will stay with us as long as you choose, and then we will procure you a small house where you can pass the rest of your days in comfort and peace. You are fortunately well provided for —'

'There is no money,' said Polly from the doorway, and would not look at her mistress who was at once grimacing and nodding her head frantically.

'What do you mean? The Captain —'

'It was all invested,' said Polly, beginning to cry again. She was sober again by now, but her emotions had been too battered for her to have any self-control. 'It was that South Sea affair, sir. The Bubble they called it. The Captain was most interested in the scheme. If we hadn't had a few pounds in one of them northern banks, sir, we would be penniless.' She added wretchedly, 'It wasn't so bad while the Captain was alive, because his regiment helped, but after he was gone —'

'Why in God's name didn't you tell me this?' demanded Mr. Shelbrooke, but still the old lady would not answer.

Then Cassandra cried again, 'Oh, but it doesn't matter. Why, Aunt Arabella, we will look after you. I know Francis shouts a great deal and looks so fierce, but his heart's as soft as butter.'

'Thank you, ma'am,' said Mr. Shelbrooke, staring at her.

'Oh, but it is, it is. I should know. After all, Aunt Arabella, I'm married to the man. And you cannot stay here, truly you cannot. They'll kill you. They're desperate people. Why won't you come? Give me one good reason. Do you think we don't like you?' demanded Cassandra, her voice going up and down the scale; she was contriving to look as if she most passionately loved Miss Parkington-Smith, whose face was as tight as a nutmeg-grater, and whose whole demeanour was one of the most genteel distaste. 'But we do, we all do,' cried Cassandra, well into the part. 'Why, Francis is always saying how sweet you are, and how tenderly his stepfather spoke of you.'

'For God's sake,' muttered her husband, but she ignored him, turning to James and saying coaxingly, 'Is that not so,

112

James? Have you not always heard the sweetest things of your Aunt Arabella?'

James, who had heard her referred to as a sour old maid and a mean-hearted bitch, reddened and gulped, but replied manfully, not looking at his brother, 'Yes. Oh yes, Cassie, of course I have.'

'You see!' said Cassandra. 'Well, that's all settled then. How nice it is! Polly shall pack your things, and you will come with us in the carriage. You have no idea how pretty the room is that's waiting for you. It is almost,' she said, speaking in a whimsical fashion that made her husband look at her sardonically then turn up his eyes, 'as if it knew you would be coming.'

There was a pause. Then Miss Parkington-Smith said coldly, 'Well then, it had better be informed that I am not coming.'

They had, none of them, not even Cassandra, anything left to say. The silence was broken only by Polly's sobbing. Outside the courtyard was still deserted, only some drunken creature was returning, and his song suddenly burst upon their ears, coming clearly through the paneless window.

> 'As I was a-walking down London,
> From Wapping to Ratcliff Highway
> I chanced to pop into a gin-shop,
> To spend a long night and day.'

'I hope you are enjoying the music,' said Mr. Shelbrooke. The reveller began a second verse: it faded into the distance as he stumbled up the Rookeries' stairs.

> 'A young doxy came rolling up to me,
> And asked if I'd money to sport.
> For a bottle of wine changed a guinea,
> And she quickly replied, "That's the sort."'

Miss Parkington-Smith cried out hysterically, 'I'm not going. I'm not going, I tell you. This is my home. This was papa's home. I've lived here all my life. I'm too old to be driven out by a lot of hired thugs and bullies. Why, the Captain would turn in his grave at the idea. To be thrown out of my own home by these dreadful, common people, and have this house, papa's house, turned into a – a—Oh, the very idea of it!'

'Is that your last word, ma'am?' asked Mr. Shelbrooke.

Miss Parkington-Smith spoke now with great firmness and pride. 'That is my last word, Francis. I am not going.'

'Very well,' said Mr. Shelbrooke. He turned to pick up his hat. Both Cassandra and James at once began to cry out, she exclaiming, 'But you can't leave the poor old soul here,' and he, 'They'll murder her, you know they will.'

Mr. Shelbrooke continued as if they had not spoken. 'Goodbye, Aunt Arabella. If you should change your mind, you have only to ask Polly or your black servant to get you a sedan chair, and we will be delighted to welcome you, whatever the hour.'

'I shall not change my mind,' said Miss Parkington-Smith, almost contemptuously. 'I wish you goodbye, Francis. And you too, dear Cassandra. As for you, young James, I hope you will continue with your schooling, for young people should improve their minds, and education is so important, is it not?'

'It is indeed,' said Mr. Shelbrooke grimly. A muscle was flickering in his cheek. He went up to her, hesitated, then kissed her shrivelled lips. They felt to him like paper. He gave her a long, hard look. 'I do not know,' he said, 'whether you are a most courageous woman, or the most damnably obstinate old fool I have ever met, but I do know this: you are up against most evil, ruthless and unprincipled people who will stop at nothing, and in this world of ours, ma'am, none of us can afford to stand alone. I am young, I believe I am reasonably strong, I have been instructed how to use my fists, and I own a pistol, but if I were in your position, I, too, would go, and instanter. I know it seems to you like running away, but even the Captain, ma'am, your venerable parent, would surely tell you that in all battles there occurs a moment when it is tactical to retreat. There is no shame in that. It is a matter of pure common sense.'

'You mean well,' said Miss Parkington-Smith unexpectedly. 'I think you are a good-hearted young man. But you don't understand.'

He raised his shoulders in a hopeless shrug. He said nothing

114

more. Only out in the hallway, having patted the sobbing Polly's hand, he paused to look up at Mokasa, who stood there, a head above him, enormous and black: he was no longer smiling and his face was wary and grave.

'Are you staying here with these two ladies?' asked Mr. Shelbrooke.

'Master,' returned the African, 'I will stay to guard them with my life, for it is the devil who awaits them, and I cannot abandon them.'

Mr. Shelbrooke's eyes moved over the massive shoulders and the neck like a tree-trunk. He said, 'Here is my pistol. You may need it. Keep it by you. And don't let anyone in. Anyone.' He added, 'You look to me as if you've a serviceable pair of fists on you, but I fear that will not be enough.' He paused. 'Are you a patron of the Fancy by any chance?'

The white teeth flashed. 'Yes, master!'

'Do you use mufflers?'

'No, master.'

'Then don't start using them tomorrow. And don't forget to keep that pistol in your pocket, and don't hesitate to use it neither.'

Then without another word he stepped into the courtyard. His family waited until they were out of Miss Parkington-Smith's earshot, then they began speaking in unison, both becoming more and more excited.

'You cannot possibly leave her there, with all those terrible creatures around.' This was Cassandra, with James crying out in counterpoint, 'I am going back. She must have someone to look after her.'

Mr. Shelbrooke halted. He looked white and drawn and grim. There was little trace left of the handsome young gallant who had been gambling his life away, who seldom came home sober, and who was reputed to play the devil with himself and all who came in contact with him. The black shadow of the Rookeries fell aslant of him so that half of him was in its darkness, and the other illumined by the crescent moon above. Already from the tenement came a rustling and a shuffling like an army of rats: he heard this, shuddered involuntarily, then his jaw set.

He roared at Cassandra, 'What the devil choice have I got?' then to James, bringing his hand down on his brother's collar and swinging him round, 'You try to go in there, and I'll break your back. So you'll look after her, will you? The perfect knight—What good do you think you can do? You're nothing but a wretched little schoolboy who has only to be thrashed and he comes snivelling home to big brother to protect him —'

Both Cassandra and James cried out at this, and by chance they spoke precisely the same words, 'That's not fair!'

'I dare say it's not,' returned Mr. Shelbrooke, beginning to stride on again, with his family trailing after him like a couple of unwilling sheep. 'But if you're fools enough to imagine there's any fairness in life, it merely proves what I've known for a long time – that you're both half-witted.'

'I think you're a coward,' cried Cassandra hysterically, and at this James gasped, for he would never dare say such a thing, he would scarcely have dared to think it.

Mr. Shelbrooke stopped dead. He looked at her, and she stared back at him, her fingers twisting together. Then he gave a brief laugh, said, 'Very well, my love, I must accept your verdict, I am a coward,' and walked on again, staring ahead: he could see dimly in the dusk the carriage waiting in Tottenham Court Road, with Jem pacing up and down beside it.

'You're brave enough when it comes to fighting duels,' said Cassandra in the quavering voice of one who, having already said the unpardonable, refuses to retract. She had picked up her skirts, and was treading carefully in the muck and stones of the roadway. 'I'm sure,' she went on, 'you show a prodigious courage at the hazard table. But when it comes to protecting a poor, miserable old lady against a crowd of ruffians —'

She broke off. James half suspected she was crying. He himself dared say nothing. He backed against the wall. He thought privately this was a bit much of Cassie: if he had said such a shocking thing, he would certainly have received the flat of Francis's hand across his cheek, and it was not fair the way women took advantage of being the weaker sex. He did not believe that Francis was a coward, yet there was something in what she had said, that echoed miserably within him, and suddenly he wanted to do something he had not done for the

116

past five years, he wanted to bawl like a girl, and there was an alarming lump in his throat that simply refused to go down. He gulped, and then his brother started to speak, calmly and clearly, still apparently in full control of his temper.

'If you will be so good,' he said, 'as to explain to me what one man can accomplish against the whole buildings, maybe you'll persuade me to change my mind. It's not as if we should be simply against that couple of bullies—Oh, of course you did not see them. You didn't miss much. But it'll not be just those two, it'll be the whole boiling of them, for indeed I swear they dare not do otherwise – and to deal with so many we should need a regiment of redcoats. There's nothing I can do that I have not already done, and you know it. Unless you expect me to get killed – and I'm damned if I'm having my throat cut just to pacify your tender conscience. Now kindly get into that carriage. Thank God we're getting away from here. If it eases you, I believe with all my heart that the old lady will change her mind – she must change her mind – and I should not be surprised if she didn't arrive on our doorstep within a very short time. And,' he added bitterly, for he was quite exhausted, and – though he would never have admitted this – his own conscience was biting into him like a branding-iron, 'I hope you enjoy yourselves, for a more cussed old devil never existed, and I swear you'll do nothing to please her.'

Neither his wife nor his brother answered him, and presently they were rolling along Tottenham Court Road.

And back in Paradise Row, Polly and Miss Parkington-Smith wretchedly avoided each other's eyes. At last Miss Parkington-Smith crept up to bed, while Mokasa set planks of wood against the broken window, and Polly shifted the dresser against the front door.

And now it was pitch dark, and the inhabitants of the Rookeries were setting about their nightly business.

EIGHT

The carriage came up to the High Street of St. Giles-in-the-Fields, just before it turned into Oxford Street. The hour was late and there were not many passers-by. From the shops and alehouses swung huge signs on their ornamental iron brackets: they creaked sadly, making a thin, wailing noise. A scavenger passed them with his handcart, ringing a bell to announce his aproach; a sedan chair could be seen going in the direction of Cavendish Square.

None of the Shelbrookes spoke a word. James was still occupied with the lump in his throat which refused to vanish.

Cassandra was swinging her foot and gazing resolutely out of the window. Mr. Shelbrooke's head was bowed, and his arms folded across his chest as if he were asleep.

And all three of them were visualizing precisely the same thing: a respectable and disagreeable old lady, in her smashed desolate house, staring up in terror at the rabble which had burst in upon her and now surrounded her.

As the carriage turned into Oxford Street, its iron-rimmed wheels clattering and slipping on the greasy cobbles, there was a pounding of horse's hooves, and a voice suddenly bellowed out at them.

'Don't be frightened, madam, but stand and deliver your money: if you speak a word, you're a goner.' The voice then added more pacifically, 'If the gentleman will kindly dismount and hand me over all the valuables, there'll be no trouble for any of us, and you can all go on your way.'

Mr. Shelbrooke sprang to his feet, his hand flying for his pistol, then drew in a harsh breath of fury, for the weapon naturally was no longer there, it was in the pocket of Mokasa. He snapped to his wife and brother, who had caught at each other's hands, and were gazing out in a mixture of terror and excitement, 'Stay exactly where you are,' then flung open the carriage door and leapt out.

He stared up into the face of the rider who had reined his horse beside the carriage, his pistol levelled. The look of anger began to be succeeded by one of utter incredulity, an incredulity reflected upon the face of the highwayman, whose pistol hand slowly fell to his side.

'Well, Zephaniah,' said Mr. Shelbrooke, breathing rather quickly, 'I see you have changed your profession since I saw you last.'

'Well now, Mr. Francis,' returned Zephaniah amiably enough, 'and how is the world treating you, sir?'

'Excellent well, thank you,' said Mr. Shelbrooke, then began to laugh, in which Zephaniah presently joined him, so that Cassandra and James, already battered and baffled by the events of the day, were left gaping at the extraordinary spectacle of the head of the household apparently enjoying a vast joke with a gentleman of the road, who had only a minute ago threatened them all with robbery and violence.

Mr. Shelbrooke stopped laughing as swiftly as he had begun. He said, 'In the circumstances, I assume that I may now send my wife and brother home?'

'Why certainly, certainly,' said Zephaniah. 'If I had known it was you, sir, one of the family as one might say, I'd never have dreamt of stopping you. All a mistake, sir. It's the bad lighting – I trust as you don't bear me any grudge.'

'Never in the world,' said Mr. Shelbrooke, 'but I want to talk with you, Zephaniah, and I hope you know some place where we may be quiet and confidential. You have done me a good turn, old friend. You're just the person I've been looking for, to give me some advice.'

He turned to Jem, who wore the air of one so much accustomed to lunacy that a little more scarce mattered. He ignored his wife's wails of interrogation and protest. 'Take them home,' he said. He added, 'Those are my orders, Jem. They are in no way to be contradicted. Is that understood?'

'Are you mad?' cried Cassandra in her ringing voice. 'Are you clean out of your wits, Francis?'

'Oh, I dare say I am,' returned Mr. Shelbrooke, bestowing a derisive grin upon her.

'This is a highwayman. He might kill you,' said Cassandra furiously.

James interposed. 'It's only old Zephaniah,' he said comfortingly. 'It's all right, Cassie. We know him. He used to be our groom. He's a good sort, Zephaniah, he wouldn't harm anyone.'

It was too much for Cassandra, whose nerves by this time were as ruined as her dress. She turned on James, berating him for speaking so highly of a villain who would have thought nothing of shooting them dead, and the sound of her scolding travelled back on the air, so that Mr. Shelbrooke, listening to it, grinned more widely than ever, then smote Zephaniah on the shoulder.

'Don't ever marry, boy,' he said. 'Stay single all your life and you'll be the happy man.'

Zephaniah gazed thoughtfully after the receding carriage. 'She's a real good-looker,' he said.

'She is,' agreed Mr. Shelbrooke. He was feeling strangely as if he had slid some six or seven years back in time: he could almost see himself strolling round the stables with young James, a stocky little boy, following like a dog relentlessly at his heels.

'A bit high-spirited like,' suggested Zephaniah.

'That is an under-statement,' said Mr. Shelbrooke.

'But you always liked the high-spirited fillies,' said Zephaniah, meditatively running one of his ribbons through his teeth, 'eh, Mr. Francis? Now what was the name of that farm lass? You was real taken with her.'

'I think we'd better not mention her,' said Mr. Shelbrooke hastily, 'for after all that was a long time ago, and I am now a respectable married man. And I am respectable too, though nobody seems to believe me. I've got to talk to you. Where can we go?'

'There's a brandy-house down Rathbone Place,' said Zephaniah. 'It's not the sort frequented by gentlemen, but then, if I remember you, Mr. Francis, you'd not be quarrelling with that, you always had a kind of taste for low company.'

'I've not changed, and it sounds exactly what we need. I gather you are not yet married, Zephaniah?'

They were strolling down towards Rathbone Place, Zephaniah leading his horse by the bridle. Mr. Shelbrooke remarked his companion's vivid attire, with the strings of bright ribbon dangling from wrist and knee, the flash of silk shirt and the brilliant cravat. But the face, oddly enough, was the same red, robust country face he had always known. He had loved that face as a boy: it went with a handful of apples, sensible homely advice, and an endless variety of country songs – not always the kind that mama's friends appreciated, but jolly songs for whistling and dancing. It was in defiance of everything an honest face: one could imagine Zephaniah robbing fat, rich citizens, but one could never see him being cruel to the defenceless and young.

Zephaniah said now, 'Well, Mr. Francis, I'm not in the kind of profession that encourages a wife, as you might say. Women are queer customers, you must admit that, they're bloody queer, always weeping and scolding and carrying on, and they don't care over-much for a husband who's out half the night, and may never come home in the morning. But,' he added thoughtfully, almost as if he were astonishing himself, 'I seen someone—Oh, she's just a slip of a lass, and perhaps she's over young for me, but I can't get her out of my mind, Mr. Francis, I just can't rid myself of the thought of her, and maybe I'll ask her and settle down after all.'

'This sounds serious,' said Mr. Shelbrooke.

'Ay, it does that. There's something about her that moves the heart. I think of her all the time. I don't know why. I lay she's no better looking than an hundred others, and she's not half so handsome as your good lady. But she reminds me of a foal we once had, that I nursed five nights through to pull it round. Your father wanted to shoot it. I wouldn't let him. It's the same with her. I couldn't bear to see her hurted.' He paused, then grinned a little shamefacedly. 'I doubt she'd let me stay on the road. Would you offer me a job again, sir?'

'Any day.'

'Well, who knows, but I might be taking you up on that, Mr. Francis, sir. This is the place. There's rough customers here, but I reckon you and I can take care of ourselves, and they've a French brandy here that's not bad drinking, not bad at all.'

They sat themselves down at a wooden table and, as they were sipping their brandy, Mr. Shelbrooke remarked, 'I think perhaps it's high time you changed your profession, friend, wife or no wife. You don't want to end by being scragged, anatomized and set on view in a glass case. I'd hate to come into Surgeons' Hall and see your confounded death's head mopping and mowing at me.'

'I'd make a fine end,' sighed Zephaniah. 'Can't you see me, Mr. Francis, standing up in the cart, and making a fine, grand speech? Why, I'd have them all in tears, and I swear half London would be out to see old Zephaniah turned off.'

'Oh, for God's sake!' snapped Mr. Shelbrooke, setting his glass down so violently that he nearly broke it. 'I can see you well enough. That's where you'll be ending in a little while, and it's not the end I'd choose for you.'

Zephaniah was eyeing him, smiling with a gentle mockery, just as he had smiled in the salad years, smiled at a bragging, fierce schoolboy who came rushing to him with some tale of woe. And the smile caught at Mr. Shelbrooke's heart so that he scowled and looked down, then speaking in a sharp, loud voice, ordered two more brandies.

'You was always one for the underdog, Mr. Francis,' said Zephaniah. 'And Master James was just the same. Oh, I remember well. You never liked to see people set down.'

'Well, I'm delighted to hear you say so,' said Mr. Shelbrooke angrily, 'for everyone, including naturally my own family, seems to consider me a bully and a coward who'd sell the world to save his skin. But never mind that. I want you to tell me something. What do you know about the Rookeries in Paradise Row?'

Zephaniah's face changed. It was no longer amiable, nor was his voice. He answered shortly, 'I lives there.'

'You live there!'

'I do. Why not? It's a stinking cesspool, but it suits me. There's no one to ask where you're going. There's no one to peach on you. There's no evidence men there. There's only fellows like myself – coiners and pickpockets and footpads and whores. They'll never tell on you. They wouldn't dare. They're as bad as you are.'

'And who is the owner of this charming place?' asked Mr. Shelbrooke then, grimly, as Zephaniah instantly turned on the innocent, jolly smile that James had already noted, 'Oh come off it, you old hypocrite. Do you think I don't know that look of yours? You always used to wear it when you didn't propose to answer me the truth. I remember it as a boy. I once asked you about a poacher my father was after. You wore the same grin, but I happened to know he was a friend of yours, I knew you were lying. Don't lie to me. This is too important. Damn your eyes, Zeph, I'm no Mr. Peachum, I'm not an evidence man. If I'd set my heart on hanging you, I've got enough evidence already to top you twice over, same as if you wanted to shoot me, you've a brace of pistols in your pocket, this very moment.'

Zephaniah stared, then laughed. 'I'd not shoot you, Mr. Francis.'

'I'd not give much for my chances if your life were at stake. Who is the owner? Who is the devil? You must know him, confound it. Doesn't he collect the rents?'

'What, him? He'd never so demean himself. He's a gentleman.'

'You make me ashamed to bear the name. Who does collect them then?'

'Oh, two bullies of his, regular strong-arm fellows. One of 'em's a real gallows-bird, and the other's a poor sort of half-man, tenpence-ha'penny in the shilling he is, only he's handy with the knife like, not having the wits to know what he's doing half the time. He's always laughing. The women are scared stiff of him. They shut the children up when he's near.'

Mr. Shelbrooke looked thoughtful, but made no comment. 'Only him – since you want to know – he does come from time to time. I seen him. I don't know his name, at least I suspicion it, but suspicion's no proof, you know that as well as me. That's the truth, Mr. Francis, so help me. He's a big fellow, well dressed. I know he's got some kind of job, to give himself a respectable air like. I think—But it's no matter what I think, and it wouldn't help you neither. Only I'm sorry for the folk as has to work for him, for he's an ugly customer, and I'd not mind getting a poke at him one dark night if I thought I'd get away with it. I know one thing about him though. He's a lousy thief-taker, sir, and there ain't no lousier profession in the whole world. There's never been any proof. If the people in the Rookeries knew for certain, his days would be numbered and you'd not need two figures neither. We don't like evidence men. But I tell you, there's no proof – all I know is it don't do no good to be on the wrong side of him. Those who come athwart him don't last long.'

Zephaniah after this was silent for so long that Mr. Shelbrooke said impatiently, 'And what exactly do you mean by that?'

'Zookers, sir, I remember there was Elms, he was a neighbour of mine above a year, a very civil man, a cutter of gloves by trade, and only a common thief in his spare time like. He was all right until the day he couldn't pay his rent, and then they picked him up, and he was indicted for stealing half a guinea and a silver Spanish dollar. He was turned off, sir, it must be near enough the year today. And there was Eliza Powell, she was a good, honest working woman, and would slave like a pack-horse, only she was mightily given to drinking, and one day when she was a bit fuddled, she gave our gentleman a piece of her mind, saying the buildings was a disgrace, not fit for honest folks to live in. I don't know all the rights and wrongs of it, but they came for her soon after, and she was transported to Botany Bay. There was no real harm in her. She was a decent sort of soul.'

'My stepfather's sister lives next door to the Rookeries,' said Mr. Shelbrooke.

Zephaniah started, slopping over his brandy. For the first time he looked genuinely astounded. 'Damn my soul, you don't mean the old lady that's got to quit? Your aunt, Mr. Francis? Her? She's a bloody silly sort of bitch, if you don't mind me saying so. She's not got a hope in hell. If he wants her out, she'll have to go. And,' added Zephaniah earnestly, 'it'll be better for her if she goes quick. If she don't, she'll go feet first, as I told that old Polly who looks after her. The gentleman wants her place for his girls. The rents of the Rookeries don't

124

bring him in enough to set him up in cravats, but the girls do. It's a strange thing, Mr. Francis,' said Zephaniah, adopting a pontifical air, and sliding the ribbons through his teeth, 'and I ain't what you might call a moral man, but I don't care over-much for that kind of thing, sir, especially as all his girls are silly country sluts, like the ones you and I have known in our time, who come up to town, thinking London's the place to make their fortunes. By the time he's done with 'em, it's his fortune they're making, and half of them down with the French faggot stick, and rotting in their graves before they're over twenty. That's what he wants your aunt's house for, and that's why she's got to instanter. I can tell you this, sir. He's coming down tomorrow morning himself, to see she's out. Oh, he won't be spoiling his gentlemanly hands – fine white hands he's got, I've seen 'em – but his bullies will do his work for him, and half the Rookeries will be helping with dogs and all.'

'Dogs!' exclaimed Mr. Shelbrooke, pushing his brandy away with such force that the glass rolled to the floor, split and smashed.

'That's what he uses, Mr. Francis, when he wants 'em out quick. There was Sarah Thomas – I heard her. "Don't let 'em get at me any more," she says, "for if you do, they'll kill me." And him with the rotten teeth says, 'You bitch, that's my design,' and then she runs from the buildings in her shift, all in a gore in the grievousest manner you saw any creature, and the dogs after her as if she was a fox, and—' He saw Mr. Shelbrooke's face. He checked himself. 'Get the old girl out, sir. Knock her on the head if you have to, but for the love of God, get her out. She's all right tonight, maybe. Everyone's out. We work nights, as you might say. But they'll start on her tomorrow morning, early. Get her out before they come. Get her out as soon as you can.'

'Yes,' said Shelbrooke, in a sick, angry voice. 'Yes. But in the devil's name how?' Then, 'Will you help me, Zephaniah?'

'No, Mr. Francis.'

'For God's sake, man —'

'No, sir.' Zephaniah's face had lost all trace of jollity. It was grim now, grim as the Rookeries. 'Polly asked me the same. I'd do a lot for you, sir, you know that, and I've nothing against the old lady, but I've got myself to think of, and I'm not in a position, as you might say, to take unnecessary risks. Believe you me, sir, if I was to raise a finger to help her, I'd land up in Newgate jail tomorrow, and there's not one of them in the buildings would dare to do anything to help me.'

'But I promised you that —'

'I'm not a baby, Mr. Francis, to depend on promises. What's a promise to the likes of me? Oh, I know you means it. You was always fond of old Zeph, even as a boy. You'd do everything in your power to save me, do you think I don't know that? Only you couldn't, boy. With all your money and your fine fancy friends, you couldn't do a bloody thing. And I'd be scragged at Tyburn, and your old lady'd be none the better off. No, Mr. Francis.' And he repeated with a savage vehemence, 'No, no, no!'

'I suppose I must accept that. But tell me this, Zeph. What would you do if you were me?'

'Oh – I think I'd take my pretty wife into the country, and forget all about it for a couple of weeks.'

Mr. Shelbrooke digested this, eyeing Zephaniah from time to time beneath his brows. Then he said abruptly, 'You imply that everyone in the Rookeries would band against her. That's so appalling that I can scarce credit it. But I always knew these people were beasts. They're not human. No human being with any decency in him could stand by and watch an old woman being murdered.'

Zephaniah had risen to his feet. He was not a tall man, but he was broadly built and conveyed an impression of size. 'Mr. Francis,' he said sternly, 'you always had enough to eat, didn't you? You always had a bed to sleep on. You always had money in your purse to buy what you wanted. You got no right to say what you've just said, no right at all, and I'm ashamed of you, sir, I'd have thought better of you.'

He paused, and Mr. Shelbrooke, thus relegated back to boyhood, stared at him. He would have taken this from no one else, but there was a burning sincerity in Zephaniah's words, even a sorrow, that kept him silent.

'These people aren't beasts,' said Zephaniah. 'They're afraid, that's all. They got nothing, and they're afraid of that

126

being taken from them. You don't have to be clever to understand that, sir, it's something you know in your guts. When
you're starved like, and your baby's so weak it can't even cry,
and your wife maybe has her belly full of the next one on the
way, you don't bother about standing up for your rights. You
ain't got no rights. You just do every bloody thing you can to
get a crust for the wife and a drop of milk for the baby, and it
don't matter if that means busting someone's head open or
knocking a fine gentleman down and stamping on him. You're
not fighting for your rights, you're fighting for breath. If you
couldn't breathe, Mr. Francis, and you was gulping for air, air
would be the only thing you'd be thinking of. You wouldn't
care if a child was starving next to you, or a woman was being
beaten to death. You'd only think that if you hadn't air you'd
die. And that's the way it is with them. One wrong step and
they're dead. Oh, we talk of the gallows, sir, we make a great
joke of it, we call it all sorts of names. We ain't just hanged, we
dance the Paddington Frisk – but we only joke because we
dussn't do anything else. The gallows is always there. On our
right and on our left, beneath our pillow, dangling from the
ceiling, and, so they tell me, there's over three hundred easy
ways of tying the noose about our necks. You'd not understand
that. How could you? Oh, if you was to murder someone, I
suppose you'd hang. But we don't have to murder. We just
exist, and we hang all the same, for no better reason.'

'It seems to me,' said Mr. Shelbrooke, 'that I owe these
people an apology. For I must admit that this point of view
has never struck me before.'

'Oh,' said Zephaniah with a sudden air of subservience that
sat most oddly on him, 'It is I who should apologize to you,
Mr. Francis. It's not my place to tell you your duty.'

'You bloody old hypocrite,' said Mr. Shelbrooke, 'where's
your cap in hand, Zeph? And don't forget to touch your fore-
lock when you speak to me.'

Zephaniah shot him a look, and Mr. Shelbrooke grinned
at him, then said seriously, 'All right. I accept what you say.
You should know, after all. But surely, in the name of reason,
if everyone in the Rookeries would combine against this –
this gentleman and his dogs, he'd be done for, and there'd be

no danger, for there'd be no one left to do any peaching.'

'Oh, you talk fairy tales for the babies,' said Zephaniah scornfully. 'I thought better of you, Mr. Francis, God's truth I did. Combine! There's only one thing in the world that'd make 'em do that, and that's if they knew for certain our gentleman was an evidence man, that it was him who laid information. And maybe that's true and maybe not, but he'll take damn good care they never find out. If you reckon on something like that happening, I can only think being married has turned your wits like. You've gone soft in the head.'

'Perhaps I have. Now you come to mention it, it wouldn't surprise me. Being married does odd things to people. Wait till it's your turn. But surely, surely, there's something to be done. You know all these people. They must trust you. You could talk to them.'

'No one in the Rookeries trusts anyone else.'

'But you could at least mention the subject —'

'No, Mr. Francis.'

'Are you sure there's nothing you can do?'

'I'm bloody sure, Mr. Francis.'

'You used to care more about people,' exclaimed Mr. Shelbrooke angrily.

And Zephaniah answered as he had answered Polly, 'I learnt not to care a long time ago.'

'God forgive me,' said Mr. Shelbrooke, 'I thought I did too.' He looked round for his reckoning. 'So there is nothing to be done.'

'Not a thing in hell,' agreed Zephaniah. 'You'd be wiser not to meddle – 'deed, sir, you would.'

Mr. Shelbrooke rose rather unsteadily to his feet. He had drunk a great deal of brandy, but his staggering was not entirely due to drink. He nodded unsmilingly at Zephaniah, then without another word walked out of the brandy-house, and set off for home which included, as he was painfully aware, a knight-errant of a brother and a dramatic amazon of a wife, both of whom were doubtless waiting up for him.

He walked up Oxford Street under the cloudy sky and crescent moon. His fob told him that it was past two o'clock. It was not held to be safe for unaccompanied and unarmed gentlemen to walk the streets so late, but Mr. Shelbrooke was far too disturbed to care, and one or two slim gentlemen out on their errands, eyed him first hopefully, then doubtfully, and finally decided to let him be.

As he came to Poland Street, he saw one of the night-walkers slipping past him. This held no interest for him, and his glance was absent-minded and cursory, then something about her struck him. He stopped, stared, then called out in mingled anger and astonishment: 'Jenny!'

She stopped, hesitated.

He saw she was preparing to dive past him, like a frightened animal. He deliberately blocked her way.

'Jenny,' he said, his voice shaking with shocked anger, 'what the devil is this?'

She was a pretty girl. He had always thought so. It was not the kind of prettiness that interested him, for he preferred something more dramatic, more sophisticated, and this was only a child scarce older than James, but pretty she was in her country way, with soft curling hair, large eyes and a trim figure. Hers had never been the kind of looks that lasted, but they were appealing and certainly played a large part in her undoing. He saw now that, though she was still pretty, she was lamentably painted, the hair crimped into a style that did not become her, and her dress vulgar, garish and over-tight. She seemed as scared as a rabbit, and her voice – it was tainted with the whining London accent – was shaking up and down the scale as she answered him, her eyes moving from side to side as if she were seeking some way of escape.

'Oh, Mr. Shelbrooke,' she said in a dreadful attempt to sound genteel, 'fancy meeting you at this time of night.'

In the circumstances this social greeting was almost indecent in its absurdity. Mr. Shelbrooke said roughly, 'What are you doing here? What have you got all that filthy muck on your face for? Did I not give you sufficient money to go home? I didn't pay you to go back on the streets again, you silly little trollop. What damned nonsense is this? Don't you want to lead a decent life? Don't you want to keep those looks of yours? Didn't I make it plain what would happen to you if you go on in this fashion?'

She began to cry. She whined, 'I can't help it, sir, honest I can't.'

'What do you mean, you can't help it?'

'He won't let me go.'

'Who's *he* and what the devil can he do to prevent you?'

'He says—' She broke off, casting a frantic look over her shoulder, as if the mysterious 'he' might suddenly appear. Then she cried out in a frantic, wailing rush, 'He'll have me sent to the House of Correction. He'll have me transported. He says I stole a ring from him.'

'And did you?' demanded Mr. Shelbrooke, staring at her.

'No! Honest to God I didn't. But he says I did. He wears lots of rings. He says if I don't do exactly what he tells me, it's the end of me. I can't do nothing. It's his word against mine. Who'd believe me?' She was sobbing now so that her words were incoherent. 'I can't help myself, Mr. Shelbrooke. You don't understand. It's all right for the likes of you. They'd listen to you. You're a gentleman. You got the right accent. You got lots of friends who'd speak up for you. But a girl like me's got no chance at all, no chance at all.'

And before he could say a word or catch hold of her, she dived past him, ran down Poland Street and, by the time he reached the corner, was well out of sight.

What with this and his conversation with Zephaniah, Mr. Shelbrooke could scarcely have been in a worse temper when he arrived home. James at least was in bed – wide awake, as it happened, but this his brother did not know – but Cassandra was waiting up for him as he had feared and was, as he saw at once, in one of her more formidable dramatic moods.

He saw her as he came up the stairs: she was leaning over the banister, her chin on her folded arms. She looked extraordinarily beautiful as always – indeed, with her hair and her colouring it was almost impossible for her to look plain – but at that moment her beauty was only a further irritation, he could not endure it, he was so damned tired, so utterly out of sorts with himself and the world.

He said wearily, his voice rough and hoarse with fatigue, 'Can't it wait till the morning?' Then he said, 'Oh, Cassie, don't quarrel with me now. I'm in a vile temper, I warn you.

Things are bad enough between us, surely, without making them worse. We shall only say a great deal that we'll both regret tomorrow. Go back to bed, there's a good girl. We can discuss everything in the morning.'

'The morning will be too late,' said Cassandra. She saw he had been drinking, and was about to reproach him, but a closer view of his grim, exhausted face warned her that this at least must remain unsaid.

He paused, halfway up the stairs. Cassandra, whose mind always functioned theatrically, thought they might look a little like Romeo and Juliet, if one could imagine the young lovers still together after the moon-romance had died. But the thoughts induced by this were frightening, and she said rather desperately, 'Francis, I swear I do not mean to nag, and I'm very sorry I called you such names, but how can I sleep when that poor old lady may be being murdered at this very moment?'

'If she is, there is nothing we can do about it,' said Mr. Shelbrooke. He realized that this sounded deplorable, but had often noticed in himself and other people that violent emotion tended to produce this kind of callous brutality, as if it were some secret defence against sentimentality.

Cassandra naturally chose to take the remark at its face value. 'Oh, of course you don't care,' she said. 'It would be too much to expect. When I think of what may be happening —' Her voice rose. 'Aren't you going to do anything, Francis, anything at all?'

'Yes,' said her husband. 'At the moment I am going to get into bed and I am going to sleep.'

'Her death will be on your conscience,' said Cassandra.

He shrugged. He continued walking up the stairs and, as he did so, Cassandra backed into her room. She said nothing more, but every graceful movement was a reproach, and the enormous green eyes fixed on him were luminous with condemnation.

Only as he reached the landing, prepared to go into his dressing-room, he stopped: for a moment they looked at each other.

Cassandra, near tears, was thinking, He does still care, and he looks so unhappy, he looks dreadful. And then, if only he would come into my room, we could comfort each other, we could stop this horrid quarrelling, we could perhaps find some way of saving that poor old soul.

And Mr. Shelbrooke was thinking, If she would only give me one small sign to show that she would like me to come to her.

Cassandra said, 'Good night, Francis.'

Mr. Shelbrooke said, 'Good night, Cassie.' He added mechanically, 'Sleep well.'

Then he went into his dressing-room and shut the door.

There was silence in the Shelbrooke household, but for a while none of them was asleep. Cassandra crept into bed, and lay there, hands beneath her head, staring up at the ceiling. She was thinking of a great many things, and Miss Parkington-Smith was one of them, but there were other things as well, such as, for instance, how hard it was that one flaming outburst of temper should in that violent second have smashed everything that had made their marriage and their life worth while.

Presently, feeling desperately wide awake and knowing that sleep was impossible, she got out of bed and went to her dressing-table, opening the bottom drawer. Under the silk and satin lay this morning's three roses, together with a crumpled note.

Cassandra did not take this out, only stared down at it. She thought, We cannot go on like this. She thought, After all, what can he expect, I am young, men are attracted to me, I was never made to lead a nunlike life. She thought, It's done all the time, it's done by almost everyone I know, it is not even fashionable to remain faithful to your husband.

And then she thought, But I don't really want anyone else, and at this she lost her temper for the twentieth time that day, shoved the drawer shut and flounced back into bed, rolling over so that her face was buried in the pillow.

But the pictures that came to her mind now were not of Francis, they were of a vinegar-faced old woman who looked as if she liked nobody and nobody liked her, and this was followed by such horrors that Cassandra began to cry in real earnest, and continued to cry for a long time.

Mr. Shelbrooke did not, of course, cry, for such was not his inclination. But he did not even get into bed or take off his clothes: he paced up and down for most of the night. He thought of Cassie a great deal, for indeed she was seldom out of his thoughts, but the greater part of his mind was occupied with a variety of schemes, each of them more preposterous than the last, and all of them concerned with the kidnapping of a foolish and obstinate old woman who had never looked truth in the face, and was certainly not going to begin now.

As for James, he did not sleep for the first hour either, but, being younger than the other two, he could not stay awake indefinitely, and fell at last into a peaceful slumber. He at least had made up his mind, for during the drive home, a sudden and astonishing idea had come into his mind, and he was resolved first thing tomorrow to find out if it could possibly be true.

NINE

James was up before any of them. Cassandra always lay late in bed in the morning, and Mr. Shelbrooke, though normally out early, had demanded coffee to be sent to his room. He too had a great decision on his mind, and he felt he could not endure at this moment either Cassie's histrionics or James's bursting curiosity.

James came noiselessly down the stairs in his stockinged feet: he was, apart from the shoes he carried in his hands, dressed to go out, and there was a penknife in his pocket. He knew that Cassie would certainly not trouble herself about him, but one never quite knew with Francis: he might suddenly develop one of his looking-after-my-little-brother moods, and appear on the landing, demanding, 'What is all this, and where do you think you're going?'

James therefore crept down as if he were a burglar, then sat down on the bottom step to put his shoes on. This accomplished, he bounded into the kitchen, flung his arms round Mrs. Bowes's neck, gave her a smacking kiss, and cried, 'I want three cups of coffee, a piece of steak, a slice of cold ham and some stewed kidney.' He added, 'I'm starving. I've not had a bite to eat since yesterday's tea, and that was only a few miserable biscuits, it wouldn't keep a parrot alive.'

Mrs. Bowes adored him, as he knew perfectly well, and would have got up to cook him a meal in the middle of the night, had he expressed a wish for it. But she glowered at him now, put on a great scolding air, and snapped, 'It's only eight o'clock. Breakfast isn't near ready yet. What's got into you, Master James? Are you so anxious to get back to school?'

James made a face at her, said, 'Not likely, not with that brute of a Frog waiting for me with his birch at the ready.' But he changed colour slightly, for school, as it happened, was precisely where he was going, and he wanted nobody to know.

He devoured a colossal breakfast, for after all he had to keep his strength up: he was about to put his head into the lion's jaws, and even St. George probably nourished himself well before attacking the dragon. He washed the steak, ham and kidneys, including half a loaf of bread, down with innumerable cups of coffee, then swung out of the house, glancing once and warily up at the windows, lest Francis might be looking out.

But Francis was far too occupied with his own problems to stare down at the street below, so James walked in the sharp morning air, through the side streets of Cavendish Square, and cut across the Fields to the hamlet of Marylebone.

He knew the time-table of the school by heart, having the kind of mind that burdens itself with every sort of minute detail in the hope that one day this might be of use to him. And in this case the details were very important indeed.

This was the French conversation day, taken by the Doctor himself, with old Rainbow at his side. James wondered casually what colour her hair was this week. The Doctor would have already assembled all the boys together, regardless of their age or abilities; from nine in the morning until two o'clock, and from three-thirty until six, every lesson would be conducted in French. The boys would be examined on their knowledge of current affairs, they were expected to discuss the latest books and plays, and not one word of English must be spoken.

It was one of the few silent classes of the week, for nobody said very much except the Doctor, and there was a great deal of nods and gestures to compensate for a remarkable lack of the French tongue. James would be conspicuously quiet, for he had no ear whatsoever for languages, and would subside, as far as was permitted, into his private dreams, while Dr. Fountaine shot foolish questions at them all, and Mrs. Fountaine waved her arms in a Gallic fashion, interpolating from time to time such remarks as, 'Et alors', and, 'Mais voyons, messieurs', in an effort to spur the flagging conversation on.

All the masters were compelled to attend this session. It was all right for Beau Frog who, whatever else one might say against him, spoke the most fluent and impeccable French, but it was hard on the science and mathematics teachers who did not speak one word. However, the Doctor insisted on their attendance, and it used to provide some light relief for the boys to watch these gentlemen sitting at the back of the class, striving to look interested and fighting with their yawns.

Mr. Fielding was of course in his element, and would engage the Doctor in some abstruse philosophic discussion which was incomprehensible to everyone else, but which naturally displayed him at his formidable best.

James felt, therefore, that he was entitled to take it for granted that Mr. Fielding would be out of the way for five hours. He did not however risk going in at the main entrance, but ran through the garden, and slipped in at the side door, making his way towards his own classroom.

The confounded parrot raised its usual squawk as he crept by: 'Pray come into the parlour and have a glass of wine.' James could gladly have wrung its withered neck, but contented himself with shooting it a bitterly hostile look. However, this was not likely to attract attention, for the parrot was an institution, it always said this to anyone who came by, and repeated the phrase so frequently that nobody listened to it any more.

James's heart was pounding as he came into the classroom, pushing the door open in a furtive way, terrified lest there should be someone there.

But the classroom was empty. The window was a little open, and faintly from upstairs could be heard the drone of the Doctor's voice. James gazed about him, wondering almost angrily why he was so frightened, why his heart was thumping so unnecessarily. Devil take it, what could happen to him? Suppose Beau Frog suddenly descended upon him, laid his great white hand that was so powerful, despite its softness, on the scruff of his neck — What then? For God's sake, what then? He would be beaten. Well, he had been beaten before, and many times. The beating would be savage, but it could not be more than that: even Beau Frog would not dare flog him into unconsciousness. It was not as if he were some orphan boy, defenceless and alone in the world, some wretched little climbing boy or an apprentice from the Workhouse, whose body could be conveniently disposed of in the River Fleet. He was James Shelbrooke, with a powerful and influential brother, and this James kept on telling himself, as he stole, leaden-

136

footed, towards Mr. Fielding's massive desk.

But nothing could quieten his insubordinate heart, nothing could dispel the strange atmosphere of fear and cruelty that seemed to surround this perfectly ordinary room with its desks, blackboard and shelves of books.

He saw his own desk, almost with surprise. It seemed an age since he had sat at it. Once he had carved 'J.S.' on it, and underneath he had drawn a succulent female form in ink: unfortunately the ink had sunk into the wood and could not be erased. He had been thrashed for that, he remembered, and in front of the entire class: he had been told moreover that he had a salacious mind and would end on the gallows.

The drawing was still there, of course. He could not resist looking at it. He would not admit to himself that this was less from curiosity than a desire to put off what he had come to do. It was in any case a poor drawing: the beating should have been less for innate viciousness than a palpable lack of artistic ability.

James looked round the room, then realized that he was simply marking time. He cursed himself, and went over at once to Mr. Fielding's desk, standing on the dais.

It was locked, of course. Trust old Beau Frog. But James had come prepared for this. He took the penknife out of his pocket and slid the blade under the desk lid. The lock after all was an old one, and so was the desk: it had probably never entered Mr. Fielding's head that any boy would dare to tamper with his belongings.

The knife slid round several times, then there was a rending sound and the desk opened.

James was almost choking by this time. His vision was so blurred that he could scarcely see what he was doing. But he noticed immediately that there were no exercise books in the desk, only packets of neatly docketed papers bound together by tape. There was nothing in the school curriculum to explain this. There was one loose paper on top. He stuffed it into his pocket. His ears were singing with terror: he could not understand this for he had never felt like this in his life.

For a second he hovered there, almost unable to move. In the silence and stillness he heard the parrot give its loud squawk of, 'Pray come into the parlour and take a glass of wine.'

And, as he heard this, his eyes dilated, he smelt a faint trace of perfume on the air.

If it had not been for that, he would probably not have heard the soft, swift steps coming down the passage. He knew those steps. He had no time to shut the desk. With the sweat pouring off him, as if this were a hanging matter, as if he were a gentleman of the road like Zeph, with the watch after him, he ran like a hare to the window, flung it open wider and put his leg across the sill.

Mr. Fielding saw the desk before he saw James, and to this James was to believe later that he owed his life. The schoolmaster's eyes were caught for a second by that wide-open lid, with the neat bundles of papers inside. Then slowly, with such a look on him as James had never seen, he turned and raised his head.

The window was narrow and James was broad. There was also a considerable drop to the garden below. But he knew from Mr. Fielding's face that this was no longer a question of a flogging, this, unbelievable as it seemed, was a question of murder. James, frantic with terror, contorted his sturdy body so as to wriggle through the frame: he was half out, half in, temporarily jammed, when Mr. Fielding leapt across the room and grabbed at his coat-tails.

James could not use his hands, for they were clinging to the sill outside. But he could use his feet, and in a paroxysm of panic, kicked out and brought the sole of his shoe smashing into that white, intent face. He did not think that once his highest ambition had been to deliver such a blow. He was past thinking coherently of anything. With a final wrench that threatened to crack his ribs, he tore his way through the frame, and landed in the garden below with a crash that seemed almost to jolt his spine through the top of his neck.

Mr. Fielding, who had reeled back from the blow, recovered himself with a speed of which James would not have considered him capable. As James frantically picked himself up, and bolted in the direction of the Fields, he saw for one split second his schoolmaster's face as he leaned out of the window.

He was to see that face in his dreams for many nights to

138

come. The great, white moon countenance, with its Roman nose and thin black moustache, was contorted with rage. The eyes were slitted with it. The fleshy mouth that could smile in so ugly a fashion was smiling no longer; it was moreover hideously cut by the heel of James's shoe so that the blood trickled over the chin. To James, in that one anguished flash of time, as he staggered up and took to his heels, the face was no longer human: there was not in it a vestige of mercy or compassion.

He could not help turning once: it was as if he were mesmerized. And he saw that Mr. Fielding was levelling a pistol at him. He thought, amazed by the utter lunacy of this, Christ, he's going to shoot me, he really means to kill me. He went down flat on his face as the bullet whistled across him, then picked himself up again, and ran and ran, no longer knowing where he was going, the sound of the shot ringing in his ears, his one craving to be out of range, to be safe again.

He believed – it was all so entirely mad, anything could happen in a world where schoolmasters aimed their pistols at naughty pupils – he believed that Mr. Fielding was coming after him. He ran long after he needed to run. He ran until his heart and lungs demanded surrender, and he fell down flat on the grass of the Fields, too weak to move, expecting that at any moment Mr. Fielding would loom over him and finish him.

But there was no sound. There was no burning flash of pain. There was nothing but the stubbly grass, the sun, now gathering heat, beating down on his neck, the twittering of some bird winging its way across the sky.

He had in his blind terror ignored the fact that Mr. Fielding was a vast man. Only sheer agony of fear had enabled him to squeeze through that window frame. For Mr. Fielding it would have been entirely impossible. He had obviously decided that by the time he had run down the stairs and crossed the garden, James would be well out of sight. He had doubtless returned to the Doctor's classroom and would be sitting there, considering his best method of revenge.

There was in any case no sign of the enemy, and presently James managed to sit up and, after investigating various portions of his body, prodding himself here and there, and stretching his limbs, he came to the conclusion that there were no holes or rents in him and that he was still alive and undamaged.

He struggled to his feet, for he was still terrified that Mr. Fielding would come looking for him. He felt very shaky, but he managed to drag himself on, and after a little while the drama of the situation was borne upon him, and instead of being afraid, he began to feel pleased with himself. Instead of shambling on weak, groggy legs, he strode quite proudly along, only he still walked away from the school, and found he was taking the same direction as on that other famous occasion : the 'Farthing Pye House' was only a hundred yards away.

He was not intending to go in, only he happened to glance over his shoulder and saw that a distant figure was coming over the hill. All his terrors revived. He began to run again, and in desperation plunged into the tavern.

It seemed to be very crowded. He stood there, a step inside, his breath coming in gasps, then peered out of the door to see that his pursuer was almost upon him, had obviously seen him and was proposing to follow him in. He gave a little cry that no one heeded, and stared in anguish at the form that darkened the doorway : he was too bemused to see it properly, indeed by this time his pride was entirely extinguished, and he screwed his eyes up tight as if this somehow would prevent his enemy from seeing him.

A familiar voice broke upon his ears, and a familiar hand descended in a great clap upon his shoulder.

'Why, Master James,' said Zephaniah, 'what are you a-doing here? You're making a practice of this, boy, you're growing to be just like your brother.'

The mist cleared from James's eyes, but another mist seemed dangerously disposed to take its place : he gave a great gasp and turned his head sharply aside, mortified by the tears of relief which, unasked for and unwanted, showed ominous signs of rolling down his cheeks.

If Zephaniah noticed this, he made no comment, only remarked, 'What you need, young master, is a quartern of strong waters,' and in a moment a mug of ale was thrust into James's shaking and sweating hand. It did the trick almost instantly, and he sat down on the bench beside Zephaniah, bestowing a shamefaced smile upon him, with the girlish tears well back in their locker.

He recovered almost at once. He thought how marvellous it was that Zeph was here. He was just the person to give advice in these unprecedented circumstances. He looked a little shyly at his friend, assuming that he had been on his nightly excursions and had come in here for a refresher.

The highwayman looked as dapper as ever, with the bright ribbons flowing around him as if he were a maypole, and the smile he bestowed in return was his usual jolly one: it was really very hard, if one had not experienced it, to imagine Zephaniah threatening people, robbing them and perhaps even shooting them.

But this at once reminded him of what had happened. He said earnestly, 'I am glad you're here, Zeph. You can help me, I'm sure. You see, Mr. Fielding has just tried to shoot me.'

Zephaniah after a pause, said, 'And why should he do that, Master James?'

James went very red. He buried his face in the mug of ale for a moment, for the story, when actually put into words, was, as so often happened, not quite so glorious as it had seemed at the beginning. It had all seemed very romantic and dramatic at the time, but to say boldly in the bright light of this summer morning that he had broken open a desk and rifled private papers – James suddenly wondered what Francis would have to say when he heard about all this. He almost certainly would hear: it was not the kind of thing Mr. Fielding would keep to himself. As he was secretly anxious for his brother's good opinion, he felt more disturbed than ever and, after a couple of abortive attempts, fell silent again.

Zephaniah said very gravely, 'Young sir, what have you been up to?'

James put his mug down on the table. Everyone around him was drinking and talking. At one table men were playing with the dice, at another they were involved in a card game. It was all very like Mr. Hogarth's drawings, but James suddenly knew that he had had enough of drama, and that this was the moment to speak the truth.

He looked up at Zephaniah, who met and held his gaze with the utmost seriousness.

James said, 'It's really to do with my Aunt Arabella. That's the old lady who won't move out, you know, she lives next to the Rookeries and they've given her notice to quit. Well, I know there's someone who's doing his best to get rid of her, and suddenly last night I had an inspiration. You know the way you do, in the middle of the night. I thought this person might be Beau – it might be Mr. Fielding. He's my schoolmaster, you see. He's a real old devil, Zeph, I think he could do anything. Oh, this isn't as silly as you may think it is. That last day at school – I ran away, you know, I don't know if my brother told you – well, I was being kept in, and everyone else was at the Pleasure Gardens. And a girl came in asking for Mr. Fielding. She was —' He hesitated. 'She was very pretty, Zeph, quite a stunner, but she was – well, you could see what kind of girl she was.' He added quickly, very much the man of the world, 'Not that that's anything against her, of course. I mean, I know there are girls like that, just as there are highwaymen like you.'

'Thank you, Master James.'

'That's all right, Zeph. I only wanted to make it clear that she wasn't a lady, at least not what we call a lady. Only she was pretty, as I said, and she was very young, and I think she was frightened. She said – she said she had a protector. She said she wanted no trucks with the likes of him. She said she was a respectable girl. Well!' cried James, rather disconcerted by the intensity of Zephaniah's gaze. 'You must admit it was strange, Zeph. He's so respectable, and he teaches us, he's supposed to instruct us in manners and morals, and a girl like that comes and leaves him such a message.' He paused. Then he said, 'I somehow thought Mr. Fielding might have something to do with the Rookeries. Of course I detest him, so I suppose I'm prejudiced – but he does wear the most extravagant clothes and perfume and things, and I don't see how a schoolmaster's salary can possibly pay for them. Anyway, I sneaked back into school, this morning, and – and I broke his desk open. Only I didn't get much chance to investigate, because he came in and saw me.'

Zephaniah said nothing.

'He potted at me,' said James, with a crack in his voice. 'I was half out of the window, and he drew his pistol and fired straight at me. Now you must admit that's a bit out, Zeph. I mean, if he'd thrashed me or knocked me down — But to try to kill me! You don't do things like that, not to someone of my age. I know I shouldn't have broken his desk open, but still I am one of his pupils, and to try to murder me—'

He stopped. He still could not quite believe what had happened, and now he had put it into words, it sounded more incredible than ever.

Zephaniah said after a silence, 'This girl, Master James. This girl who you say was so pretty. Didn't she tell you her name?'

'Oh yes,' said James.

'And what was it?'

'Jenny.' James peered up at Zephaniah through the smoke and blur of people. He could not see the highwayman's face, for his head was turned so that his three-cornered hat obscured it. He grew a little afraid. He said, 'I don't know if it makes any difference, but I did get one thing out of Mr. Fielding's desk. I put it in my pocket. It was a loose sheet of paper. It was as if he had thrown it in without having time to put it in its proper place. Would you like to see it? I haven't looked at it myself yet.'

'We'll both have a glim at it,' said Zephaniah.

James dug it out of his pocket, smoothed it out and, with a propitiatory air, laid it on the table. Both boy and highwayman bent their heads to examine it. It was clear enough. It was written in a neat print, and ran as follows:

'To be indicted for Breaking and Entering: Miss Jenny Trantum, aged seventeen, profession street-walker. Charged with stealing one Ring, belonging to Robert Fielding, also with Breaking and Entering the Shop Premises at Vigo Street, and stealing 2 Gowns, value 20s., 2 Petticoats value 2s., a pair of Sheets, value 15s., 2 Pieces of Silk, value 10s., a Gold Ring, a Trunk, 3 Shirts, 2 Shifts, 2 Girdles, 3 Caps, a Silk Mantle, 24 Clouts, 2 Aprons, a Coat and a Silk Handkerchief, all the Property of the Proprietress of the said Premises.'

There was a little note scrawled after this in Mr. Fielding's writing: 'To come up before the London Sessions in a week's time.' And then there was his signature.

James was about to remark that she hadn't half been going it, when the quality of Zephaniah's silence checked him, made him stare into his friend's face. His expression was such that James could only call to mind the old phrase: he looked as if he had seen a ghost.

James said timidly, 'I don't quite understand, Zeph. What does this mean exactly?'

'I'll tell you what it means,' said Zephaniah. If he had ever been a jolly man, he was one no longer. 'It means the rope, young master. It means the Tyburn cart and a hanging, with all London out to see.'

James thought of the pretty young girl with her whining cockney voice, who had been so afraid. He said incredulously, 'They can't hang her — She's not much older than me.'

Then suddenly he realized that the rude note he had left for his schoolmaster had probably precipitated this; he broke off, going a little green.

'Her age don't make one hell of a difference,' said Zephaniah roughly. 'If you steals property over the value of five shillings, you hang, and here —' He jabbed at the figures with his fore-finger. '— Twenty, two, fifteen, ten – that's forty-seven shillings, ain't it? And there's more beside.'

'Perhaps,' said James, 'she didn't really do it.'

'I don't reckon she did,' said Zephaniah, 'but that don't make much difference, not with Mr. Bloody Fielding standing there as evidence.' His face contorted. 'The bastard! The lousy, peaching son of a whore!' He broke off, caught at James's arm, jerking him to his feet. He bestowed a smile on him, and the smile was fierce and bitter, yet held a kind of be-wildered resignation. 'Master James,' he said, 'you're looking on a fool, boy – a damned, bloody, blithering fool. I'm a-going to tell you something, young sir, that I've never told a living soul. I wanted money, see, I wanted a devil of a lot of money, and I didn't choose to spend the rest of my days saying, "Yes, sir, No, sir", always at the gentlemen's beck and call. Oh, I mean nothing against your brother, nor your dad. They never

144

did me no harm. They always acted fair and square to me. But it wasn't enough, so I kicked over the traces and I went my own road, and I told myself I didn't give a damn no longer for anyone or anything. I'd bloody well take what I could get, and if it wasn't given me, why, I'd say, "Cocky, what's a-clock?" and ram my pistol down their gullets, and if that wasn't enough, give 'em a pill to send 'em to the graveyard. And now — Oh, I always swore I'd never run my head into a noose as long as I could avoid it. I dare say it comes in the end, you can't keep ill company and hope to die in your bed, but I meant it to go on for as long as possible. And now, Master James, I'm going to put my head in that noose, and all for a lass I only met a few days ago, a bit of a lass no better nor worse than an hundred others that vile rogue has sent to their damnation. Only there's something about her that's different to me, see, and this time he's not getting away with it, not if it means that poor old bastard, Zephaniah Clarke, has to swing high above the people.'

He paused. James was too dazed to say a word.

Zephaniah looked again at the sheet of paper. He said slowly, 'I dunno. I dunno at all.' He picked up one of his ribbons and slid it meditatively through his teeth. 'Mostly they can't read nor write. Only — We don't stick at much, cully. Murderers, thieves, whores, that's all one to us in the Rookeries. But we don't like evidence men. We don't like them one little bit. If a fellow cuts another's throat, we looks the other way. If a chap what should know better brings in the country girls who're too simple to see what he's doing of, we mayn't care for it much, but it's a way of making money, and money's all that matters to most of us. But turning evidence —' His voice rose. 'It's today they're throwing the old lady out, ain't it?'

'Yes,' said James with a catch at his voice.

'Then I think I'd better be getting along,' said Zephaniah in an airy fashion so strangely in contrast to his preceding speech that James could hardly contain his curiosity. He made as if to go, only pausing to ask, 'What about your brother, Master James? Isn't he coming down to the Rookeries to see the fun?'

'Francis?' said James, a little dazed by this and not compre-

145

hending it at all. 'Oh no, Zeph. Francis won't be coming. He says he can't do anything.'

'Ah!' said Zephaniah, and grinned.

'After all,' said James defensively, 'there's not much he can do, is there?'

'Of course not,' said Zephaniah. He was still grinning, as if something amused him enormously. 'And it's nothing important, as you might say. Just an old woman being knocked on the head like, and thrown to the dogs.'

'Zeph!'

'A real cussed old bitch she is too, saving your presence, sir – never did anyone a good turn in her life, and fair nags the life out of Polly, the lord only knows why she stays with her, poor old soul, for she don't get no money, and she gets precious little else. I dare say it's a mercy the old girl's put out of the way. Well, I'll be getting along, cully. The Rookeries are my home, after all, and I like to keep my eye on what's going on.'

James noted the new form of address. It was an unusual familiarity from Zephaniah, and seemed to denote that he was pleased with himself. He cried out joyfully, 'I'll come with you, Zeph.'

'Oh no you won't, young master.' Zephaniah turned on him. 'This ain't going to be anything for the likes of you. You're going straight home, that's where you're going, and if I catch you anywhere near the Rookeries, I'll break your neck for you.'

'Oh, Zephaniah!' protested James, furious, not so much at the threat, which did not impress him, but at the implication that he was too young to run into danger.

But Zephaniah only said, 'Now run off home. Do what I tell you, boy.' He seized James by the shoulders and swung him round, giving him a shove with his knee. 'That's the way you go. Off with you now.'

The look in his eye and the firmness of his voice made James sullenly and reluctantly do as he was told. He began slowly to walk back in the direction of Marylebone, while Zephaniah with a wave of his hand and a bright flutter of ribbons, strode off towards Tottenham Court Road.

It was only then that James realized that Zephaniah had taken Mr. Fielding's paper with him.

However, this did not seem to him particularly important, for there were other matters in his mind, and far more urgent. He walked on, looking from time to time across his shoulder: as he walked he kicked at the grass beneath his feet, and muttered various imprecations, all connected with Zephaniah's dictatorial ways and strange misunderstanding of James Shelbrooke's adult status.

By this time Zephaniah was well out of sight, but James still walked on until he came to the reservoir of Marylebone Basin. Then he branched off by Mortimer Street, and began to run strongly and swiftly, taking the footpath across the fields that would bring him out at Tottenham Court Road.

And as he did this, Mr. Shelbrooke was knocking at his wife's door.

Cassandra answered him in so languid a voice that he was astounded. She possessed superlative health; he had never known her ill, and her vitality was such that she could dance all night and show no trace of fatigue the next day. But now she was lying back in bed, with the curtains drawn, and from what he could make out of her in the gloom, her face was a ghastly white.

He had more than enough to preoccupy him, but Cassie in so wan and listless a state alarmed him so much that he almost forgot what he was about to do.

He exclaimed, 'For God's sake, darling, what is the matter?'

She muttered in a thin, querulous voice quite unlike her normal tones, 'Oh, don't fuss, Francis. And don't come near me. I can't endure it. I don't want anyone. I wish to be alone.'

'I beg your pardon,' said Mr. Shelbrooke. His voice was stiff with hurt and affront. He moved back as quickly as if she had spat at him.

She shot him one swift glance, then turned her face away. She said, 'I didn't mean that — Only I have so dreadful a headache, and even the sound of people's voices makes it worse.'

'I'll call the physician immediately,' he began, but she at once interrupted and, if he had not been so distraught with everything, he might have remarked that her voice was suddenly strong again.

147

'All I need,' she said, 'is to be left alone. Completely alone. I shall be well again by the evening.' Her voice tailed off into its former thin whine. 'I have always believed that fasting is the best cure. You know that. I shall sleep and I shall eat nothing, and I swear that will do me more good than any amount of blood-letting and soothing syrups. Oh, Francis,' sighed Cassandra, 'will you not let me sleep? I feel utterly exhausted.'

He retreated to the door, still eyeing her in bewilderment. He had never known Cassie behave in such a way. She often indulged in tantrums, but never in the vapours. He said, 'At least let me send your maid up to you.'

She gave a great cry. It was the cry she had once produced with great effect when playing Lady Macbeth. She had in point of fact made a shocking mess of the role, for she was hopeless in high tragedy, but one or two of the more violent scenes had been effective, if only for the wild beauty of her person and the remarkable volume of her voice.

Mr. Shelbrooke had never seen her performance in this particular role: his own personal problems were so overwhelming that Cassandra in the hysterics was the last straw: he could not summon up the patience to deal with her.

'Will you go away!' she cried, then with a plaintive sob, 'Oh, Francis, forgive me, but can't you see I'm too ill to be badgered like this. I assure you I will be quite recovered by the time you come home. I believe I am better already. All I need is three hours' sleep.'

'I cannot leave you like this,' protested Mr. Shelbrooke. He was still hurt, and this was not improved by her turning away from him and closing her eyes. He said stiffly, 'Very well. If you insist. I will tell James to keep an eye on you.'

'Thank you,' said Cassandra, so faintly that it was as if the last vestige of her strength had left her. 'Goodbye, Francis.' Her eyes opened. 'Are you going to your Club?'

'Later,' said her husband. 'I have some – some business to see to first. In the City. I dare say I shall spend the afternoon at the tables, unless of course you would prefer me —'

'Oh, no,' said Cassandra. 'No. I must be alone.' And she turned her face into the pillow, so that Mr. Shelbrooke who was, for some inexplicable reason, not entirely convinced that

148

she was as ill as she pretended, stared at her for a while, then moved quietly from the room.

He banged on James's door, but James apparently had gone out. This seemed to him in no way extraordinary for James liked to roam about the town, so, with a last look at Cassandra's door, he went down to his own study.

He examined his pistols to make sure they were loaded, and selected for himself a stout stick from the rack. Then, after a brief hesitation, he poured himself out a glass of wine, which he drank at a gulp.

He said, 'Damn the obstinate old bitch!' Then, after a second glass of wine, 'Damn her. Damn her to hell.'

Then he let himself out of the house in Hanover Square, and started to walk in the direction of Tottenham Court Road.

Cassandra, fidgeting and kicking her feet under the blankets, as if she could not bear to stay still, waited until she heard the bang of the front door. Then she leapt out of bed and ran to the window, looking out. Far down below she could see her husband walking, as he had said, in the direction of the City; he seldom took the carriage when on his own, for he had been brought up in the country and welcomed the chance to stretch his long legs.

She poured out some water from the ewer, and washed off the white powder she had liberally daubed on her face. Her complexion at once revealed itself in its natural brilliance. Then, her eyes shining, she knelt down by the oak chest in the corner, and lifted up its lid.

There they lay, all the costumes she had once worn, wrapped carefully in paper. 'Who knows after all what may happen?' she had once told Francis pertly, in the earliest days of their married life. 'You may find yourself a doxy you love more than me. You may kill your man and have to flee the country, or lay your all, myself included, upon the hazard table, and throw ames-ace. You may live to thank God for a wife who can earn her own living, so that you can desert her at your pleasure, or else depend on her to support you. I am not going to throw these lovely things away. They are mine. I adore them. And one day perhaps I shall have need of them.'

She could not resist, even in this emergency, looking

through them, letting their folds slip softly through her fingers. The material was in most cases coarse enough, and the jewels and ornaments were cheap paste, but each gown was a memory, triumph or failure, each reminded her of the exciting days of the past.

Here was Polly Peachum – Polly, her favourite part. It would be appropriate enough to wear today, but she could not walk through the town dressed like Polly, it would be courting disaster. She laid it back in the chest, making a comic little grimace of regret and, as she did so, hummed:

> *'But he so teaz'd me,*
> *And he so pleased me,*
> *What I did, you must have done.'*

And this, of course, this saucy bit of sprigged muslin, was the Country Wife. Francis had seen her in the part, and spoken very roughly to her about it. 'It is the grossest indecency,' he said, with that extraordinary prudishness only to be seen in men who were by nature free in both speech and behaviour, 'I do not wish you ever again to act in so obscene a role.'

Oh well— She had never acted it again, though she had loved the part, it had appealed to all the extravagance in her nature.

But this— Ah this! This was Rosalind, her darling Rosalind, her best part, her greatest success. Cassandra knew well enough that the success had been due more to her slender figure, her red hair and her talent for carrying men's clothes than to any gift for speaking poetry, but nonetheless it had been a success, and now she spoke the lines slowly, as if she only half remembered them, slitting her eyes, and adopting instinctively a swaggering attitude in front of the mirror.

' "Men," ' said Cassandra softly, ' "have died from time to time, and worms have eaten them, but not for love." ' Then she struck a swaggering posture, looked saucily up at an imaginary Orlando, and declaimed, ' "A lean cheek, which you have not; a blue eye and sunken, which you have not; an unquestionable – an unquestionable —" '

But the rich words had slipped out of her mind; she stood

150

there scowling, the shirt and breeches hanging over her arm, and at this moment the clock in the hall chimed ten o'clock.

She gave a little cry, leapt away from the mirror and tore off her night-gown. In two minutes – she had not learnt to change quickly for nothing – a slim girlish boy pirouetted round, and Cassandra, gazing joyously at her reflection as she coiled her hair up, to push it under a cap, saw that the clothes still fitted reasonably well, though her figure was undoubtedly a little plumper, owing to a great deal of rich food and too much relaxing in the chaise-longue.

She slipped one of Francis's jackets round her shoulders, for this after all was not the stage, it was London in full daylight, and there was, it was impossible to deny, an androgynous air to her that in her Vauxhall Gardens day she had not noticed.

Indeed, as she was about to leave, she eyed herself a little doubtfully. Somehow she was not quite so boyish as she had imagined herself to be. She must remember not to raise her arms, for that would make plain contours unusual in the opposite sex. There was also the betrayal of her slender waist, not noticeable on the stage, where in any case the audience was prepared to accept the transformation as traditional, but possibly rather startling on a London morning.

For a moment Cassandra, easing her arms in the over-tight shirt, wondered if she were not being foolish, if she were not permitting her love of drama to run away with her, as Francis always told her. But the thought of going alone into the Rookeries as a woman plain and simple was even more alarming, so she shrugged, practised a couple of manly strides and decided that at the worst she would be regarded as one of those strange effeminate beings occasionally to be seen at the fashionable assemblies, and so heartily despised by her husband who, with the usual masculine tolerance, said they made him feel sick.

But she did not want to think of Francis at all. His temper had never been one of his best points, and if he found out what she was about to do, he would certainly blow and blast her to pieces : this was not only blank disobedience, it was also remarkably dangerous.

' "Oh, I'll see thee hang'd on Sunday first," ' said Cassandra loudly, quoting from another play which had suited her down to the ground, and on this note of defiance, she crept out of her room, making sure that James was not hanging around, or her maid come up to see how she was, slipped down the stairs, then came out, a little apprehensively, into the street.

She felt a little as if she were setting forth on some criminal occasion. But a passer-by walked past her, without so much as turning his head, and this put heart into her: she set off swiftly in the Oxford Street direction, rejoicing in the freedom of limbs unencumbered by petticoats, and singing a little song to herself as she went.

And so by stages the entire Shelbrooke family converged upon the Rookeries in Paradise Row, together with a great many other people.

TEN

James was the first of the family to arrive, though Zephaniah had preceded him by half an hour.

He really had no idea at all of what he was going to do. He was a strong lad for his age, and big-built, but he had sense enough to know that the people he was up against would, if he obstructed them, put their foot upon him and crush him like an insect. He was also troubled with a strong feeling of guilt, for this whole proceeding was rank disobedience, and Francis, an amiable brother in most respects, despite his short temper, was not going to take kindly to this at all, especially as not even James himself could pretend there was no danger involved.

There was also Zephaniah. But James had every intention of dodging Zephaniah, and various rather snobbish remarks were whirling in his brain, such as: He has no right to order me around, and, He's only a common highwayman, and, Just because he knew me as a little boy, he seems to think — None of this really helped, and it seemed to James remarkably unfair that he should be the sole member of his family to take on so perilous an undertaking, and yet be obstructed at every turn by interfering grown-ups.

He came into the courtyard of the Rookeries. He did not know what he would find. He half expected it to be filled with a howling rabble, armed with sticks and stones. But there was no one there at all, and somehow this was more disturbing than anything else. There was an atmosphere to this dark, silent, stinking place, where the sunlight never penetrated, where the water perpetually dripped through cracked tiles and eroded eaves, that chilled his soul. The absence of people and the absence of sound was unnatural. A black cat crept out from behind a corner, and James, who liked all animals, and would have been grateful for its company, called it eagerly then, because his voice sounded so unnaturally loud, checked himself, glancing nervously across his shoulder.

The cat did not help him. This was no soft pussy to sit on a cushion and be fed with cream: this was a true inmate of the Rookeries, wild and savage and thin as string. As James crouched down, holding out his hand, it backed, hissed with narrowed eyes and flattened ears, then streaked into safety.

James, feeling rebuffed, looked towards Miss Parkington-Smith's house. That was silent too, and shuttered. There was not a gleam of light to be seen through the windows: Mokasa must have piled the planks against the broken pane.

James wondered what the old lady could be doing now. She must be very much afraid. A dreadful thought struck him that perhaps she was already gone, perhaps even dead. He screwed up his eyes. He gave himself a mental kick. He muttered sternly to himself, James Shelbrooke, you are a coward, then with feet that seemed to have leaden weights attached to them, walked slowly towards the house.

It was at this point that he first became aware of the sobbing. It was certainly not Miss Parkington-Smith, nor Polly either, though for one fearful minute he thought it might be the latter, bewailing her mistress's untimely end. But it was plainly not, it was a violent, childish sobbing, almost hysterical, and at least it was a human sound, it denoted feeling, it was better than the bleak, cruel inhumanity of this dead-end dwelling.

James swung round, then exclaimed, 'Jenny!'

She raised her blubbered face. She must have been crying herself sick. She did not look a naughty lady at all, at that moment she seemed more like a terrified child, hopelessly at odds with everything. She was plainly scared out of her senses. She was running across the courtyard like a hen, stumbling from one side to the other, and howling at the top of her voice as if she were at the end of her endurance.

James was thankful for the chance of action. He said again, 'Jenny,' and coming up to her, caught at her arm.

She gave a scream of pure panic, snatching her arm away. She began to run again, but he easily outpaced her with his longer legs. He said urgently, 'Jenny, what is it? What's happened? I'll not hurt you, Jenny. I'm James. Don't you remember me? Why don't you tell me what all this is about?'

154

She stopped then. She let her hands fall to her sides. James had never seen a more woebegone face, nor one more filled with terror and desolation. She looked about twelve. All the paint had been washed from her cheeks. Her hair, which she had attempted to curl in a fashionable, provocative manner, hung in bedraggled rats'-tails about her, and her bright, cheap clothes were torn and spattered with mud.

'I'm done for,' she said.

'Gammon!' said James.

'They'll hang me. I can't even plead my belly. I ain't got a chance. They'll be coming for me any moment now. *He* said so. He says he's got all the evidence.'

James did not ask who *he* was, for by this time he believed he knew only too well. A great rage stirred within him, such as had never been induced by the pain of the rod. He said, rather wretchedly, 'Oh, Jenny, you've been stealing things, haven't you?'

She raised her head proudly. 'No!' she said, then her voice soaring up in indignation, 'That I have not then. I never stole anything in my life. I never even nicked a handkerchief off of anyone. I'm an honest girl,' said Jenny, then began to sob again. 'I don't want to hang. It's not fair. They don't have the right.'

James hesitated. He was quite at a loss, for he had never in his life been faced with such a situation. Then at last he spoke, in his most practical manner, trying in this fashion to conceal the fear that was threatening to numb him again. 'I tell you what,' he said, 'you've got your room here, haven't you? Let's go there, and we can talk things over. We can't just stand here after all, with everyone listening to us.'

And as he said this, he glanced round him again: surely it was unnatural for the place to be so deserted. He had the impression that somehow it was not deserted at all: it was full of hidden people, still and listening like himself, waiting with cold, hard looks for the moment to spring out and attack. A shudder went through him, though the day was warm enough. He said again, almost frantically. 'Oh, Jenny, do let's go. I don't like it here very much. Where is your room?'

She shot him a strange, wary look, that came oddly from that dripping, childish face. It was the look of one who knew little, yet had learnt one thing in bitterness, that all men were the same, whatever their age or class, they all wanted one thing only, and afterwards they would kick you away and forget about you.

But nobody could look at James's ingenuous, baffled countenance and imagine such things. Not even the worst deceiver could contrive to look so supremely innocent. Jenny gave a giggle that was half a sob, said, 'You're a softy, ain't you? You ain't out of the egg yet.'

'I am fifteen,' retorted James, with angry hauteur.

'Oh you!' She spoke with an almost tender contempt. 'You don't know nothing. They didn't ought to let you out alone.'

'Well, you're one to talk!' cried James, furious at this insult to his manhood. 'They let you out alone, and just look what happens to you.'

She stared at him. It was almost as if there were an echo in her ears of another time, not so long ago after all, yet a million light-years away, when a smaller, childish Jenny had argued and fought with someone like James: *You are, I'm not, you are, I'm not —*

'Yah!' she said, as she might have said then, and she stuck her foot out so that James, coming nearer her, tripped over it and nearly measured his length on the cobbles.

'If you were a boy,' he said threateningly, 'I'd thump you for that.'

'But I'm not a boy, see?' said Jenny, making big eyes at him, then, forgetting for that brief moment the gulf between them, the horror that awaited her, burst into giggling and began to run towards the entrance into the Rookeries. 'You can't catch me!' she called out, 'for all you're a blooming boy.'

He dived after her. He completely forgot about Miss Parkington-Smith. 'Can't I just!' he said. 'Why, you don't even know how to run.' And he rushed up the stairs after her clattering heels.

*

Mr. Shelbrooke, blissfully unaware that his half-brother had not only disobeyed him but was also right inside the Rookeries, in the company of a girl of doubtful reputation, did not hesitate as James had done, but made his way at once to Miss Parkington-Smith's house.

He was both desperate and angry, and as always Cassandra was deep-set within his mind. He wondered still if she were really ill, but the rudeness of the rebuff she had given him was such that his anxiety was submerged in rage. He tried to brush her away from him. He decided that in some way or another he must kidnap his aunt; this time he would put up with no nonsense, he would even, if necessary, carry her out. He could not quite see himself stunning her into unconsciousness, and he had a suspicion that he might have to do this to get her away, but he was resolved not to put up with any more of her old-maidish stupidity: if she refused to be rescued, she should be rescued against her will.

It was in this truculent frame of mind that he stormed up to the house in Paradise Row.

Like James, he was taken aback by the silence. He did not like it. The inhabitants of the Rookeries did most of their living at night, yet on his last visit he had been aware of a vast, surging life within the building. Now, like James, he sensed that life was still there, but it was watching like some giant beast of prey, and there was not a voice, not a footstep, not a cry, not an oath, not even a wail from one of the many babies dragging out there their famished lives.

But he was older than James, and moreover he was well armed. He came up to the house and banged on the door. He could not see into the parlour, because the window was blocked up, but like a thief in the night he leaned his ear against the door, hoping to hear the sound of footsteps, or at least an anxious voice demanding who was there.

There was not a step. There was not a sound. Mr. Shelbrooke, with the hair pricking on his head, shouted through the keyhole.

'Aunt Arabella!' he called. 'It's Francis. Your nephew. Let me in.' And again, 'Let me in, do you hear me?'

Whether or not she heard, she did not answer. But certainly everyone else in the Rookeries heard Mr. Shelbrooke's powerful lungs, and there was a rustling and a stirring about him, all

157

the more ominous because it was silent.

He banged again, bruising his knuckles. 'Polly!' he called. 'What the devil's going on here? *Polly!*'

He bethought himself of the blackamoor, but did not know his name, so he continued to call Polly until his voice was quite hoarse, and always there was the same dead silence, until at last, like his brother, his imagination began to function in a shocking and melodramatic way, so that the hushed house became littered with bodies, lying in their blood.

With regard to Polly at least, he was perfectly correct, only she was not lying in her blood and she was not lifeless: she had passed out cold after finishing the rest of the bottle of gin.

Polly's courage was gone and her spirit temporarily broken. Her disappointment when Miss Parkington-Smith had refused to leave with her relatives had been so monstrous that she had no strength left in her. She was a country woman, she was faithful and loyal to the last degree, but this kind of town warfare terrified her: never in her worst nightmares had she imagined herself and her mistress driven out by wicked men who would not hesitate to use force. And when Mr. Francis left, with his pretty wife and young brother, she felt entirely deserted, and not even the sight of Mokasa, with his huge fists and Mr. Shelbrooke's pistol, could restore her.

She did not speak again to her mistress. What was the use? She fled back to her kitchen, and there for a long time she sat, crying softly and rocking herself to and fro. Miss Parkington-Smith had not called her. She was up in her bedroom, with the door locked. She might have been dead for all the sign she gave of living: it seemed to Polly, now in the blackest depths of despair, that they would all be dead soon, anyway, so it scarcely mattered.

But it never entered her head to leave, herself.

Nobody tried to break in again during the night, but there was a fantastic noise around them from dusk to dawn, and every fresh thud or yell made Polly shudder afresh, as she huddled there.

The girls next door seemed, from the sound of them, to be breaking up their furniture, and they were all certainly dead drunk. There were perpetual bangings on the wall, scrabblings at the planked-up windows, sounds as if people were standing by the door, peering through the keyhole, scratching on the wood with their nails. There was a constant scurrying of footsteps that did not cease till dawn, and filth and slops were hurled at the house, so that the stench, coming through the gaps in the hoarding, rose to Polly's nostrils and made her retch.

When daylight came, the noise stopped abruptly, but to Polly this seemed merely the indrawn breath before the battle proper began, and her nerves were shattered, she was whimpering with fear, prepared to go on her knees to the invaders, to beg them to spare her mistress and herself.

From Miss Parkington-Smith there was still not a sound.

At last Polly rose to feet that would scarcely support her, picked up the half-finished bottle of gin, and in a couple of hours had finished it down to the last drop.

She hardly knew what she was doing. She had eaten nothing for a long time. All she knew was that the first lovely gulp quietened the trembling that convulsed her, the second spread a soft, warm glow throughout her chilled body, and after the third she no longer cared what happened to any of them. When the dizziness came upon her, she thought vaguely that it was a passing indisposition: she flung open the kitchen window for some air. But the air had a different effect from what she expected, and in due course she let the empty bottle fall from her hand and with a foolish smile gently subsided to the floor, where she lay snoring while Mr. Shelbrooke was knocking, oblivious of him, of her mistress upstairs, of the danger that awaited them.

Mokasa, of course, heard Mr. Shelbrooke plainly enough. If he had been called by name, he might have realized who it was. But he had only spoken once to the gentleman, he was a simple, single-purposed man whose one thought was to protect the household, and he clung firmly to Mr. Shelbrooke's last injunction, which was not to open the door to anyone. So he stood there, vast, immobile and black as an iron pole and, though Mr. Shelbrooke did not know it, there was merely the thickness of the door between them, and there was more than once a danger of a period being put to Mr. Shelbrooke's existence through his own pistol, which was cocked and held at such an angle that the bullet would have gone through his head.

As for Miss Parkington-Smith, she, of course, heard the knocking and shouting, and knew perfectly well who it was, but her face was set in lines of genteel obstinacy, it was tight with it, pink with it: she was not going to move for anyone and, being as shrewd as she was cussed, she had a fair idea of what Mr. Shelbrooke would do if he were allowed inside. So she lay on her bed, in her dressing-gown, and every time Mr. Shelbrooke banged, she nodded her silly old head, and every time he roared out her name, she gave an affected wince as if it really were just too much being bawled at like this: only, when there was silence and he had presumably departed, did her obstinate face briefly collapse, so that she looked old and ill and afraid.

But she did not attempt to call him back. He wanted to get her out, and she was not going to move, for anything or anyone in the world.

The Captain would never have permitted such sacrilege.

Mr. Shelbrooke at the end considered breaking the door down; he even got so far as setting his shoulder against it. This was the moment when he came nearest to having his brains blown out. But he decided that the shock of such an entry would possibly send his aunt completely out of her wits, so he changed his mind, thus saving his life, and with a last glare at the house which seemed to him to have developed a character of its own, as difficult as that of its mistress, he strode off, thinking he would find Zephaniah.

Zephaniah had refused to help, but at least he might be able to advise. And Mr. Shelbrooke, with his hand fingering the comforting pistol in his pocket, set foot at last in the Rookeries, about to make the acquaintance of those whom he had once summed up as brute beasts without a trace of humanity in them, rough creatures who did not even possess the pack instinct of the wolves they most resembled.

*

It was Cassandra who was the last of the Shelbrooke family to make her appearance at the Rookeries. She arrived not quite so self-confident as when she had started.

Her progress had been a difficult one. The men she met on her journey – and she had had the sense to take the side-streets and footpaths – had not been so unobservant as the first passer-by. They had stared at this pretty youth with his dancing stride; several had whistled at her, and one of them had followed her for a great deal of the distance, and had only been dislodged by despairing tactics: Cassandra had dived into a shop entrance and flattened herself against the door until he passed by.

She realized at last that Orlando had been a fool: no man, especially a lover, with his wits about him, could possibly be deceived by his female in male attire. Not only were there the more obvious distinctions, but small matters such as wrists and neck and the fashion of moving the legs made it quite impossible for any womanly woman to deceive for any length of time – though it was rumoured that one lady in Marlborough's army had achieved the impossible throughout his campaigns.

She could not, thought Cassandra, have been a very female female.

She came, a little self-consciously, into the Rookeries court-yard. She did not think to look around for her husband and young brother-in-law, for it never for a single moment entered her head that they could be there.

She went at once to Miss Parkington-Smith's house. She was more diplomatic in her approach than Mr. Shelbrooke. She knocked twice at the door and, like him, received no answer. She assumed quite correctly that Miss Parkington-Smith was up in her room, had heard her perfectly well and was refusing to answer. Cassandra could understand this. The old lady was now in the state where she had declared her in-dependence and could not possibly go back on her word with-out losing face. This to Cassandra seemed entirely reasonable: it was the way she would have acted herself; indeed her present unhappy situation with her husband was entirely due to the same kind of false pride.

She did not consider Polly at all, except to assume she would be too frightened to answer. As for Mokasa, she had forgotten all about him.

She did not, therefore, waste time on knocking uselessly at the door, but slipped quietly round to the back of the house where she was delighted to perceive that the kitchen window was wide open. She was an agile girl, and pleasantly unhampered by petticoats: it was the work of a second to hoist herself on to the sill and jump down. She shut the window, thinking it imprudent to leave it open to all intruders, and then her eye was caught by Polly, still lying there prone and snoring away, her cheeks flushed and a smile on her lips.

Cassandra gazed down at her. It was easy enough to see what was the matter. Her husband often returned from his Club quite elevated, and during her stage career she had lost most of her illusions with regard to strong waters. Besides, she noticed the bottle that had rolled into the corner. She studied Polly thoughtfully for a while, then propped her head upon a cushion: privately she thought it was as well that Polly had taken this way out, for being prone to tears and the hysterics, she would be worse than useless in a crisis. Then she poured out a glass of milk, set some biscuits on a plate, and came out into the hall, to walk almost into Mokasa, who was gazing at her in the utmost astonishment.

'Good morning,' said Cassandra civilly, and began to walk up the stairs.

'Madam!' he called after her.

'What is it?' said Cassandra, turning her head and bestowing on him a kind, if absent-minded, smile.

His gaze moved from her face to her legs: his enormous dark eyes dilated in amazement. 'Madam,' he said, 'you cannot enter. She has locked the door. She will admit no one.'

'Oh,' said Cassandra calmly, 'she will admit me.' She nodded at him and continued on her way up, all in so assured a fashion that the negro did not know what to do. He knew this was Mrs. Francis, and he could not for the life of him understand why she was wearing breeches, but then the ways of white people were so extraordinary that he was past being astonished by anything. He came from a world where children were loved and petted, where the old were respected and looked after till they died: the Rookeries, and what was now about to happen, were to him incomprehensible. These extra-

162

ordinary people beat and starved their children: as for the aged, they were insulted and threatened and turned out into the street. Mokasa had been so young when taken from his native forests that he scarce remembered them, yet sometimes he longed for the dream of them, in this country of violence, foul language and strong waters: all this seemed to be masked under the name of Christianity, yet bore no relation to the beautiful creed the missionaries had taught him.

So he shrugged his massive shoulders, turned up his eyes, thus displaying their brilliant whites, and resumed his vigil in the hall, the pistol always in his hand.

Cassandra tapped at the door. There was no answer, but then she expected none.

She called softly through the keyhole. She used her voice to its utmost advantage: the husky contralto came through with a sweetness that would have melted the hardest heart.

'Aunt Arabella,' she said, 'it's me. Cassie. Francis's wife, you know. Will you please let me in, dearest aunt, for I have come all this way especially to see you.'

There was a pause, then shuffling footsteps. Miss Parkington-Smith's voice came shrilly through to her. 'Are you alone?' it inquired.

'Yes, Aunt,' said Cassandra, smiling to herself.

'Are you sure Francis isn't with you?'

'Of course he isn't. He doesn't even know I'm here.'

The key turned in the lock. The handle moved. Miss Parkington-Smith, still wearing her nightcap, her face twisted with suspicion, opened the door a fragment so that she could peer out. Then seeing that Cassandra spoke the truth, she flung it wide, and Cassandra stepped inside, to have the door instantly locked behind her.

'They are trying to get me away,' said Miss Parkington-Smith.

'Well, they're not going to, are they?' returned Cassandra cheerfully, and at this the old lady, clutching her dressing-gown to her, collapsed on to the bed; she did not cry, for she belonged to a generation where such displays were only conducted in private, but there was a desolation and fear to her that wrung Cassandra's heart: she at once knelt beside her as

163

she had done before, and took the rheumaticky hand gently in both of hers.

'You won't let them take me away, will you?' muttered Miss Parkington-Smith fretfully.

'Of course not.'

'You promise?'

'I promise, Aunt.'

'I am not going,' said Miss Parkington-Smith.

'And quite right too, Aunt Bella,' said Cassandra. She added, 'You don't mind my calling you that, do you? Aunt Arabella sounds so stuffy.' Then she proffered the milk and biscuits, which the old lady accepted with some surprise and considerable eagerness, for she had eaten nothing since yesterday's terrible tea-party.

Miss Parkington-Smith chewed the biscuits for a while, nibbling as always with her front teeth, then examined the beautiful and kindly young face gazing up at her.

'You're a good child,' she said grudgingly, 'but I do not know why you are wearing such extraordinary clothes.'

'Well,' admitted Cassandra, 'neither do I, really. I dare say I am over-dramatic. Francis always tells me so. Only it reminds me of the old days when I played Rosalind. But I see now it was foolish of me, because I don't look like a boy at all, and all it has done is to make me even more conspicuous. But it doesn't matter now, does it? I only wanted to see you. I didn't want you to be alone. It's so frightening to be alone. Sometimes one needs people just to talk to. I thought we could talk for a while, and let those horrid creatures outside do whatever they want to do. It won't worry us, will it? We shall just talk and forget all about them. Tell me,' said Cassandra, 'about yourself when you were young, Aunt Bella. Tell me all about your papa, the Captain, and the officers who used to call. Did you flirt with them? Did you go dancing with them? Did you make a map of your papa's campaigns, and follow wherever he was going?'

A number of strange things were happening to Miss Parkington-Smith's face. Perhaps it was because for the first time since Jack walked out of the house, she had been called Bella. The lines of resentment, primness and disapproval were almost softening. She looked again at Cassandra, and gave her a half-smile: this was someone who really understood.

'He was a very great man,' she said. And at those words there rose before Cassandra's vision a hero, stern, courageous, handsome, defending his country to the last drop of his military blood, not the cantankerous, drunken boor that the Captain had really been: in the light of this illusion it seemed to her romantic mind that a bugle was blowing faintly on the air.

'He was born in 1650,' said Miss Parkington-Smith, with the air of one imparting a fact of the utmost importance. 'He remembered so well the time when dear King Charles came back to his rightful throne. He always detested those horrid upstarts – Roundheads we called them, you know. They beheaded the King, Charles's father. My dear papa was always so very patriotic, always on the side of the right, and quite devoted to his King and country. I declare he would have cut any traitor's throat with his own hand. That shocking Monmouth! Of course he was a – he was not legitimate, you know. The girl, Lucy Walters or Waters, it is not important, she was only a slut, of course, and I don't suppose for one moment she told the truth. I dare say if the truth was known, he was no relative at all.'

This made little sense to Cassandra who was only interested in history when she was acting it, but she was amazed by the liveliness of Miss Parkington-Smith's withered countenance, and she gave the hand an encouraging pat, gazing at her always with the beautiful green eyes that had knocked Mr. Shelbrooke so violently off course that he had never been the same man since. Miss Parkington-Smith remarked the magnificence of those eyes herself, and it was as if a hard knot inside her began painfully to unravel. She went on talking, and the thin voice spoke of this strange melange of past history and her own girlhood, an intermingling of fact and fiction, seen through the haze of more than sixty years.

Outside in the courtyard of the Rookeries the silence was broken. There were ugly noises: the trampling of feet, harsh voices, thuds and crashes, and away in the distance the barking of a dog. Cassandra heard them. But she did not so much as shiver, for this would at once have communicated her fear to the old lady. She gazed steadfastly up at Miss Parkington-Smith; her smile did not waver, and the hands clasping the old lady's remained cool and firm.

For the first time in her life Cassandra was playing her part with conviction: this time she must not fluff her lines.

'Go on, Aunt Bella,' she said. 'Oh, pray do go on. This is so interesting. You are telling me things I've never heard of before.'

Miss Parkington-Smith needed no encouragement: she was well away. The names of battles studded her conversation like black pearls and Cassandra, who had once derided this, listened with fascination: Sedgemoor, Ramillies, Blenheim, Oudenarde, Malplaquet. The glories of the past, great victories, the gallant and young who fell, never to rise again. Little fragments of history thrown in. 'I once met Prince Eugene —' And, 'I never understood the evil things they said about the dear Duke, especially after all he had done for his country. Abigail Hill – a cousin of the Duchess, you know, ah, there was a woman, Sarah was her name – a sly piece, Abigail.' And, 'He had a wonderful funeral. I stood in the crowd. I cried my eyes out. Such a great, great man.' And, 'Don't believe the nasty things they say of him, my dear – we will never see his like again, they don't make men like that nowadays.'

And who Abigail was, Cassandra had no idea, and sometimes she was not sure whether Miss Parkington-Smith was speaking of Marlborough or of her father. But it did not matter; what interested her was that from beneath the battles and the great names and the glory, there emerged a shy, plain, prim little girl who men never looked at twice: a disagreeable young woman with an acid tongue, who never compromised, who never made friends, yet who kept two altars in her heart that could not be destroyed: one for her father and one for the great Duke himself. There might perhaps have been heartbreaks, there might have been agonizing rebuffs: Arabella was after all a girl like other girls and had a heart like other hearts, but this Miss Parkington-Smith did not mention. If ever there had been some young ensign who broke that primness down, Cassandra was never to hear of it, only her romantic heart as always functioned overtime, and she was already visualizing the gallant boy going to his death in the Low Countries, while Arabella wept into her pillow alone.

In this she was entirely wrong. There had never been such an ensign, dead or alive. There had been a rigid propriety in the young Arabella harder to face than the enemy bayonets: no one had ever presumed to storm the fortress.

But to Cassandra it was all very grand and sad, and the tears made her eyes shine, so that Miss Parkington-Smith was positively glowing with the warmth she felt towards this young woman in her peculiar garb.

'People,' she remarked in her most genteel voice, 'have sometimes wondered why I did not marry. But I always tell them the same thing. My life, I tell them, was devoted to dear papa, and when he passed on, I knew I could never again meet a man in any way comparable to him.'

And this was indeed marvellous, considering papa had bullied the life out of her, but then it was a long time ago, and Miss Parkington-Smith sincerely believed every word she was saying.

'Papa,' she went on, 'taught me a great deal about men.' She uttered the last word as if she were speaking of some strange, not quite respectable, animal. 'So you see, my dear, though I have never married, I have had considerable experience of the opposite sex.'

'Oh I'm sure, Aunt Bella,' murmured Cassandra, 'I'm sure you know far more than I do.'

'Men,' said Miss Parkington-Smith – it really was quite odd the emphasis she put on this word so that the monosyllable assumed polysyllabic proportions – 'Men need humouring, my dear. They so often say things they do not mean. They are sometimes quite violent. But one should not pay too much attention. I am sure that many marriages are wrecked because the wives are a trifle – now how shall I put it? – a trifle over-sensitive.'

Cassandra was no longer smiling. Her experience of men exceeded anything that Miss Parkington-Smith could have dreamed up in a nightmare: she had seen them drunk, lecherous and sodden with self-pity. She had learnt at the very beginning that a young woman on her own, especially one on the stage, was automatically regarded as easy prey. She had learnt to say no with the utmost charm, and she also learnt how to say it with the utmost brutality. She had no illusions left about any of them, with the possible exception of Francis, but now she listened as if this were something vital to her: her eyes were fixed on Miss Parkington-Smith with an almost painful intensity.

'One must treat them like children,' said Miss Parkington-Smith, uttering this far from original statement with the greatest benevolence. 'One must forgive. Papa was the dearest of men, but sometimes when he was tired he would say a word that might be a little hurtful.'

Cassandra in her mind added a bottle of port and a handful of army oaths to papa's exhaustion, but the Captain no longer interested her, nor Marlborough neither. She said slowly, 'You think that even if one is hurt, one should just forget all about it?'

'Of course,' said Miss Parkington-Smith. She added, with an almost patronizing smile, 'After all, if one doesn't, one is doubly hurt oneself, and that is foolish, is it not?'

'Yes,' said Cassandra. 'Yes.' And she smiled back, her widest and most ravishing smile, then, much to Miss Parkington-Smith's astonishment, kissed her. 'And now,' she said, 'tell me more about your dear papa's campaigns.'

But this she was never to hear. Downstairs the noise had achieved such proportions that it could not possibly be ignored any longer. There was a great bashing at the door, followed by two pistol shots and a yell of pain. Cassandra and Miss Parkington-Smith fell silent. Neither of them moved. Cassandra still knelt there, with the thin hand in hers, and Miss Parkington-Smith sat very upright, staring ahead.

She said only one thing more, and that came out in a whisper. 'I am not going,' she said.

That was all.

*

Mr. Shelbrooke came up the Rookeries staircase. There was no banister. It had been broken years ago. The fragments of it still lay in the cellar, for nobody had bothered to remove them, and the rats and mice played and scuttered round them, burrowing through the dirt and filth that had accumulated there for many years, so that the stench rose to the top of the building.

In this hot weather the putrid odour was almost suffocating, but Mr. Shelbrooke paid it no attention and still continued on his way up.

There were four storeys to the Rookeries. The cellar, which he could see by looking down the well of the staircase, was also inhabited. There was nobody there now, but at night there were as many as forty, and this accommodation was shared with asses and pigs. After the first floor, the broken staircase with its worn treads was dangerous to climb, and Mr. Shelbrooke could not help wondering how many of the infants survived their first excursion out, for a fall here would result in broken bones if not a broken neck.

The doors of all the rooms were open, so that he could see inside. This was presumably to let in the air, but the stench came with it, and he was horrified yet not surprised to see that many of the inhabitants were sick and lying on their straw, some with the marks of a burning fever upon them. The healthy denizens seemed mostly to be out; a few sat by the window, staring, doing nothing.

Mr. Shelbrooke looked in each room to see if Zephaniah were there but, though he was by now on the third floor, could perceive no sign of him. He grew more and more aware of the terrible poverty and barrenness of all these dwellings: the landlord could have done nothing to them for over twenty years. The window frames and door-posts were perfectly black with soot and dirt, the walls were neither painted nor whitewashed for many years together; patches of paper or a rag covered the windows where the glass was broken, but obviously could not prevent the rooms from being over-hot in summer and freezing in winter.

It was the sight of the children that appalled him. His own stupid, ill-bred words came back at him like barbs. These at least were innocent, they were not brutes, they could not be condemned for their sins. Some of them lay there too weak and exhausted to move, others, wise with wicked wisdom, stared at him with bold impudence, pricing him as a coney for their catching: it was their only hope of survival in a world out to crush, and they would not survive long, for the mark of the gallows lay plainly across them. None of them smiled; they all looked as if smiling were alien to them. He saw their bony arms and legs, the filthy rags that covered them, their heads crawling with vermin: the sickness came up in his throat so that for a moment he leaned against the sweating, greasy wall to steady himself.

He came up to the landing window and there paused. There was no glass here, either. God knows what it must be like in mid-winter. He stared down into the back courtyard that he had not yet seen. He saw that a ditch had been dug there, and that a sluggish water, perhaps from one of the tributaries of the Fleet, flowed through it, carrying its burden from the slaughter-houses, the fell-mongers, the drainage from the dye-houses: a mixture of scum, sewage and carrion which was in both appearance and smell so nauseating that he drew back, only to come quickly to the window again, calling: 'Zephaniah!' There was no mistaking that sturdy figure with its bright, incongruous ribbons: Zephaniah strode past with an air to him as if he were back in the countryside and not breathing in infection with every step.

Mr. Shelbrooke called his name again, and was about to descend the stairs in a rush, but Zephaniah, giving him a cheerful wave, beckoned him to stay where he was.

So he stood there, still leaning against the wall, then by degrees became aware of a great noise and confusion down below. He saw too that one of the drabs on the ground floor had followed his progress and had dragged herself up, half asleep, to take a further look at him. He had already seen her and her companions sleeping away their night's activities, but now he gazed with a kind of appalled acceptance at this girl who could not yet be in her twenties, yet who showed every sign of disease, who smelt already of corruption, who coughed with every step she took, and who for his benefit had slapped the paint on her gaunt, pocked cheeks.

He shook his head at her. When she burst into wild laughter and shrieked some kind of obscene invitation at him, he turned away, thinking of that poor, silly slut of his who would, if she persisted in staying, in a little while find this her ending.

Zephaniah came swiftly up the stairs, and seeing what was happening, gave the girl a push, telling her roughly to go back to her room. 'There's nothing here for you,' he told her, and when she answered lewdly and impudently, shoved her again so that he all but sent her over the broken staircase: she ran down, shouting abuse at him.

'Well, Mr. Francis?' he said.

'Well, Zephaniah?' said Mr. Shelbrooke, giving him a grim, unamused smile. He heard the row below; it was more deafening than ever. He could hardly bear to stand there talking, but he must know before he charged into battle if this beribboned man were an ally or an enemy.

'They've started,' said Zephaniah, then grabbing Mr. Shelbrooke's arm, 'No! Don't you be a bloody fool, sir. Your old lady's all right. She's got company, like.' And here he gave his companion a twisted, mocking smile. 'My Jenny, she's got company too, so they tell me. Quite a gathering as you might say, sir.'

'I don't know what the devil you're talking about,' roared Mr. Shelbrooke who, what with a sleepless night, his terror of what might be happening to his abominable aunt and the sights he had just seen, was out of all control. 'I dare say we haven't much chance against what sounds like an infernal mob of them, but at least I can pick off half a dozen, at least I can make some effort to get that obstinate old bitch away.'

Zephaniah was no longer looking at him. He was peering down the stairs, listening to the sounds which had reached diabolical heights. There was a savage grin on his lips. 'He's come,' he said.

'Who?' demanded Mr. Shelbrooke, exasperated beyond all reason by this seeming detachment. He added furiously, 'You've always been a friend to me, Zeph, and I wish you no harm, but if you're not going to help, at least you need not hinder. I warn you, friend, if you do not let me pass, I shall be compelled to use this.' And he drew the pistol from his pocket and levelled it at the highwayman's head.

Zephaniah only grinned the wider. He did not so much as

flinch. He made no attempt to reach for his own weapon. 'Now, Mr. Francis,' he said, as if he were speaking to the schoolboy of long ago. 'Now, sir, don't be hasty, never be hasty. It's out of your hands, boy. There's nothing left for you to do. Look! Look for yourself.' And he jerked Mr. Shelbrooke into the adjoining room, stepping over a sleeping baby and kicking a mangy dog out of the way. 'Look, I tell you.'

Mr. Shelbrooke looked out of the window. It was an extraordinary scene. His long-sighted eyes could make out clearly the rotten-toothed bully who had threatened him yesterday, and even as he looked, one of the men in the crowd – for it was like a battle scene, with men, women and children everywhere – lunged at him, and the tough disappeared in a tangle of flailing fists, cudgels and stones, never to reappear. The dogs were there, great mastiffs trained and starved into savagery: even as Mr. Shelbrooke perceived this, one was shot down. He could scarce distinguish what was happening, but he could not miss the fierce intentness of the fighting faces: it seemed to him as if the entire population of the Rookeries, male and female, were repulsing the would-be evicters.

Then he saw on the outskirts of the courtyard another figure which seemed to be staring as aghast as himself, and he exclaimed in amazed disbelief. 'But that,' he cried out, his voice soaring up, 'that's Mr. Fielding. That's my young brother's schoolmaster.'

'I do not think,' said Zephaniah, passing a ribbon through his teeth, and leaning idly there as if this were all in the day's work, 'he'll be doing his schoolmastering much longer. Not when the whores get at him. They don't like him peaching on one of them. Especially as she'd never be here except for him.'

Mr. Shelbrooke stared at him. Then he said as calmly as he could, 'I'm going down whether you like it or not. But I still wish to know who are my friends and who my enemies. What is all this? You said you could not and would not help. I remember distinctly. It's not the kind of thing one forgets.'

'Did you not say,' said Zephaniah, 'that if they all combined – I reckon that was your word, Mr. Francis, you being an educated man like – the others'd not have a dog's chance?'

'I did indeed, and you said that was a fairy story!'

'Ay, so I did, so I did. But then there's my Jenny who you was so kind to, sir, and there's this.'

He held out the paper James had stolen from Mr. Fielding's desk and, while Mr. Shelbrooke was reading it, went on speaking, almost as if to himself.

'They'll put up with anything, sir, except that. That's what I said to—But never mind. We've always known there was a Peachum here. We've suspicioned, but we was never sure. Now we are. We remember, sir, that there's many gone to the gallows as shouldn't have gone, many transported to Botany Bay as should still be here. I could give you all the names, sir, if you was interested. There's John Tyler who stole a penknife and thirty-five shillings. And William West who stole twenty-six yards of striped linen. There's Martha Negus, she took some ribbons. It's all the same. It's not what they did. It's that they came athwart him, him down there. He'll not endure that. He won't be crossed. He's the master here. He brings out the girls and rakes in the money. But he didn't ought to have put that in writing, indeed he didn't. And I took good care they all seen it. Most of 'em can't read nor write, but I can, sir, because your good father taught me, and I read it out to them all, I read it out loud and clear so that they all understood.'

He stood back so that Mr. Shelbrooke could pass. He was smiling no longer. 'You can go down if you choose, Mr. Francis. But don't fret about your old lady. She's all right. They got other things on their minds now than old ladies. Go on, sir. I want to see my Jenny, though I dare say your young brother's looking after her well enough.'

Mr. Shelbrooke was almost down the stairs before the full impact of those last words came upon him. But by that time he was in the full mêlée, and could only struggle to fight his way through the crowd so that he could reach Mr. Fielding, with whom he had an entirely personal score to settle.

However this, as it happened, was never to be.

*

James and Jenny sat on the bed in her room and looked shyly at each other. They talked quietly, with long pauses be-

173

tween their words. They talked of themselves, without commenting on each other's remarks, yet somehow the words blended, made a pattern.

'It was a farm,' Jenny said, twisting her fingers together as she spoke. The nails, James noted, were bitten to the quick. 'I liked it there. But I thought London would be so grand. I could work for some fine lady, I would earn piles and piles of money, and then I'd marry a lord.'

'There's not much in a lord,' said James. 'I dare say you could do better than that. I lived in the country too. I liked it, but I like town better. There's more to do. There's the playhouse and concerts and boxing and cocking. I like all those things. I like playing cards too, but my brother won't let me.'

'It was a lady who met the stagecoach,' said Jenny. 'I didn't know. I was that excited. She seemed such a nice lady. She asked me if I was looking for work, and she said she knew someone who had just the right job for me.'

'I shall do the Grand Tour,' said James. 'Francis promised me. I only have to wait three more years.'

'She took me to a gentleman,' said Jenny. She gave a faint, hiccuping sob. 'It was him. That Mr. Fielding. And after that —' She broke off, eyeing James, then burst out in a kind of anguish, 'But you'd not understand. You're only a baby —'

'I tell you I'm not! And I do understand.'

'Do you, cocky?' She gave him a watery smile. 'Your brother did, anyways. He was real good to me, your brother. He's a real gentleman. I thought I was going home at last. Only *he* was furious, and now he's going to top me, for something I didn't do, for something I didn't do —'

And she started to cry again, rocking from side to side, while James patted her shoulder rather warily, muttering, 'Oh don't, Jenny, don't, don't! It'll be all right, I tell you, it'll be all right. My brother will see to it. My brother can do anything if he gives his mind to it. It'll be all right. You must stop crying. It's not good for you to cry like that.' Then he exclaimed in despair, 'Oh, Jenny, whatever am I going to do with you?'

She could not stop. She sobbed hysterically, rubbing her sleeve across her eyes, 'I don't see that he can do a bloody thing. And old Zeph wants to marry me too, but he can't do anything neither, nobody can, and I don't want to hang, I don't, I don't —'

James stared helplessly at her, not knowing how to comfort, quite out of his depths in this black and shadowed world where they hanged little girls for petty theft. He offered her his handkerchief, but she did not seem even to see it. And at last, feeling very self-conscious and hoping no one would see them, he put his arm round her, first gingerly then tightly, while she wept on his shoulder, and there for a time they stayed, the girl who knew too much and the boy who knew so little, and perhaps in that interval James grew up for he no longer minded the absurdity of the situation, only felt choked with grief and anger that such things could happen and he be so helpless to prevent them.

It was she who moved away at last, and wishing not to embarrass her, he rose to his feet and went across to the broken, dirty window, peering down into the courtyard.

Then he gave a great shout. 'Jenny, come here! There's a devil of a rumpus going on. Oh, I do believe it's Beau Frog – Jenny!'

But Jenny was not looking at him. She had turned to the door and was moving timorously towards Zephaniah, who stood there, smiling down at her.

'It's all right, lass,' he said. 'It's all right. You don't never need to be frightened again. My little Jenny—Don't you have a kiss for me, sweet, for by Christ I've earned it.'

James, a little red round the back of the neck, continued to stare down, then gave a gasp, convinced he had had a glimpse of his brother fighting his way through the crowd: he leaned out at a highly dangerous angle, wild with excitement and convinced from this and Zephaniah's words that his aunt was saved.

*

Mr. Fielding could not understand at all what was happening. He had sent out his usual gang of rogues and ruffians to get this tiresome old woman thrown into the street. There were a dozen of them, more than usual, in case the family made trouble. But he did not really expect any difficulty, for the gentlemen of the *ton* seldom cared to involve themselves in so

175

sordid a business; as for the inhabitants of the Rookeries they were well trained by now, and knew better than to interfere with him.

He saw now, and only too plainly, that he was mistaken. The blood rushed into his pale face. The whole lot of them were out, including old Jack, the Musical Shrimp Man, who was not singing now, Simon with his one-eyed dog yapping at his heels, and even, as far as he could make out, all the girls. They were armed too, with every kind of implement, and some of them had pistols and blunderbusses, snatched from some illegal hoard. He could see no sign of his henchman, the dogs had vanished – presumably shot down – and the mob was now fighting indiscriminately like the wolves they were, maddened with fury and lust of battle, and surging dangerously near him.

He stared at them in rage mixed with a frank bewilderment, for such a thing had never happened before, he could not begin to comprehend why they were all so out of hand.

He was not immediately afraid. He had never been a coward, chiefly because he had so deep-rooted a contempt for his fellow human beings. His long mouth curled in the utmost disgust and distaste. He thought savagely that he knew how to deal with them. There would be a fine number of indictments at the next sessions. He would take one in ten for this, and they could count themseves fortunate that he did not take more. He would teach them a lesson, by God, that they would not forget and, as he thought of this, a hot flush of blood surged through his veins, his heart beat a paean of triumph, and he fell briefly into a scarlet dream of revenge, so immersed in this that he was unaware until too late that the fighting had suddenly ceased, and that a small section of the mob was advancing upon him.

He realized his danger, raised a blanched face, and snatched out his pistol, only to have it knocked from his hand by a carefully aimed stone.

He stared into the faces of his enemies. They did not speak. They only walked silently towards him. It was not the men. It was the girls. It was the girls from the ground floor.

He knew each one. He knew them very well. He had met them a year ago, two years ago, three—Not more. They seldom lasted more. He remembered them all. He had always had an excellent memory.

There was Lucy. She had been a pretty thing, with her fair complexion and black hair. The hair was dyed now, falling out, dirty, verminous, the complexion blotched, there were running sores at the corners of her painted mouth. There was Hannah. Hannah had been a real beauty, and a girl of breeding too, her lover had deserted her, her family had turned her out, she had nowhere to go, for herself and her child. Well, the baby was dead, and Hannah soon would be dead too, she had the consumption, like so many of them, and was already skin and bone. There was Elizabeth. And Jane. And Molly. And Barbara—

They were almost on him. Suddenly and horrifyingly he could not move. He had to go on looking, looking into their dreadful faces, and behind those faces with their sores and scars and paint and powder, were the fresh young faces of the girls they had once been, the little country girls who had come so joyfully to London where the streets were all paved with gold.

Then Mr. Fielding began to scream.

ELEVEN

Mr. and Mrs. Francis Shelbrooke, with young James at their side, were setting out for tea with Miss Parkington-Smith.

Mr. and Mrs. Francis Shelbrooke sat close together at one side of the carriage; they were holding hands. James, a little way away from them and gazing out of the window as they trundled up Oxford Street, thought, This is how it was last time, it's as if nothing had happened in between, all that fighting and killing was just a nightmare, it cannot be real.

He swung round to put this interesting point of metaphysics to Cassie, who enjoyed discussions and never treated him like a child, only to see that his brother was kissing her cheek: they quickly moved apart, and he as quickly stared out of the window again.

Well, perhaps it was not as if nothing had happened. It was not quite the same. Things never were. For instance, he, James Shelbrooke, was going next week to a new school, a cramming establishment, to prepare him for the university. 'You've got the brains,' Francis told him, adding, in case this sounded fulsome, 'more or less. You just don't work. You're a lazy little hound. The Manor House is no good for you. They waste far too much time on French, the discipline seems to me remarkably lax, and you seem to have far too much opportunity for walking out whenever you feel like it. Now you are going to work, and there'll be no nonsense about it whatsoever.'

All this was pronounced in a severe and elder-brotherly tone, with Cassie winking at him in the background, and James merely said, 'Yes, Francis', and 'No, Francis', as the occasion demanded. It was a pity in a way. Now that old Beau Frog would never come back again – he wondered what exactly had happened, for Francis, looking a little white and grim, had refused to discuss it – he would not have minded returning to a school where he could do pretty much as he chose, and where from time to time he could wander off in the direction of the

178

'Farthing Pye House', and have a chat with old Zephaniah.

But he had forgotten, of course Zeph would no longer be there. Zeph was marrying his Jenny, that funny, silly little girl who seemed to require a schoolboy and a highwayman to act as joint knights-errant.

For a second James's round, amiable face changed, grew secretive. He could still feel the sharp bones of those thin shoulders beneath his hands. And he would never to the end of his days forget that sudden glimpse of a world he had never dreamed existed, like the black entrance to some passage-way in hell. He closed his eyes. He did not want to think of it, not now, later yes, but not now. He would think of Zephaniah instead.

Zephaniah was leaving, indeed had already left, the Rookeries. Zephaniah was shortly about to take on a new job, found for him by Francis who seemed to derive an enormous amusement from the idea whenever it was mentioned. Zephaniah was going to become a turnpike-man, living with Jenny in a cottage behind the high, white gate: whenever he heard the sound of hooves or wheels, he would have to run out, crying, 'Pike-Gate, hallo!'

Francis, whenever this was mentioned, invariably subsided into shouts of helpless laughter.

James personally did not find it particularly amusing, and had already memorized the turnpike charges, so that he could occasionally take over the job: a penny ha'penny for a rider on horseback, fourpence ha'penny for a cart or carriage, and one and six for a four-in-hand.

'I fear your earnings will go down sadly,' Francis said to Zephaniah. But Zephaniah merely grinned, ran one of the ribbons through his filed teeth, and said, 'It's better than the triple tree, Mr. Francis. The road has done me justice, sir, but love has been my ruin, as you might say, and now I'm turned respectable, like many an unfortunate man before me.'

'I'll lay you'll prove a terror to all the highwaymen,' said Mr. Shelbrooke.

'I will that, Mr. Francis,' returned Zephaniah placidly. 'There's not one will get through my turnpike, sir, and if he tries it on, I'll shoot him down like the dog he is. None of that nasty carry-on while I'm in charge,' said Zephaniah, adding, 'It's disgraceful that honest folks can't travel in safety. I don't know what's the matter with us these days, I'm sure, there's no chance for any of us.'

Then they both began laughing again, as if they were schoolboys, not full-grown men, and James, feeling far older than the pair of them, turned a contemptuous back on them.

No. Things were definitely not the same.

And Cassie and Francis — They were embracing again. You would think they had been married long enough to keep this kind of thing for the decent privacy of their own home. But oh no, given the slightest chance, and there they were kissing and cuddling and carrying on, and Francis hardly ever went to his Club these days, and Cassie was looking so outrageously lovely that it was hardly respectable to go out with her. It was true, of course, that they were much more agreeable to live with: Francis never lost his temper now more than three or four times a week, and Cassie, always prone to spoiling, would have given any casual passer-by the world on a platter if he had so much as expressed a wish for it.

But then, after that appalling, amazing and – it had to be admitted – gloriously exciting day, nothing had gone as might have been expected.

They had all met in the courtyard. By that time they were all so exhausted that they simply gazed at each other without astonishment or reproaches. Zephaniah had procured them a carriage to go back home, and they had collapsed into it, Cassandra in her absurd boy's outfit, her red hair falling out of the cap, her face white and dazed, Mr. Shelbrooke, battered, mud-stained and breathing in great gasps as if he scarce had the strength left even for that, and James himself, who had fallen fast asleep the moment they set off.

James, when they arrived at Hanover Square and he had tumbled out on to the pavement, expected the rating of a lifetime and perhaps worse, but Mr. Shelbrooke only looked at him, and said in a blurred, thick voice 'You're a confoundedly disobedient brat, but I believe that disgraceful old aunt of ours owes her life to you.' Then he said in more normal tones, 'God, you're filthy!'

'So are you,' retorted James, half asleep but with enough spirit left to reply to such a stupid accusation.

'Faith, and so I am,' said his brother and laughed. 'A fine crew of ruffians we all look, and no mistake.' Then he said briskly, 'You are going to straight to bed.'

'Oh no,' protested James: there was nothing in the world that he wanted more at that moment than sleep, but he could not let this pass without some kind of reply.

'You,' repeated Mr. Shelbrooke, 'are going straight to bed. I'll have Mrs. Bowes send you up some supper. It should by rights be bread and water, but I dare say she'll add a little chicken and wine to it. Go on. I've had enough of you for one day. Hurry up now.'

James, so bleary with sleep that he could hardly keep his eyes open, turned a dim glance on Cassie who normally took his part, but she hardly seemed to have heard what was said, she was not looking at him at all, only gazing at Francis.

So he said 'Oh all right,' in a grumbling tone, then his brother surprisingly clapped a hand on his shoulder and gave him a great push forward so that he went towards the door at a run.

'Good night, James darling,' said Cassandra, but he did not even hear her.

'He's half asleep already,' said Mr. Shelbrooke. He was standing in the hall, looking down at the table. There were two letters there, one for him and one for his wife: beside the latter was a rather faded bunch of three roses. He picked up his own letter, studying the address. 'This is from mama,' he said; 'What in God's name has she been up to now?' He turned his gaze on to his wife who was still pacing up and down in her preposterous clothes, and said, 'For pity's sake, Cassie! Do you really mean to tell me you walked to Paradise Row, dressed like that? Who's been sending you roses?'

'Oh, one of my admirers, I expect. Throw them away. They're withered. They smell.' Cassandra, brushing the flowers aside, with a faint colour burning her cheeks, walked into the drawing-room, and flung herself into a chair, with her breeched legs asprawl. Her eyes flickered up to Mr. Shelbrooke's dirty and unshaven countenance, then away. 'Yes, Francis, I walked all the way. Dressed like this.'

'It's a wonder you were not hauled off to Bridewell. Of all the idiotic things – I thought you had more sense, indeed I did.'

'I thought,' said Cassandra, her head flung back against the cushions, 'that it would save me from the unwelcome attentions of the gentlemen.' She added pensively, 'It didn't. They seemed to follow me even more.'

Mr. Shelbrooke turned up his eyes. Cassandra in her present attitude, with her arms beneath her head so that the over-tight shirt was strained to its utmost, looked as masculine as the Venus de Milo. He came nearer her. 'Sometimes,' he said, a little thickly, 'I believe you are almost half-witted.'

'Well,' said Cassandra, surveying him through half-closed lids, 'if I had worn petticoats, I doubt if I could have climbed through the kitchen window.'

'You climbed through —!'

'Oh, I'm not so missish as you think. What has your mama to tell us? I'm sure she could climb through any window.'

'It wouldn't surprise me at all. And what did you do when you had climbed through the window?'

'I had a long, long talk with dear Aunt Bella.'

'If dear Aunt Bella knew how I longed to wring her neck —And what in God's name did you talk about?'

'Men.'

'Christ!' said Mr. Shelbrooke.

'I was a little astonished, myself. Oh, Francis, pour us both out some wine. I think I need lots and lots of wine. I think I want to get drunk, rolling, roaring drunk. Like Polly. Poor Polly. She was wiser than I ever believed she could be. Aunt Bella, I mean. She is such a silly old lady, really, but perhaps it was because she was so frightened, or perhaps it was simply that no one had ever let her talk so much before.'

Mr. Shelbrooke, who had brought out the decanter, poured two glasses of wine. He offered her one which she accepted in a languid manner. Her eyes, however, were not languid at all: they were glinting with amusement and devilment. 'Oh,' she said on a sigh, 'this is so wonderful.' She took a deep draught of the wine. 'What has your mama to say? Do open the letter, Francis.'

He did so, his eyes always on her. He glanced cursorily at the large, bold, black writing of the dowager Mrs. Shelbrooke, then swore unrepeatably, turning a wild countenance on his wife who nearly dropped her glass and exclaimed, 'What has she done now? Oh, do tell me, Francis, you must tell me.'

'She's married again. It's the General. The poor devil!'

Cassandra burst into fits of laughter. She said when she could speak again, 'Oh, how can you say such a thing? She always makes such a success of her husbands.'

'She always seems to kill them off,' said Mr. Shelbrooke, adding, 'What can she expect? She overworks them. And he's an old man. He'll never last.'

'Francis!'

He wandered round the room, the letter in one hand, the glass in the other. Then he came back to her, standing over her. He said irrelevantly, 'For a famiy so determined not to embroil itself, we haven't done so badly.' Then, 'How dare you! Of all the lunatic behaviour—You might have been killed.'

'I suppose,' said Cassandra, 'there might be other ways of killing ourselves off.' She swivelled her glass round, admiring the ruby glow of the wine, then suddenly put the glass down, whispering, 'Oh, Francis!' at exactly the same moment as he exclaimed her name. He instantly came to kneel beside her, his hands reaching out for her, and she began to cry in a weak, comfortable fashion, muttering, 'Oh, how stupid we've been, how stupid – I swear your lunatic mama has more sense in one little finger than the pair of us together. And what a lovely way to be killed off—Aunt Bella said we were stupid, I don't know why we had to be so stupid, do you?'

'God knows,' said Mr. Shelbrooke, his arms tightly round her. 'Oh, God knows—And what could she possibly have to tell you, this absurd old maid, for all she's ever said to me is some blasted account of her father who was, as all the world knows, a drunken boor and an intolerable bore—Oh, Cassie, how I've missed you —'

But he was never to hear what exactly Miss Parkington-

183

Smith had said, for he had by this time lost all interest in her, and presently they went upstairs together, their arms around each other, both dizzy with emotion, exhaustion and wine.

On the landing he made as if to follow her into her room, only there had been so many rebuffs and even now he was not quite sure. He hesitated, watching her as she leaned against the half-open door, in her swaggering boy's attitude, the slender legs astride, her arms impudently akimbo.

He exclaimed in a confusion of rage and laughter and desire, 'What the devil is all this play-acting? Do I have to stand here in the cold while you play out your Beatrice or Juliet or whatever the hell it is?'

'Rosalind,' said Cassandra. Then she raised her chin as if she were speaking to the gallery. Her voice came, high and clear. ' "A lean cheek, which you have not; a blue eye and sunken, which you have not; an unquestionable – an – an —' Then she gave a great cry of triumph. 'An unquestionable spirit, which you have not —'

He did not answer. He only smiled at her, a great, wide smile that stopped her speech as if she had been gagged. Then silently but in a great rush he came to her, and the door slammed behind them.

In all battles, as he had once remarked to Miss Parkington-Smith, there occur tactical moments: like the great Marlborough at Blenheim he knew at last that this was not the time for retreat, but for advance and victory.

And Cheri was delighted, for he was a dog of habit, and his favourite resting place was not his own basket, but his master's dressing-room bed.

*

'I think,' said Miss Parkington-Smith, 'that the table looks most agreeable.'

'Yes, ma'am,' said Polly, beaming, for this was like old times. There was the pretty china (sent by Mr. Francis), the spoons presented by Zephaniah (she did not ask where they came from) and the nice new furniture which Mr. Francis had had delivered – 'We have no room for it,' he said. 'You would be doing me a favour to accept it.'

184

It was true that the room was not quite as it had once been. The glass in the windows had not yet been replaced, but the boarding was concealed by handsome velvet curtains – these were from Mr. Francis's mother in the country; there were mats in place of the carpet, and until this morning there had still been that sad, blackened space where once the Captain had hung in his glory.

Only just before luncheon, Miss Parkington-Smith, who was hopping round the place like a pleased and agitated little bird, had chanced to open her desk, and there had discovered a small crayon sketch of dear papa, done by one of his young ensigns.

And at once the sketch went up on the wall. It looked a trifle absurd, and by no means filled the space of the original painting, but the sword and pistols helped, and really the general effect was quite striking.

So at least it seemed to James, as they entered the parlour, ushered in by Mokasa, a beaming Mokasa, who had apparently decided to stay with Miss Parkington-Smith, in case any further trouble occurred, and who now acted as her handyman, chopping wood, scrubbing floors and doing most of the shopping, for Polly enjoyed ordering him about as much as he seemed to enjoy living with a family again.

'Who is that, Aunt Arabella?' demanded James, as his brother and sister-in-law, wearing fashionable clothes and a remarkably social air, settled themselves at the table.

'That child, is your dear grandfather,' said Miss Parkington-Smith, smiling in a way that, for her, might almost be described as beaming, though her small, thin mouth was not made for such exaggeration. She turned her head to gaze at it again with the utmost pride. 'I beg of you, Francis, to take a closer look. It is so like him. Dear papa! How pleased he would be to see you all here in this house. The drawing was done by a young ensign. I do not remember his name, but I believe – yes, I am certain – he was killed at Oudenarde. Poor boy!'

Mr. Shelbrooke rose to examine the picture, and Cassandra followed him, to peer over his shoulder. For a second their hands linked. He looked in silence. His mouth twitched once. Then he turned a perfectly grave face on his aunt.

'An excellent drawing,' he said, 'and, I am sure, an admirable likeness.' He did not meet Cassandra's eyes, but he trod on James's foot as he took his place again, for he suspected that his young brother, who had also taken a closer look at the picture, was about to speak with his usual frankness.

'Oh, indeed, indeed!' cried Miss Parkington-Smith, then, 'Do try one of these little cakes, dear Cassandra. I am sure you will enjoy them. They are Polly's baking.'

James, who had opened his mouth to speak, was silent and inserted a cake instead.

The portrait was possibly the excellent likeness that Miss Parkington-Smith had claimed it to be, only the young ensign possessed something entirely foreign to the lady – a sense of humour, coupled unmistakably with an intense loathing of his superior officer.

It was a caricature of a stupid, choleric face that stared out at them: the face of a gross, self-important, greedy bully, plainly addicted to port wine.

'I am so happy,' said Miss Parkington-Smith, 'to have a picture of dearest papa up on the wall again.'

There was a brief silence, then Cassandra exclaimed, 'Oh, Aunt Bella, isn't it wonderful to be sitting here like this? No more shouting and swearing, no more horrid men beating on the door —'

'Oh, really,' said Miss Parkington-Smith, drinking her bowl of tea with both little fingers outstretched, 'I never took it seriously. Not for a single moment.'

'Did you not, ma'am?' said Mr. Shelbrooke with a dangerous glint in his dark eyes: he ignored the pressure of his wife's fingers on his arm.

'Now don't be absurd, Francis,' cried Miss Parkington-Smith quite pettishly. 'It was all bluster. I knew that from the beginning. It's always the same with that class of person. The Captain used to say so, and he was perfectly right as always. "The common people," he said, "shout and threaten, but they are too stupid and cowardly to do anything." I was never afraid. After all, this has always been my home. I knew they could never move me out. It just required a little determination and – why yes, I will admit it – a little courage. After all, I was born into the army. Dear papa always said one should never retreat in the face of the enemy.'

She bestowed a small, prim smile on the three people who had risked their lives to come to her rescue. She said, 'Of course, this is not quite what I have been accustomed to. Some of the people next-door are really quite tiresome. But I have always kept myself to myself. I am perfectly content to remain as I am.'

Mr. Shelbrooke said carefully, his foot beneath the table tapping, 'These people – these tiresome people saved your life, Aunt.'

'Oh, fiddle!' said Miss Parkington-Smith. 'I believe there was something of a confusion, but —'

'Confusion!'

'But then the common people are so rowdy, are they not? Another cake, James?'

'I am hoping,' said Mr. Shelbrooke, 'to be able to do something for these people. They live in the most deplorable conditions. It amazes me that they remain human at all. As for this traffic in girls, it is high time Parliament —'

'So interesting,' said Miss Parkington-Smith vaguely. 'You were always quite a hothead, Francis, if I remember. But you must not be too revolutionary. The Almighty after all must have known what He was doing to place us all in our right station of life. I remember – now, this will interest you, dear Cassandra – after the Treaty, Utrecht you know, the end of the war when papa retired, we had to engage a new batman – that's the army term, you know, for a valet – and we discovered that one of the young men who applied for the post was a follower of that dreadful man, Wesley —'

And so she went on talking in her thin, quick, quavering voice: she wore a new grey paduasoy, with the family pendant hanging on her flat bosom; her hair was neatly piled, and the little crippled hands moved perpetually, as if she were arranging some unseen bunch of flowers.

She remarked, some time later, 'You will be pleased to know that we have a new landlord.'

Mr. Shelbrooke who had seen what was left of Mr. Fielding – and it was remarkably little – looked down. Cassandra who, though she had not been a witness, had some idea of what had occurred, went rather pale and refused the cake that Miss Parkington-Smith was trying to press on her; James followed suit, suddenly wishing he were back home.

Miss Parkington-Smith said playfully, 'I thought you young people had such vast appetites—Come, James! Oh, of course I was speaking of the new landlord. He seems quite the gentleman. He was in the army, of course. He came to pay his respects. I may say, I was favourably impressed.'

And so indeed she might have been, for Mr. Shelbrooke had already had a word with the gentleman in question, making it quite plain that it would be to his interest to let the old lady stay until the end of her days. But he said nothing, and even Cassandra was reduced to silence. Indeed, Miss Parkington-Smith had said very little to her throughout the afternoon, only remarking at the end in a bright, waspish voice, 'Such a pretty dress, my dear. I am afraid I am too old to appreciate the more advanced fashions. But you look charming, and I am glad to see your gown is not cut too low.'

'Thank you, dear Aunt Bella,' said Cassandra, who had done some hard work with pins and ribbons to produce so genteel an effect. She reached out and laid her hand on Miss Parkington-Smith's wrist: the old lady trembled for a second, and her eyes moved furtively aside. 'I love you very much, Aunt,' said Cassandra warmly, 'for you taught me something I should have had the sense to know, only I didn't. I can never thank you enough, never.'

For a brief flash of time Miss Parkington-Smith's face changed. Perhaps she was thinking of a young woman who had knelt beside her, talked so comfortingly of the dear days that were gone, stayed by her when her spirit was almost extinguished. In that flash, a timorous, childish person peered from behind the pale, cold eyes. But then it was gone. She said in her quick voice, 'I am devoted to you, dear child. It is so pleasant to have you all in my little house. Papa would be quite delighted.'

When they left, an hour later, they walked through the courtyard of the Rookeries, Cassandra with her hand through her husband's arm, while James wandered ahead of them, peering in his usual inquisitive fashion, round corners and down alleyways.

Then Mr. Shelbrooke drew Cassandra against him, and kissed her heartily, as if this were the only reality: she clung to him, crying, 'Oh, you mustn't blame her, Francis, you mustn't. She can't help it. She just doesn't know. She doesn't know anything.'

'For someone who doesn't know,' said Mr. Shelbrooke with a sigh that was half a laugh, then was not a laugh at all, 'she has certainly caused a most extraordinary upheaval.'

But James, who was still too young for this particular brand of reality, could only stare about him, trying to find some sense in what was so entirely senseless.

There was no trace of the battle. They had carted away what remained of Mr. Fielding, who would never wield his rod again. The Rookeries were shuttered and dark, waiting for the night before they came to life. In the ground-floor rooms the girls slept. Perhaps they had already forgotten their vengeance, perhaps it was after all only a minor incident in the tapestry of their brief, garish, violent lives. The children were sleeping away their hunger, and the men – coiners, thieves, pickpockets, highwaymen, beggars – dozed, head on chest, forgetting the three-cornered ending that awaited them.

It's so stupid, thought James, why are people like this, don't they ever learn? And so brooding, he all but cannoned into one of the Rookeries children who scurried across the courtyard. It was a little boy who might have been anything from six to fifteen: it was impossible to say, for his face had been old when he was born, and the stunted body might be any age.

He looked at James, and James looked at him: two boys from opposite ends of the world.

The child gave him a wide, gat-toothed grin, and James, for some unknown reason, made him a small bow, then watched as he disappeared round the corner.

His brother was calling him. James turned to go, then, as if words would still the turmoil within him, said aloud, 'It's all ridiculous.'

Then he ran off to join Francis and Cassandra, to set off on their journey home.

*

Miss Parkington-Smith, who had fallen into a light doze – for she was old and had had an exhausting day – woke to see Polly coming in with the candles, a rejoicing Polly, for young Mr. Francis had handed her a large sum of money and told her there would be more of it whenever it was required.

The old lady smiled and nodded in the gentle light. They were wax candles, such as they had not had for many years, but she did not even remark this: it was simply another thing that was her due, to be taken for granted.

'I think they enjoyed their tea, ma'am,' said Polly.

'Naturally,' said Miss Parkington-Smith. 'I am sure they appreciated my courtesy in inviting them.' She looked around her with the utmost pride and satisfaction. 'They admired my home, of course. How glad I am that it has always been kept as papa liked it. I shall never leave it,' said Miss Parkington-Smith.

Mayflower Historical Fiction for your enjoyment